OUR EYES AT NIGHT

Also by M Dressler

The Last Ghost Series
The Last to See Me
I See You So Close

The Deadwood Beetle
The Medusa Tree
The Floodmakers
The Wedding of Anna F.

OUR EYES AT NIGHT

A NOVEL

M DRESSLER

ARCADE PUBLISHING • NEW YORK

First Edition

This is a work of fiction. Names, places, characters, and incidents are either the products of the author's imagination or are used fictitiously.

Arcade Publishing books may be purchased in bulk at special discounts for sales promotion, corporate gifts, fund-raising, or educational purposes. Special editions can also be created to specifications. For details, contact the Special Sales Department, Arcade Publishing, 307 West 36th Street, 11th Floor, New York, NY 10018 or arcade@skyhorsepublishing.com.

Arcade Publishing® is a registered trademark of Skyhorse Publishing, Inc.®, a Delaware corporation.

Visit our website at www.arcadepub.com.
Visit the author's site at mdressler.com.

10 9 8 7 6 5 4 3 2 1

Library of Congress Cataloging-in-Publication Data is available on file.
Library of Congress Control Number: 2021949493

Cover design by Erin Seaward-Hiatt
Cover photography: © Tatiana Maksimova / Getty Images (woman); © Diana Robinson Photography / Getty Images (Middle Drinks Canyon); © Adam Hynes / 500px / Getty Images (The Milky Way)

ISBN: 978-1-950994-23-6
Ebook ISBN: 978-1-950994-43-4

Printed in the United States of America

We settle for *soul* and *body*, but here I am,
something more—*and so are you*

OUR EYES AT NIGHT

Prologue

When Tom Grunn, the last resident left in Briscoe, Utah, saw, at the far edge of town, an abandoned house being suddenly gussied up, made over with salvaged wood and straightened-out flashing, he could only shrug at first and wish the foolish squatters well. It wasn't, he reflected, the first time this high, lonely, desert plateau had attracted dreamers, adventurers, off-the-gridders. Remote country tended to—or, at least it used to—suck in idealists, people of few resources but energetic imaginations, most of them doomed to fail. Before this latest batch of wanderers had shown up, the hard, dry scruff had hosted, in reverse order, frackers, bikers, miners, Mormons, sheepherders, soldiers, the Navajo, and the Ute. And long before these, ancient, rock-etching cliff dwellers. The slot canyons and scarred cliffs of the Four Corners had seen them all.

What was notable about these new arrivals, though, apart from the fact that Grunn hadn't seen them or any of their faces yet, was the timing of their experiment, which wasn't only foolish, but dangerous. The former fracking zones were still busily causing earthquakes. The wells in this part of the county had been running dry. Still, it wasn't until Grunn noticed that some of what was being nailed and framed up had actually been stolen, scavenged from recently vacated properties, places abandoned when the land became more valuable for what lay underneath it than for the baked ground on top, that his white-whiskered frown deepened. It was one thing, he thought, to build your folly out of materials you got by your own sweat. It was a whole other thing to tear pieces out of the carcass of a town while it was still squirming, a little ashamed of the way it had sold out.

Stealing was the word he was mulling over as he went to check on the junkyard behind his decaying barn. He'd been saving and selling scrap back there for years, since before his wife had died of liver cancer. "Architectural elements" Doris had always called them, trying to dress them up. Truth was, he just liked to keep things other people got rid of. It made a man feel scrupulous. Moral. Safe. He knew every piece of wainscoting and curled shingle out there in the old corral, preserved by the dry heat or else by the corrugated steel roof he'd thrown up to babysit some of the gentler items. No one had ever messed with any of it, not without his permission. He'd gone off that morning to Cortez, Colorado, driving over the state line for a last run of supplies for the road, but it was clear that while he was away someone had come in and made off with three good joists and some solid timber. Whoever had done it must have thought he was already packed up and gone—when he was only nearly or almost so.

Grunn swore and trudged back to his pickup truck and sped through what had been, even at its brightest hour, the meager outpost of his native town. He crossed the closed railway line, heading toward former cattle range, stopping finally at a weedy plat just shy of a sunken cattle guard. The squatters' house lay on the other side of this barrier, at the end of a ruin of gravel road, hardly visible for the cheatgrass and Russian thistle tangling over it.

Out of his truck he leapt, and stood and stared.

Fast work the strangers had been doing. One story had risen to two since he'd last looked. Windows had been glazed with old, rippled glass and excrescences tacked around freshened eaves—funny, curlicued scrolls, additions more common, he knew, in the nineteenth and twentieth centuries than in the twenty-first. He recognized two of the turned, cracked porch posts. Those had been toothpicked from the heap behind his barn.

Plain thievery. He flexed his hands, his temper outpacing the heat. Old Poston, the rail manager who had once owned this property, he might be long gone, but he, Grunn, was still here, wasn't he? For a few more hours, anyway. And while he was still here, and even if it wasn't for much longer, no one had a right to assume his, or his former neighbors', belongings. He marched forward in his boots, ready to call out the trespassers and with a .45 in his back pocket if he needed it. Some things in the West just weren't open to discussion. He lifted one foot above the cattle grate.

And there he fell back, thrown off balance.

It was like a wall of ice. Like some unseen barrier, a meat locker's door, had slammed in his face. He tried again to walk forward, to push through the invisible blockage, the unyielding, unreasonable weight. He heard no sound, but felt a pressure. Again he was shoved back. He stumbled and looked down. His feet were still under him, but his knees wavered.

And his hands were trembling. In 104 degrees of heat.

From the other side of the cattle guard he heard a childish whispering.

He looks so funny now, Miss. Doesn't he?

Impossible. There had been no children in Briscoe, not for years. And where was that other murmur coming from? A muted, older voice, female, saying:

Hush now. Be careful. Let's see what the intruder does.

He inched backward, away. Slowly.

Then faster.

Better . . . better get on over to the county sheriff and report this, he thought. Ghosts were still illegal in these United States of America, even if there weren't so many left now, and even if other countries, other places, were careless enough to give them a pass. Phantoms, to Grunn's, to any decent person's mind, had no business being anywhere. Even out here in the middle of nowhere where there wasn't much business left to be had.

He would call this in. Definitely. It was his duty. Probably the last thing he would ever do for this town where he had once lived so happily.

If only he hadn't thought again of his wife. "When I've gone," Doris had whispered from her hospice pillow, her eyes yellowed with jaundice, "I'll know better than to wander back across the line between life and death. I know it isn't allowed. I'll stay put. But just in case you need to hear it, you remember: we were lucky to be alive and live in this beautiful, wild place and never see any real trouble, though surely we could have, the way so many others endured it. We were lucky to be left alone and in peace together, by the living and the dead. Sometimes I wonder how we managed it. For a while, anyway. With all the tragedies some places see."

To honor her simplicity and kindness, then, and for no other reason—certainly not the childish laughter following him—Tom Grunn hurried back to his truck and decided, *Just go.* What did it matter now, anyhow? Everything was finished in Briscoe. Whoever had come here, belatedly, foolishly, they'd just fade away, too, in the end, as everything else did under this blazing sun. The desert, it devoured. Even the dead, he thought as he fired his engine, would do no better here than the living had trying to scratch out a home in this place that had seen the unhoming of so many. After his wife's death, Grunn had gone to her grave and wept to her, inconsolably: *There's nothing for me to do here anymore. No way to fashion a living. Nothing to occupy a man. Hardly even a phone signal, and no neighbors left to bitch about it to.* Not in this rising heat, with more and more people escaping, retreating every day to oases of green, as even he, with at last some money in his pocket from the government, *forgive me, please forgive me, honey,* was about to do.

Let the vultures have what was left. "Who cares?" he said aloud, and gunned it.

Behind him, in his rearview, the squatters' house seemed to retreat as well, the thorny weeds in front of it growing smaller and smaller, quivering, while all around the desert wind charged at the sage and the blackbrush and the pale desert primroses, which stood their ground, as he had not, white skirts licking against the red earth.

Part One

THE HUNTER

1

Philip Pratt felt himself finally beginning to enjoy his work again, especially now that he'd taken up an assignment in a good-sized metropolis.

In this sparkling city by its Great Salt Lake, on a quickly warming June morning, he sat lounging at a sidewalk café on the shady side of a busy street not too far from the civic center. He'd spent several good, productive days ferreting out a ghostly remnant in the Utah Governor's Mansion. Revivifying, it was, getting some intensely focused work done. No longer chasing after a chimera, *the one that got away.*

The haunt in the Governor's Mansion had been a vagrant male, forty-nine years old, recently killed after falling asleep inside a construction dumpster tipped into a sanitation vehicle—like many cities with a rising population, this one was full of overflowing bins of detritus, building sites fringed with cranes, churning cement trucks. The haunting had begun soon after the man's death. The governor's wife had reported to her security detail seeing an unauthorized guest on the staircases leading to the upper stories of the house. She had recognized the poor man, as many had, from the news—he'd been a well-known Olympic skier before becoming an addict and then drug counselor. The First Lady, a good politician, had persuaded her husband to publicize both the haunting and the removal as a way to express deep sympathy for two pressing issues at once while at the same time giving it as her opinion—correctly, to Pratt's mind—that the afterlife of the spirit was even more painful than his lived life had been, and so it would be inhumane to prolong it.

Pratt, called in as he always was thanks to his reputation for thorough work, was able to reassure the governor, the city, and the prying press that the cleaning would be meticulous and humane. What he didn't share was that such cases—souls who might have been on a path to death but who did not, at that moment, intend to die—were often pitiable, their confusion in the afterlife so much like their confusion in life—*where am I, how did this happen, why did this happen, how did I get here?*—that hunting them became a quick, melancholy exercise, like chasing after a leaking balloon.

Once he'd arrived, been introduced to the governor, and been let into the mansion, confirming the housekeeping staff as well the family were vacating (though not, usefully, the entire security detail), Pratt had slowly gone over the place—a lavish, almost gaudy nineteenth-century palace, with an opulent, curving double staircase as its centerpiece. The stairway had been the location of the first visitation. He took readings there as well as on the first floor and then went up to the labyrinthine second. After an hour he had concluded, with the intuitive skill he charged substantial fees for, that the poor man had taken shelter on the second story behind a paneled wall. There the ghost's unguarded energy, which

Pratt felt like a fist reaching inside his chest, was strongest in a room being used as a small library.

The paneled end of the room, where the ghost's charge was strongest, offered no obvious access point, not without destroying some antique maple chair rails. Happily, a security guard knew the name of the city's heritage officer, Praveena Ayer, a very professional voice on the other end of Pratt's cell phone who explained to him that during a Christmas fire early on in the millennium, parts of the house had suffered smoke damage, and at that time certain rooms had been renovated and foreshortened to accommodate access space for cables and modern technology.

"I could come to the mansion with the original plans," she had offered.

"It's better I come over to you," he said and thanked her. The fewer intrusions at a site the better, Pratt had learned the hard way, over the years. Collateral damage during hauntings was extremely rare; but it happened, and it had happened to him. Now he took care and only allowed security or law enforcement to accompany him during cleanings. He agreed with Ms. Ayer that they would meet at her office in thirty minutes.

He'd found her in a bright, sunlit space at City Hall, where she'd unscrolled original blueprints from the house on a lighted panel, showing him exactly the place that had been created for fiber-optic and other necessary lines that had been common at the time, and where an access panel was hidden, behind a maple bureau. She was surprised security had forgotten about it. But then everything was wireless now.

Her elegant wrists under her colorful blouse rolled the prints away.

"I should be able to get to that fairly easily, then," he confirmed.

"Yes," she said. "It should slot right out."

"Perfect. I can't thank you enough for your prompt assistance. Sorry for the trouble."

"It's no trouble at all. And I hope everything goes smoothly. I know the governor and his family will appreciate it." She smiled, the encouraging beam of one living being reassuring another: everything is going fine, we are all on the right track, don't worry.

Praveena. Such a beautiful name, Pratt had thought, driving back to the mansion.

With the bureau shoved aside and the panel summarily removed, matters went forward appropriately and quickly. He knew the job would be an easy one now. All ghosts sought shelter; most mistook how safe their shelter was. They might appear on staircases but generally fled open fields for darker corners. The remnant of the Olympic skier, his spirit hollowed out by some sadness that had probably excavated him long before his death, was easily spotted once Pratt had squeezed into the access passage. There the ghost leaned, his pale, translucent cheek resting against the breakers of a dusty junction box, as though he'd become exhausted from having to draw on his own, depleting current.

"It's hard," Pratt said kindly, approaching him, "what you're feeling."

"It is," the hollow whisper answered. "Help me."

"That's what I've come for."

"No one listens to me."

"I know."

"Not even here. I thought they might. In this place."

"I understand."

"How is anyone supposed to live like this?"

You aren't, Pratt could have said but didn't. He made an effort, wherever possible, to avoid cruelty, especially with any soul so obviously ready to be released. It was different with the resistant ones. Sometimes every strategy had to be employed to hold a stubborn ghost still for its sentence. But usually there was no reason to be harsh, unfeeling. The people living in this house had every right to live undisturbed. But the dead *were* the disturbed, the pitiable. It was Pratt's task to bring peace to all.

"I have," he offered it, "something in my hand that will help you."

Like children, the weak ones. They always wanted to look. And that was their undoing.

Pratt raised his arm. A brief, fearfully bright flash. A quick cry from the dead, soft and loud at once, like the sound of a firework before it gives itself over to light and destruction.

And it was done.

Pratt had pulled down his jacket sleeve, concealing again the metal cuff that was both his weapon and his bond. He brushed the ash and dust from his chest and exited the wall space, calling in the security guard to come seal it behind him. Then he left the mansion by a rear door to avoid the press or any gawkers lurking nearby, anyone unexpected or unnecessary.

And if there were, at moments like this one, a fleeting sensation, a rapid blinking—he sometimes thought he caught a glimpse of a familiar face, someone watching him, closely, reproachfully—he reminded himself this had always been an aftereffect of the intense physical nature of his work and its burst of fire: a lingering halo in the eye.

And if, sometimes, even understanding this, he still out of habit looked over his shoulder, he told himself that at least he had been getting better lately at checking the impulse to go after shadows that had, each time, proven to be nothing more than hallucinations, his memories on guilty parade.

Self-control is the next stage after self-doubt, Pratt considered now, sipping an iced tea at the café near the civic center not so far from where Praveena Ayer worked in her bright office—no dark, cramped passageways for her. He felt both rested and comfortable this day, sitting in the noon sun. More at ease than he had been in a long time. Chasing after some single-minded obsession, as he'd been doing—it had proved to be the wrong path. You might take a wrong turn, but then you corrected, because life was too short to repeat errors.

In any case, Pratt thought as he leaned back in his chair, after a man's been working long enough in obscure locations chasing after a fugitive spirit nobody other than himself really believes could exist, what that man really needs is charm and culture and living company. Someone you could talk to. Connect with.

He lingered under the café umbrella, peaceful, watching passersby as they tenderly touched their phones to parking meters, carried takeout into the office building across the street, leapt out of the way of a cyclist about to swerve around an open car door. Life was too short, yes, it was, not to pay attention to such small, sweet details. He stretched his healed leg out from under the table. The pain and limp that had once bothered him, the result of the haunting two years ago that he had now decided to put behind him, were a thing of the past. The air going in and out of his lungs was warm, but not searing. His senses were clear after yesterday's bracing job at the governor's residence. Sometimes the things a man feared might come to pass did not. There had been, fortunately, no revolution of ghosts and their supporters, as he had once worried. No elusive, ghostly leader had emerged to change the rules of what counted as life. The number of overall disturbances in this state—and around the nation, in fact—had continued to fall. Soon everyone who passed or would pass from this life would accept and know the truth: the era of hauntings, of remnants, was largely over, and there was no point trying to hang on in a world that had enough trouble confronting current dangers. Only so many crises can be managed at once.

It would mean less business, in the end, for a ghost hunter. And maybe even an end to an entire industry one day, after the last ghost was put down. But there would be more peace, perhaps. Pratt looked down at his phone. Maybe there would be more time for other pursuits, and perhaps even time to correct things, change course, in middle age, before a man ended up being some craggy-bearded lonely bastard.

"Sir?" came the waiter again, a young man with a bald, shaved head. Odd how some people were attracted to a skeletal look. "Can I get you anything else?"

"Still waiting for my friend," Pratt answered, annoyed the young man hadn't remembered he'd already said so. *I am waiting for Praveena Ayer,* he wanted to say, *a friend of mine of only twenty-four hours, but it's fascinating how far we've already come.*

Look what happens, Pratt thought as he nodded the waiter away, when you allowed yourself to keep your eyes open and fall in step with a new place, a fresh face.

At the close of his work at the governor's residence he had called Ms. Ayer back, and she'd obligingly accepted his invitation to dinner that night. A pleasant evening it had been, too, marked by a refreshing honesty—or in any case enough honesty, he'd guessed and hoped, to hint that more might be possible, eventually.

"Let's get all our work questions out of the way," she'd said and smiled after the salad course. "How we came to do what we do."

He'd smiled back. "So how did you come be an archivist?"

"Escape. I had a difficult childhood. Not the most difficult, I'm aware, but not pleasant." Her voice was pleasant, though, with a lilt in the middle of her sentences that each time landed in a calm place. "My father was—is—an alcoholic. Unsafe and unpredictable. I hid in the safety of books and history, stories that were already finished. Then I graduated into preservation, records. I like to be around order, tidiness. I always knew I'd do something library related. And you? Did you always know you would be cleaning ghosts?"

How much am I willing to share? Pratt thought, then said: "I had a knack, when I was a child, for not being afraid of the space under my bed." That much was true. He'd understood, early on, that fear was giving control over to something outside the self, something that might or might not be present. If you controlled that fear, in you, if you took the pounding in your heart not as an alarm but as a meter, then your bed remained yours alone. Only it turned out that a lonely bed wasn't always what you wanted. "I wasn't afraid of looking underneath," he went on, "and if something was there, of drawing it out. Because it seemed to me then the best way to deal with something unwanted is to really look at it, and then—smash it."

This much of his life he had told to others, matter-of-factly, in the past. But no more than this.

"It sounds like it was the same with you, Praveena. If something is unbearable, then you find a way not to bear it?"

"Yes. Exactly. So, what was your first ghost then? Did it come out from under your bed?"

At this point, with a client, he usually changed the subject to the haunt currently being dealt with, since his personal history had no bearing on the task at hand—the present was all that mattered. But Praveena Ayer wasn't a client. And the ghost she had helped him settle was no more now than an emptiness sealed up behind a closed wall.

"It was my grandfather," he said.

"Your grandfather was your first ghost cleaning?" She seemed astonished and concerned, leaning forward. "A family member?"

Her face made it clear she was already thinking: it must have been terrible.

It hadn't been, in the end. Pratt went so far as to share with her that the old man had come out from under his bed, yes, but had left him alone, going instead to his baby sister's crib, where she slept at the other end of the room. He'd been seven years old at the time. His parents, when he told them who had been coming every night, had insisted he was only dreaming about Grandfather, missing him. It was long before any of the current technologies had been invented; the living, then, were still in doubt as to how many ghosts roamed the earth, or even if ghosts were real at all. And in any case, *why*—his parents had tried to reassure him—*why would your grandfather, when he had been such a kind, decent man in life, come back night after night to pull the blanket away from your baby sister? It's just a bad dream, Philip.*

"He would take the blanket, pull it to him, and then drop it on the floor. Every night. After he'd gone, I'd put the blanket back."

"My God. What happened? What did you do?"

"I decided—or it struck me, as a child—that the dead weren't so kind and decent after all. My grandfather wasn't acting lovingly, in my eyes. What he was doing, it seemed selfish to me. So I asked myself, why would he selfishly take a baby blanket? Did he want to be a baby again? Was he trying to cover his old, dead body with it? Maybe he was cold, or maybe he didn't want to see himself? Before he came the next night, I went to my mother's vanity table and stole a picture of him, young and strong. When he came out from under my bed again, I was standing by my sister's crib. Holding the picture up in front of me. Of my grandfather."

"Why did you do that?"

"I wanted to show him what he was. That he couldn't have that, he wasn't that, he wasn't my grandfather anymore. And that coming to our room and being angry about it wasn't going to help him."

"But you were just a boy. How could you know to do that?"

It wasn't the whole story. But it was enough, for the moment. He didn't want to startle her. "I assume it's that . . . I was just old enough to know that shame is a powerful force, and young enough to be cruel about it, too. When he started whimpering, like a shivering, wet animal, I laughed out loud, because I thought it was strange and funny. Then he screamed at me. My parents woke and ran into the room. My mother froze, seeing her father like that. Exposed. Naked and shriveled, the way he'd died in the bathtub. It must have made it even more shameful for him. He cried out and went to pieces right in front of us and never came back. That was the lesson of that night. That a haunting can become unbearable for the haunt. Make a ghost bear the burden he wants you to bear . . . and you'll find most of them can't." For the rest, there was the weapon at his wrist.

"Incredible." She was shaking her head, still concerned. "But it must have been awful for you, the whole experience."

"Ah, but the nights were peaceful after that."

"Yes. And your mother and father must have been grateful."

"No, as a matter of fact. They, we, never spoke about it. It was too much for my mother." Later, he understood: people don't always thank you for imagining how to help them. He rarely saw what was now left of his family, on the other side of the country. His work disturbed them. If he would give even his own family no quarter . . .

Praveena Ayer didn't seem disturbed. She'd studied him with her clear, dark eyes, eyes he was fully beginning to admire. "I think what it is," she speculated, "is that people don't want to be confronted with the past—but they also don't want to do the real work moving the past into its place requires. They don't like either erasing it or looking at it. They don't want to be involved. I'm so sorry, Philip. Maybe there's still time, I hope there is, for your family to come to understand."

She'd reached out her elegant hand a little way across the table. Her skin, that was what life looked like. All life.

And like a different kind of life, too, all at once.

Was Praveena Ayer, Pratt had wondered then and sat wondering now, a person who had found a way to shed her own ghosts and so wouldn't call on him later to do some work she would come to hate him for?

And, he thought as he waited in the bright noon sun of the café to see her again, if you were going to ask questions, why not ask some good, invigorating ones? What if Praveena Ayer were the kind of person a ghost hunter could come to trust with his life's work? And even, at some point, perhaps, decide to grow old with, as he retired from his life's mission, letting someone else, the next generation, guard the borders, the boundaries, manage, patrol, what should and shouldn't be crossing over. What kind of life might be possible for two people who knew, in different ways, how to negotiate history?

Perhaps she was tired, too, more tired than she let on, of drawings and maps and arcane details. And dreamed of a future separate from the past. Something more restful?

He held this question in mind, smiling a little at its presumption but still savoring it, and still savoring the memory of her hand, stretched out across the restaurant table, as a breeze skipped down the street and tangled in the cloth napkin lying across his lap. He checked his phone again. She must be running late. From the little he knew of her, he guessed this wasn't a normal pattern for her. They seemed so much the same—punctual, organized, professional.

Pratt checked the time again. Another ten minutes gone. Some vague anxiety had begun to stir in his throat. He was gifted, or cursed, with a hunter's sensitivity. The air shifted, a quiver ran through it suddenly, like the passing of a commuter train. When he heard the siren's wail only a block or two away, he stood and broke into a run. The bald, skeletal waiter shouted after him, *Sir, you haven't paid your—*

A private taxi lay crushed under the gray cement truck fallen on top of it. Police and pedestrians, at the corners of the intersection, encircled the accident, watching as paramedics bent down and spoke through the car's crumpled windows. The driver of the cement mixer was being helped out through his shattered windshield. A second ambulance was arriving.

Flashing the credential at his wrist, Pratt pushed through the people between him and the scene. In his official capacity he was allowed access to any location where there might be a fatality. He rushed toward the crushed car. A paramedic, grim-faced, was pulling away, waving to someone behind Pratt. Pratt dove under the man's arm and dropped to his knees and peered past a wrinkled curtain of glass.

Inside, the driver, a young man, lay dead with his eyes open. His head rested on Praveena Ayer's lap. Praveena's compressed body was folded over his at a broken angle, her head twisted to one side and resting on top of the dead man's. She was still awake.

"Oh, there you are," she said, calmly.

Pratt shoved aside the dangling curtain, getting as close as possible. He needed to whisper to her words, a plea, he'd never before spoken in his life.

"Fight. Fight, please," he said into her dark, darkening eyes. "Don't go. Rage. Fight. Fight. That's how they do it. If you do, I won't hurt you, I promise you. Come. Come. Please."

"I took an Uber because I was running late . . . I'm so sorry."

"Please. Come." He hardly understood what he was saying. He only knew they couldn't be finished, not yet, not yet, there was so much still to say, to confide, to understand. Why hadn't he trusted her, already, with more of the truth, of his life? Why had he hesitated, when it was obvious she had been someone of compassion and care? Now it didn't matter, now all that mattered, what he needed from her, was for her to rage, rage against the dying spark. It was the only way forward for them now, enough rage and passion to undo death, yes, yes, why not, he wanted it, please, he felt it now, rage, need, in his gut, rage and blood welling inside him, in his heart, enough for both of them, it had to be, come on, come on.

She lay crushed, the light dying in her eyes.

"Don't," he insisted. "Don't."

He saw the spirit inside her fold like a room without walls, giving in.

Going. Gone.

Then he was being pulled back.

For an instant, Pratt was confused. He allowed himself to be handled, reined in. Then he felt himself shouting, his hands flailing. He flung the paramedic's grip off, his own hands shaking with all the rage and fight the dead woman beneath them had failed to muster. Why had Praveena Ayer failed him? Why hadn't she listened to him? He dimly saw police officers, gaping faces, gawkers. He heard himself telling them to get back, screaming on the outside as well as in, move, move, but there she lay still, folded, bloody, inert, the good, the decent, the friendly gone while evil still stalked the earth, unpunished and unfinished everywhere.

Suddenly, his heart accelerated, the meter of it soaring. He wheeled, hopeful.

No. It was the dead driver's spirit oozing out from between Praveena Ayer's head and knees.

His instinct had flared not for a new friend but for the familiar stranger.

Because all ghosts were the same.

Needy.

Selfish.

Wrong.

Habit centered him. He raised his weapon. He could have accepted a dead woman as a ghost a moment ago, yes, settled for some illusion of life if she had chosen it, somehow, only a few seconds ago. He would have. But not now. That was over, it already seemed to be a lifetime ago, a life that would now never be lived, and here was the truth, as always, in front of him: the dead have no choices.

Let them all burn.

Pratt heard the crowd gasp.

He himself felt, a second after . . . empty. Staring down at the spirit's ashy film floating in a gutter. He was careful not to look anywhere else, to look back, where the look on her face would already be congealing.

You thought, for a moment, he told himself, *there might be exceptions to some rules.*

That a hunter might not always hunt alone.

That the present, this time, would depart from the past.

It didn't. The past only severed itself from the present.

Or had to be made to.

2

A few days later, Pratt awoke in the apartment he'd leased at the edge of the city with its view of the drying salt lake. He got out of bed. He went into the bathroom. He showered, he sloughed skin. He dressed. He walked, detached, into the living room.

There were cut roses wilting in a vase on a sideboard. Not condolences for his loss. It wasn't right to say he had suffered one. He hadn't accompanied her body to the morgue. He'd had no right there either. He'd made his report about the ghost he had finished on site to the police officers on duty. Then he'd come back here, cleaned up, ordered dinner. He'd fallen into a cold sleep.

He was careful not to come across any news or announcement of funeral services. What good would it have done to attend? He had dinner with her only once. They hadn't really known each other. There had been no chance, no time.

The thing about life was that it demanded life, he told himself, sitting down carefully at the computer. He had avoided work for three days because every morning had felt like a stifling cloth thrown in his face. A man needed to breathe.

Life was precious. Death was natural.

He got up to throw the fading flowers away. The roses had come from the governor's office, along with a letter of gratitude informing Pratt that he would be receiving a special state commendation.

Ridiculous. There had been nothing special about the assignment he had finished at the mansion, nor about the unexpected job he had done a few blocks away from a sunlit café. He checked his messages now. The work must go on. There had been nothing extraordinary about the past week, except that the only person he'd begun to care for in years had left him without a struggle—apparently finding nothing *commendable* enough about him to fight for.

Also ridiculous. Such self-pity was strange and new to Pratt, and it needed to be expunged. He found himself, at nine in the morning, wanting a drink, but ignored the impulse. He hadn't touched a drop since his injuries, never knowing for certain if whiskey had played a role in the way a haunting had gone so badly two years ago.

Yet he hadn't failed this time. He could honestly say that. It was simply that there would be no knowing now what might have followed. Living was no guarantee of failure or success. It was simply calculations, correct or incorrect. *Yes* or *no*? *This* or *that*? *Here* or *there*?

Taxi or *walk*?

He stared at the corner where the governor's roses slumped in the trash can. A man who didn't keep at something useful would shrivel. And then, like a ghost, he would have no business taking up space in the world.

He went back to his screen, facing fresh griefs, the glow of others' fears and dreads.

Addressing the backlog, he opened another email.

Dear Mr. Pratt,

Thanks in advance for your help. My name is Sherry Hogan, and I write to you as the sheriff of Masters County here in the southern part of Utah. We hear you have done great work for the Governor and are hoping that while you're among us you might consider coming down and looking at a problem we seem to be dealing with here. It's a bit difficult to explain without you actually being on the ground, but basically, we think we have a group haunting on some private property. We're a small, out of the way place and so maybe not up to your usual standard, but we do have a good budget for security issues and of course you come highly recommended. If you would be interested in coming to take a look it would be much appreciated, and we would do our best to make you comfortable. We're more or less a straight drive south, then east to Canyon Country (we don't have an airport). Attached is the location; my contact info; and a contract from the county, should we agree to work together. It is my concern and understanding that group hauntings aren't only rare but also unstable—which is of course why we are anxious for your input and expertise as soon as possible. Thank you for your consideration and hoping to connect with you soon.

Sherry Hogan
Masters County Sheriff's Office

Pratt immediately began a response—*I will be pleased to consider your invitation.* He had waited three days to start again.

Three full days. No presence had come to stand softly at his shoulder. No drumbeat had come to his heart when he raised his hand to it—the signal that told him whether a spirit was nearby.

He was alone.

So.

3

Philip Pratt took a taxi to the nearest car dealership and splurged on a new four-wheel drive for the trip south. The SUV was expensive, luxurious, indulgent. *Life is precious,* he said to himself again. *Take pleasure wherever you can.* He entered the destination into the navigation system and drove out of the city.

The landscape slowly changed. The city was left behind. The flat salt valley, at first flanked by jagged mountains, gave way to lower, bluer, then loftier gray peaks. The sky above seemed to float like a bright panel standing on its edge. Only a few towns interrupted his journey. He reached the peak of a range, a place suitably called Summit, and there stopped at a gas station flanked by the square foundations of vanished buildings. A cashier stood behind a counter filled with hunting knives; above the man spanned a wall lined with the taxidermied heads of wild animals, their eyes looking down at Pratt polished and glassy and vacant.

"Elk?" Pratt asked.

"Yup," the man said.

"Enjoy the hunt?"

"Not much else to do up here, so yeah."

"How is it? Working alone on top of a mountain?"

"You get used to it, I guess." The man's face was lined and bland.

"You do," Pratt said. "Yes."

"My feeling is, if you can't get used to something, you better quit it."

"Exactly. My feeling, too. Ever have any trouble with ghosts up here?"

"Not really. Nothing here for 'em except snacks and gasoline." Now a bland grin. "Not the kind of fuel they need, right?"

"Right," Pratt said, counting his change. "And," he added for a bit more conversation with a living person, "the dead don't like open, exposed spaces. Like mountaintops." He gestured out the windows. "They want a nest, something to shelter in. Pretend they're still living. Pretend they have a home." Always good to educate the public.

He looked out past the empty dome of his car.

The man said, "Used to be homes around here. All gone now."

"Just as well for you, if you don't want hauntings."

The cashier finally warmed up, laughing. "Guess you never worked a gas station in the middle of nowhere. If you did, you might like some company that doesn't just pass through, hardly even sees you."

"I see you," Pratt said quickly, helpfully.

"But in five minutes you won't, will you? Whoosh. I'm gone. Me, I'm the ghost."

"Don't say that."

"Why not?"

"Because living is—real. Honorable. It has integrity. Heft and worth."

29

"But it can be boring, too."

"Not as boring, trust me, as the alternative."

"If you say so. Well. Have a safe trip wherever you're headed."

"Down to the canyonlands."

"Nice down there, if you get a place that still has water."

The mountains, fascinatingly, appeared to erode and sink, giving way to calcined mesas banded in white and orange. Pratt drove on and on, down into the flattening landscape, past more humble flashes of civilization, until, as the hours passed, these became fewer and fewer and his guidance system instructed him to cut away from the current road and cross an unmarked, sage-crusted range. Among the hummocks of badlands, hot-looking—though he was comfortably cool in his air conditioning—and sometimes blinding patterns of yellow-gray vegetation humped by. Among these nothing seemed to move, though he did spot small mounds of what looked like prairie dog villages spread out across a wide plain, and once he thought he caught a glimpse of a hoofed animal, a pronghorn, maybe, some miniature relative of the stuffed heads he had seen two hours before.

A bullet-riddled sign marked the turnoff to the town called Briscoe, where the sheriff had directed him to meet her. The asphalt turned narrower and full of potholes. Banks of low tumbleweed crowded the shoulder, and cracks filled with tar meandered across sections of pavement, the black filler trying to extend the life of something that obviously had little life left in it. A red butte flanked the road, closed in, then opened out and fell away, like a train turning and leaving.

Pratt had agreed to rendezvous with Sheriff Hogan at two o'clock in the center of Briscoe in front of a closed grocery store. She had alerted him the place was derelict, but it was still the best way for them to find each other—go much farther, she'd said, and GPS tended to falter. She'd suggested she get there first and wait for him.

He spotted her Bronco, black as she'd described, and pulled up alongside it. She was standing in the shade of a faded awning above the entrance to the chained and boarded-up market. Torn material flapped over her head like shredding skin. The heat was so intense as Pratt left the air-conditioned comfort of his SUV that he felt his head adjusting, his chin dipping, even as he raised his hand in greeting.

The sheriff, small, dark, compact-looking under a wide-brimmed ranger-style hat, came forward.

"Mr. Pratt?"

"Sheriff Hogan."

She nodded and held out her hand, too. He took it briefly. Her palm was uncomfortably hot. Or maybe it was too soon to recall a hand reaching out across a table.

"The drive down all right for you?" she said in a clipped, steady voice.

"Stunning, actually. Beautiful country you have here." He meant it. The heat might be terrible, but his eyes, his other senses, felt as though they might be refreshed in this part of the world.

"Never been to the Four Corners before? Well, welcome then. This is—or was—the town of Briscoe. Used to be a happening little place about a hundred years ago. Now, well, you see . . ."

She waved a short-sleeved, muscled arm comfortably.

"Abandoned?" Pratt asked and nodded, squinting down the ragged row of boarded and sagging structures. Hard to tell what

31

some of them had been. One perhaps the post office. Another a restaurant.

"Pretty much. Town sort of lost its purpose. Ranchers used to come down from the higher country to get their mail and supplies here. Used to be a rail line and people passing through from bigger towns. When the rail and mail died, people moved away to bigger places. Then the outbreaks a few years ago sort of sped things up. Water started drying up, too. People sold their land for mineral rights. Most of this is still owned by an extraction company."

"And they foot the bill for most of the services around here?" Including his own, Pratt speculated. The wealthy generally paid his high fees.

She seemed surprised by his question. "No. We still take care of our own business out here. We manage all right. Take care of each other. In fact, a former resident is the one who called this in, a man by the name of Tom Grunn. He said he hadn't wanted to at first, sat on his worry for a bit."

"Why would he do that?"

She smiled again. A strong, straight smile. "Another thing we do around here is not jump the gun. Things aren't always as they appear in the desert. The wind can sound like a hundred different things. The light plays funny tricks on you. The heat. But the worry finally got the better of Tom. He told me he stopped by an abandoned house and that something he couldn't see slammed him back cold and stopped him in his tracks. And he also said he heard voices. More than one."

The dead already giving their clues away. As they tended to do. Foolish, needy things that they were. "Good. And where"—Pratt took out his notebook and began making notes; he was old-fashioned, and paper was solid—"is Mr. Grunn now? I'd like to talk to him."

"Retired to Denver. You can certainly call him if you like—although I already wrote everything up." She showed him her own pad. "I questioned him, and he doesn't know more than I already told you. He just told me I'd better check it out, and I have, and it seems pretty clear, in some ways, what's going on, as you'll see when I get you on over there. Ready to follow?"

Another good sign. He preferred clients who moved things along, felt no need for dramatics or hand-wringing. A ghost is a ghost, sad, trouble, but nothing more.

"I am ready and at your disposal, sheriff."

"Thanks so much for getting here so fast." She smiled again. A cheerful person, apparently, out here in the rust and ruin. "We so appreciate your interest and attention. I mean someone of your caliber. Okay, watch out as we go along, will you, the road is paved at first, then graveled, not in good shape. Stay back if you don't want that pretty new rig of yours all dinged up."

A hint of condescension in her voice, or maybe a bit of laughter—but it was still good-natured, Pratt thought. And good advice. The road was falling to pieces. He stayed well back of the grit kicked up by the Bronco as they headed past the wasted edge of the town, where the sunken roofs of the houses looked starved. Here and there a cinderblock or adobe structure stood upright, but with doors and windows missing or open. Abandoned American flags sagged, left in tatters. Junked cars tilted in side yards. Refrigerators gaped in dry grass. Plenty of openings, Pratt noted, and plenty of shelters, for a ghost or ghosts, although it was, in his experience, unusual for a haunting to be conducted in such a lonely location. The dead want to haunt the living. What they craved most, the majority of them, was an audience. Influence.

He drove carefully over a set of defunct-looking train tracks, then continued following the Bronco as the sheriff turned toward an even drier stretch of plateau. He saw the house well before he saw the turnoff that must lead to it. A thing out of place. Out of time. His chest tightened. His senses flickered to life again. *Whenever there is something,* he'd told himself ever since he was that seven-year-old boy facing the naked ghost of his grandfather, *something that expects you to be afraid, afraid enough that you won't do anything about it . . . do something.*

The Bronco stopped short of a cattle guard with barbed-wire fencing on either side. Beyond the piped grill was an overgrown dirt road, impassable for its choke of weeds and brush, not much more to it than a vague red rut.

The sheriff got out of her vehicle. Pratt did the same. His eyes stayed fixed on the house.

"So, what do you think?" she said.

"Interesting."

Long experience had taught him: play each haunting close to the vest. Don't share the excitement, the fascination, which might only serve to rile and worry a client. Wait to see what task was at hand. And whether the job would be a quick or a slow one.

Hogan said beside him, "Sort of hard to miss, right? Doesn't look like anything else around here. Tom Grunn told me he stood right here and could go no further. He told me to be careful, because he'd made out voices, some young ones and an older one. But like I said, he was frozen out, couldn't get in. Thing is, when I got here, nothing got in my way at all. Plus, I do feel something's here, somehow, but I haven't heard a single thing, at least not yet. But your ears will be better than mine."

He took out his notebook again, calmly. "Do you trust Mr. Grunn's version of events?"

"I have no reason not to. Ol' Tom isn't nutty. He lost his wife a while back, sadly, and he hasn't been in a good way since, but I mean, you take one look at this and it's obvious it isn't . . . normal."

No. It wasn't. What had obviously been a rather ordinary one-story ranch house appeared to have become . . . a kind of feast. The lower half of the house, from this distance, looked to be a pinkish stucco, framed in a drab style out of the 1960s. Yet a Corinthian-columned porch loomed over it like a Greek, open-mouthed animal. A fantastical second story had been built above this, with raw, stripped boards neatly laid into place, and dormers thrusting forward, pure Victorian excess, snouted windows skirted with bull's-eyed frames, antique glass liquid with ripples. A chimney of fresh, red stones pinnacled the house, like something out of the English countryside. The roof was steeply pitched and covered in a mix of wooden shingles of different lengths.

"Tom said this—renovation—all happened pretty quickly," the sheriff continued. "It must have. This used to be the old rail manager's house—it was called Old Poston's House—and was just a faded pink adobe. Now it's all thrown up and mashed together like a jigsaw puzzle that doesn't fit." She seemed excited by it, too, but also keeping her cool. "What I want to know is, who did this? Tom says he knows where it all came from. It's salvage, including stuff stolen from his place. But who did the salvaging?"

"That is the question." Pratt nodded, still keeping his notes close.

"Wait till you see the inside, though." She hopped the cattle guard and led the way, her boots ankling around the dry weed and sagebrush, the kicked scent of it scrubbing the air, as though she trailed a perfume. It wasn't any issue, she pointed out, getting past where Tom Grunn had been halted.

"Careful on the porch, though," she said. "Everything looks nailed on pretty solid, but I can't vouch the original frame was ever made to bear so much load. I guess," she almost laughed, "if you're dead, you don't worry too much about anything falling down on your head."

"So you think this was built by the dead," Pratt said, non-committal. It wasn't, technically, impossible. The dead were able to move things. But not at such scale. Not usually. He was reserving judgment.

"Actually, I think it got built by squatters, and maybe ghosts scared them off and took it over. We still get what we call dirt-baggers out here from time to time. Maybe they got spooked by something, the way Tom did. See what you think."

She pushed open the sanded front door. Inside was hot, sti-fling semidarkness. Pratt's forehead and eyes needed a moment to adjust. Long curtains hung at deep windows. A wide-planked floor creaked underfoot. As his gaze took in more of the gloom, Pratt could make out the high ceiling, freshly and solidly joisted and beamed. The original ceiling must have been removed to cre-ate this open, lofty space. To the left, an unfinished staircase led up to a gallery and a row of hollow, dormered windows. The stairs didn't appear safe for use. The second floor was still mere scaf-folding, though parts of a banister seemed finished. All but one section, which looked to have been abandoned in mid-framing, as though the work had been interrupted.

Someone had been going to a great deal of trouble, Pratt thought, building something so lively on the outskirts of a dead town.

Hogan said, following Pratt's eyes upward, "I assume all that up there was salvaged, too. Or stolen, according to Tom. But over here is what you'll really want to see. Check this out."

They walked across the cleanly swept floor toward an elaborately mantled fireplace—also obviously not original. The hearth was old dark stone, but the mantel itself was freshly white-painted wood and framed with columns to match the elaborate porch outside. Above it, written just over its wooden shelf as though for a motto, some small, carefully executed black lettering:

We dead did this

"Well now," Pratt said.

"'We.' That's why I thought group haunting. With this and what Tom said about the voices. But please tell me"—she lowered her chin—"if I'm wrong. I'd like to be. Or I'd like to think they're gone. We've never had a bunch of them all at once around here. Just loners, now and then. And not for a long while now, not since people left town. I've never seen anything like this. Have you?"

Pratt had seen written communications, yes. They weren't all that uncommon. But he had never seen so bold a claim as this one. So clear, so blunt—it almost seemed forced. Almost unbelievable. He took photos to accompany his notes. Then lifted his hand to the shelf. Underneath his finger, the black calligraphy was smooth, dry. There was no charge to pick up at the moment, no energy near it. The beating in his chest was steady and calm, too. No leaping, crushing sensation; not the weight he felt whenever he was near the dead or close behind them.

"Let me take a few readings around this room," he said.

Hand lifted to his chest, eyes and ears attuned, he circled and inspected. The room was entirely, carefully empty. He touched bare, beaded-board walls. Wide windowsills. He stroked the curtains. Searching for any lingering, fine, gray dust. And felt it. There. The residue of the dead. He noted another film, too, sandier, like the desert itself. Probably blown in through cracks. The living world and the dead world side by side. He parted the curtains to look out at the searing view. The shock of light was so bright he turned away.

"There have been ghosts here," he said to the waiting sheriff. "Or perhaps one pretending to be more than one." The smarter ones indulged in such tricks, stratagems. "Pretending to have done all this."

"Pretending to have done all what?"

"The renovations. Laying claim to something belonging to the living." It was what ghosts did above all. Their stock in trade. A governor's mansion. They took what didn't belong to them.

"So you don't think a ghost or ghosts . . . '*did*' this?" She pointed to the writing.

It was unlikely. A ghost might slide furniture across a room. Might break a mirror. Turn a picture upside down. Jerk a blanket away from your shivering body. Tug the rug out from under your feet.

"There is no ghost," he explained to Hogan, "that can design, plan, build on this scale. They simply don't have the capacity for it. They don't have the mind for it, the way we do. Their forte is small tricks." And damage, more than creation. Breaking things—including, once, a balcony he'd stood on. And thus the bones in his right leg. "They play games, like children. And destroy things. Because they can't make their way out of what has happened to them. They don't plot on a grand scale. So something else has been at work here. Someone," he went on, "could have built this and then left it, or been chased off, as you suggest. Or else someone"—this was his old fear, coming back but muted, now that he'd gotten the better of it—"could have been assisting this haunting. Aiding and abetting it." The way some people—though not many, not really, only the gullible, the easily persuaded, the fragile—now and again did. "In any case, a ghost or ghosts has definitely been here."

"But are any here right now?" She backed away slightly, her hand at her hip, her holster. A habit, Pratt guessed. That gun would do her no good.

"No, I don't feel anything at all. Not in this room. Let's keep going."

"But what about that?" She pointed at the lettering again. "What does it mean?"

"I don't know yet. It could be a trick. Or a taunt."

"You think so?" She frowned under her ranger's hat. "To me it feels more like . . . pride. Like, 'Look what we did.' That cursive's like something you'd see on a plaque. Or a marker. But that's just my gut. Whatever you say I'll go with. There's another room this way."

A kitchen space. A bright room, whitewashed, with a scrubbed, tiled floor. Curtainless windows. More intense heat. Again Pratt pressed his chest. No presence. No alarm. One wall was covered in nails and hooks, and from these hung a few interesting objects: a harness, a wooden bowl, a woven blanket.

But no furniture, oven, or stove. Cabinets empty of plates and spoons.

"Were these things"—he nodded at the wall and hooks— "here during your first inspection?"

She nodded back, with certainty. "I don't know if all of this was in here in Old Poston's time, or if it was brought in later. But I definitely know this mule harness was here. Poston used to collect historic stuff, and I remember this harness. It came from a canyon not far from here called Briscoe Canyon. Bill Briscoe, he was a freed slave who came into these parts after the Mormons tried it out and didn't last a year. But Briscoe, he brought in mules, kept to the canyon, and made himself useful doing pack work and trading supplies to anybody, Native American or otherwise, at least until the soldiers—there used to be forts around here—and then later the ranchers didn't leave anybody alone. And this"—she pointed at but didn't touch the shallow, carved bowl—"this is the kind of thing white people used, early on, pioneers. But over here, now, this is real Navajo." She indicated the blanket, but didn't touch it. "You know by the pattern and the quality, plus that's a spirit line, there, that thread that looks like a mistake or like it's not finished, the wrong color, leading to the very edge. My grandmother was Navajo. That line of color is so the energy and life force of the weaver isn't closed off and trapped inside the borders of the design. The life force has a way out."

Objects at a haunting sometimes meant something, sometimes nothing at all. Sometimes they were tricks, staged props, designed to confuse. He'd also known them to be honest clues, "tells" from ghosts who wanted to communicate, who craved some sort of connection or order again. Then there were those who craved chaos and created it. And those who disguised their inner chaos as outward orderliness. The poltergeist rearranging all the china in the cabinet.

The ghost that left him a rose, sealed inside a glass ball. Childish ghosts in a schoolroom, their slates all in a row on their desks.

Yet the dead were all chaotic, no matter how or what they spoke or signaled. They were lost, as all chaos is lost and without true order. Pratt's job, he reminded himself each time, was to see through it all, and restore order.

He was open to the insights of local law enforcement, and so he nodded again at the sheriff, respectfully. But sometimes law officers actually obstructed, without meaning to, the work he was trying to do, or were even sometimes willfully obstructive—resentful of his overriding jurisdiction, or simply afraid of what he was trying to find and wanting nothing to do with it.

Sheriff Hogan, however, didn't seem to be afraid.

"So, Mr. Pratt, where do you think we stand right now?"

The right question to ask.

"I'll give you a quick summary of my thoughts," he said. "There's a great deal going on inside this house. By which I mean, there's a lot of busyness inside all this emptiness. And vice versa. What I mostly sense here, however, is absence. Which is odd for a place that seems, in certain ways, to have been made ready for inhabitants."

"Couldn't it be just squatters? And that's what Tom Grunn heard? Not ghosts at all? Just people who worried about being chased off, so they made this place seem scary?"

"It could. Except for the cold you said he described, and not being able to approach the house."

"Maybe all in his head. He just got scared, and gave up." She considered the idea, but didn't seem convinced by it.

"And then there's something else," Pratt went on, "that does point in the direction of the dead, or at least the dead aided by the living."

41

"What?"

"Look around. There are no bedrooms in this house. Nor does there seem to be any intent to build any. There are no bathrooms. There's nothing to sit on in this kitchen, dine on, eat with. There are no living comforts here. It's only the dead who need no rest, no bath, no nourishment."

"Damn. You're right."

"Does this," he indicated an old-fashioned Dutch door at the rear of the kitchen, "lead out to a backyard?"

She seemed distracted suddenly, as if thinking. Going over all of her assumptions, perhaps. Good.

"Sure," she said abruptly. "If you can call it that. Nothing but desert now."

They stepped out again into fierce light, but with a breath of breeze. He sensed the sheriff, still tense, preoccupied, behind him. Behind the house there were tools, neatly stacked against and under sawhorses. If there had been sawdust on the ground, it had been tidied, or blown away into the brush and sand. He saw the ruin of a picket fence, and beyond it the skeletons of what looked like juniper trees.

"Not much to see here," he observed.

"Believe it or not," Hogan, attentive again, said, "people used to try orchards out here. Back when there was more water."

"Hard to picture it."

"And vineyards. You still see the Y-shaped stakes sometimes. Like the old wooden grave markers."

The only movement Pratt sensed was a little farther off, a juniper tree at some distance. Its skeleton was dark, draped, fluttering.

"What kinds of birds are those, sheriff?"

"Black and white means magpies. Funny to see them out here, though, and roosting like that. They don't tend to congregate. Loners. Super smart. They like to play with things. They make toys out of anything shiny you leave lying around. Maybe they liked the busyness around here."

The checkered birds moved and darted around the branches, as though organizing themselves. Like items in a closet. After a long, busy moment they settled into a clearer form. A triangular shape. Like a long black skirt. Above it white flashes, like the sleeves of a blouse. And at the top, light and dark, a few birds, dancing like a laughing face.

His heart clenched.

Impossible. It was only his old obsession flaring. And yet . . .

His chest.

The weight.

He took two steps toward the sagging picket fence. He tripped over a fallen slat, caught himself on his hands on the ground, lifted his neck to see. The birds were all scattering now, with flying calls, their wings rising through the air, breaking apart the clear image, with sharp flaps.

"You all right there?" Hogan bent down.

"Yes. Fine." He stood, embarrassed, then not. It was all right. The hunter must take every sign seriously. Not only the first reading of a thing—you had to be open to every single sign. The pressure in his chest was real, unmistakable. It was fading now.

Something had been there. Watching, perhaps, from behind the tree. The birds could have been attracted to its energy, and if so, he was onto something now, might even have it by the tail, because it had made a mistake. The way ghosts, like living criminals, always did.

The birds formed a pointed shape in the sky as they fled. What was a flock of blackbirds called? The word eluded him. Not a murmuration. A murder? Like crows. A murder heading due east.

"There was a presence with them," he decided to tell the sheriff, let her in on his thinking.

"Them?"

"The birds," he said, slightly impatient. His work always involved catching people up to what he was already guessing. "Can you tell me what lies in that direction?"

"East that way? Little place called Castle Mesa."

"What's there?"

"Not much. A bit more life than Briscoe. And more death," she said, suddenly struck. "The local cemetery is there."

"Have you visited it lately?"

"Not lately."

"You didn't think you should?"

"You know, I've studied your work, Mr. Pratt," she said carefully, maybe also a hair impatient with him. "I do that before I hire a contractor. And you've said cemeteries aren't the place to look for ghosts. That they hate them."

"They do," he said, because it was true. "But that doesn't mean they aren't useful. There's nothing else relevant out that way? Would you say the cemetery is the most prominent feature in that direction?"

"Other than the mesa itself, I absolutely would. I can take you there, if you want. Do you think there's something about what we just saw that—?"

"It's possible. Before we head there, I need to ask you a question, sheriff." He always posed this as tactfully, as gently as he could. "Do you have anyone at that cemetery . . . people of your

own, there? Any reason you might feel uncomfortable?" Any officer who accompanied him farther toward death on a hunt needed
to be clearheaded, an asset, not a liability.

"None at all. Why?"

"What about your grandmother? You mentioned her inside.
It sounded like she'd passed."

"She's not buried around here," she said easily. "We took Grams
out to Mexican Hat, to be with her mother's side of the family, a
long time ago, back in 2002. Just right after your profession got
all its technology. But she wasn't worried—since you seem to be
about to ask. She's never haunted me or anyone. Navajo don't do
that. The good Navajo dead don't, anyway. It's not the tradition."

Though tradition didn't always matter, Pratt had found. The
dead, by definition, defy rules.

But he was reassured. The sheriff was clear, competent. He
felt his heart settling into the hunt even as his excitement, his
energy, rose. He was on the scent, now. The job was underway.
And he would get the job done. Since the turn of the millennium,
how to end a haunting had been settled technology, even if the
actual mechanism of how a spirit rose still wasn't, after all these
years, clear . . . why it was some corpses became ghosts and others
couldn't manage it, couldn't, like Praveena Ayer, untangle themselves from the wreckage. . .

He gave himself a mental shake. Even if it hadn't yet been
established why some who died haunted and others didn't, what to
do with the end result couldn't be in any question.

"Let's go," he said.

"To the cemetery?"

"Unless you'd rather simply direct me to it. Do you have other
calls to attend to?"

45

"Look around." The sheriff laughed, but as they walked around the exterior of the house, she grew serious again, and seemed to be watching him, closely. "Not many other calls these days. So I'll be going with you. But can I ask you something? If Tom Grunn was right and what he heard was a group, and you're right and they're not here now, that means a bunch of them could be moving around out here. So how do you catch a bunch of them moving around?"

"I haven't determined it is a group." At the beginning of every hunt, the hunter keeps his mind clear. Free.

"But either way? If it or they aren't in this house anymore, how do you track them down?"

"It's lucky," he said as they approached their cars, "that death is on our side, sheriff. Most ghosts want to be laid to rest. They just don't *know* they do. Induce them—find the right bait, touch the right nerve, call their bluff or test their nerve—and they'll come to you and even hold still. Why? Because eternity, emptiness, the loneliness of it, is pure agony."

He turned for one last look at the mad puzzle of a house. "Right there tells us exactly where ghostly death leads," he said. "It leads to abandoned, unfinished rooms. An emptiness that mimics life, but isn't. If you're a ghost, you're abandoned in the end, and unfinished. In time you will cry out for someone to notice this. And for closure."

"Then the writing on the fireplace in there is like a cry for help."

"Yes, if this is a standard haunting."

"And if it isn't?"

"Then it's a form of denial. 'We dead did this' as pure fantasy. Because the dead don't actually *do* anything. They can't. They're dead. All the dead can do is . . . recycle."

"You seem pretty confident," Hogan said as they reached their trucks.

"I am."

"Do you always catch your man?"

"Do you always catch yours?"

She nodded her hat. "Not always. But usually."

He didn't doubt it. "And why is that?"

"Big desert, Mr. Pratt. Lots of places to hide. But it's still a desert. Not exactly hospitable."

"Bingo."

"I will say one thing for the dead, though."

"What's that?"

She looked back again. "They make life more interesting."

They did, Pratt thought, until they didn't. And then you hunted the next one.

"One more question, Mr. Pratt."

"Shoot, sheriff."

"Even if it or they aren't here now, surely they could come right back, after we leave?"

"But they won't."

"Why not?"

"Because," he said, picturing the flight of magpies, "the game is underway."

4

The gravel road met a junction, and solid pavement. Pratt, still following Hogan, turned south, the heated asphalt rippling between them.

They came in ten minutes to Castle Mesa. It seemed to be a suburb—if that word could even be used out here, Pratt thought—of Briscoe. A smaller collection of battered adobe and trailer homes, but with more signs of life around them: bright metal blinds in the windows, land scraped and cleared around sealed front doors, over-turned buckets and plastic children's toys in the dirt yards.

They passed through the tiny hamlet—no one in sight anywhere—and at a beaten tin sign, CASTLE MESA CEMETERY, turned down a red road lined with surprisingly soft-looking, pale flowers. Primroses, they'd be called in most places. Low to the ground. Adapted.

Unexpected place, the desert, Pratt thought. He couldn't imagine living here himself, but he admired the sight of life doing its best in hard conditions.

A wrought iron fence at the end of the road marked the graveyard boundary. He braked and skidded to a stop in the dirt. Through the cloud billowing against his windshield, the size of the place was hard to estimate, at first. Not large, a few acres, rambling between junipers and sage.

Hogan got out of her truck, slamming her door. Then didn't move for some reason. He looked past her, over the fence, toward the headstones, some fallen. Faded satin flowers trembled at the foot of others.

"What is it?" he asked, getting out and approaching her.

She was visibly angry. "You see all the stones down?"

Nothing unusual in an old cemetery.

"It's never been like this. Never." She hurried through the iron gate, her boots kicking up chaff.

"Tell me what you see," he said, staying close to her—and sensing some luck already blooming. The dead didn't like cemeteries. But they liked notice.

"The big ones are the ones that are all down." She shook her head and swore.

She wove and turned, leading him through the dry, tangled plots. She was right. Not every grave had been vandalized. Those with flat stones, modest, affordable, sat untouched. It was the markers of taller granite and marble, the ones that had balanced on square pedestals, that lay face down in the dust.

"Five of them," she said, disgusted.

"Different eras and styles," Pratt noted, bending down and touching their backs, gently.

"Meth heads. With nothing better to do. God damn junkies."

A gray residue came away on his palms.

"I don't think so, sheriff. Not junkies." At least, not the ordinary kind.

The odd thing was that the dead usually respected their own. They didn't spit in the mirror, so to speak.

But they were known to rage and destroy. And this was rage. He still felt it, clawing at his chest, tingling against his fingers.

"This was a manifestation of anger by the dead," he told her.

She stared. "How can you know that?"

"Practice."

"You feel it. That fast."

"Yes."

"But these stones weigh a ton." She dropped down beside him, shaking her head, still angry, still not quite believing, it seemed. "And you said the dead couldn't *do* anything."

"This isn't really doing anything. You said it yourself. It's something a bored tweaker would do."

"So then why not tweakers?"

"Ask yourself: could the living do this? Without any equipment or assistance?"

He saw the calculations running through her mind.

"No way."

"And there's more. The charge here is angry, as I say. There wasn't any anger back at the house. There's plenty of it here. A strong charge. A remnant of a remnant's pain."

"Okay." She seemed to be taking it all in, swallowing it down. "I'm not sure I should feel any better about it being the dead over junkies, but it looks to me like you're feeling better about it, for some reason. Why? What do you think is going on? Is it connected to the Poston house?"

"A guess, at this point, but yes. Possibly." He'd been at this professionally for thirty years. There were few coincidences around the dead. Once you picked up the trail of rage, the dead started talking, whether they wanted to or not.

He stood and walked. Hogan followed.

"These taller markers," he said and pointed, "my hunch is it felt good to knock them down." When you're angry, didn't it feel delicious to lash out? He'd known what rage was. He'd blasted the taxi driver that had crawled out from Praveena Ayer's lap. He had been violently angry, then, in the past. He could admit it. "Anger can feel invigorating . . . as in, giving the sensation of life and health. Something definitely felt invigorated, or reinvigorated, here. Plus, imagine the bonus, letting loose on a cemetery. If you're dead, you want to feel alive—and you want to repudiate death, too. So, boom. Throw a marker down. Delicious."

"Two birds with one stone," said Hogan, grasping it.

"Pretty striking, you have to admit." And fascinating. And not impossible. "Interesting that the shorter and the flat stones were left undisturbed."

"Less bang for the buck?" Hogan said dryly.

There was also this to remember, Pratt thought as he took more notes: the dead never wanted to get too close to earth. They loved heights, loftiness, attics, turrets, tall buildings, mansions, structures with steeples, or, occasionally, deep caves, steeples reversed, underground. As long as they were deeper than six feet.

"Any chance you know whose graves these were?" he paused mid-scribble.

"No. I don't have any people here, like I said. I only check now and then for security reasons. I can't tell you for certain about any of these, not with their names in the dirt." She was calmer now, and seemed almost apologetic for her outburst earlier. "Not without putting a call in and getting some kind of plot map. But I can do that. I'll need to find out who's tending this place now, if anyone is. It changes pretty often. I'll radio the county office. I need to make a report." She turned away, toward her truck, still seeming to hide some embarrassment.

The work often brought discomfort, one way or another. There was no getting around it. Often a shadow started to fall between him and a client. He hoped that wasn't happening now.

"It would be good," he said encouragingly, "to know the names on the markers not just for your report but in case there's any significance, apart from the height of the monuments, as to why these were struck down and not others."

"I'm on it right now. Back in a sec."

The work had to go on. Even when it left clients vulnerable or unhappy. Pratt walked back to each grave again, checking the fallen stones. Each time, it was like resting his hand on the back of a hot blank slate. The names on the front, whatever they had been, gave nothing away. They'd been driven down into and were facing, eating into, the dry, barren soil.

He summoned his experience of other gravesites. Typically, a plot felt heavy and cold under his fingers. Usually, he could sense the coffin below: the weight of nothingness, with nothing left to stir inside it, to stir his chest. The vast majority of graves were dull and quiet and unassuming. Only the grave of a haunt that wanted to rise will vibrate with a particular, telltale rhythm, a chaotic energy with no poles to guide it. It was always the one thing or the other: the dull, cold nothingness of a soul at rest, or the murmur of the restless.

Of the five graves that had been vandalized, two, under his calibrating hand, felt cold and dull. Three were neither dull nor murmuring. A clean, scraped sensation hovered below the fallen granite monuments. Empty. Hollow.

Hogan was coming back.

"I've got one of my deputies working on finding who's got the cemetery map," she said, all business and efficiency now. "Things have gotten a little disorganized with so many people moving away. Sorry I can't tell you exactly how long it's going to take, but let's hope not more than twenty-four hours. In the meantime, I do need to write up a report about the vandalism or whatever I'm going to call this, with what you've told me so far about it. If you can give me a few minutes—"

"Of course, of course. But there's something more I need to tell you."

She froze. "What—" she said.

"I was about to explain."

She was reaching for her gun, instinctively.

Nothing he was about to say merited her dread. "Sheriff?"

"Mr. Pratt. I think you might want to turn around. Very slowly."

He felt an energy shudder through him. A subtle wave.

He turned.

A wan woman was standing there. Yellow veil of skin. White fog of hair.

"Jesus." He heard Hogan choke behind him. "That's Doris Grunn."

"Doris Grunn?"

"Tom Grunn's wife. She died a couple of years ago. I forgot he put her here."

Why so weak an energy? A spirit that wants to rise will pulse.

"Back away, please," he said to Hogan.

He heard her say, "I'm so sorry. I'm so, so sorry, Doris."

The dead hovered, unmoving, ten feet away. Flashing, flickering with unhappiness.

He gave the weapon at his wrist a turn.

The remnant looked at it. Then stared down at the granite marker below her.

"Me," it said.

"Doris," Pratt said, kindly.

"Yes. I'm Doris." A thin voice.

"I'm a friend. Do you know why you're here?"

"I'm in despair."

"Do you know why you despair?"

He stepped closer.

The first, necessary stage: make the dead feel their misery more acutely.

"I woke," the remnant moaned. "After I thought I was done."

The next step: be gentle yet firm.

"You were done. You are done, Doris."

"I told Tom so." She nodded confused. "I lay myself down."

He heard Hogan breathing quickly behind him.

"What happened, Doris? Can you tell me?"

"I don't know. I'm here. I'm tired."

"Did something wake you? Was it the falling of that stone?" It had to be the most likely explanation for this ghost rising, unwillingly, it seemed, two years after her death—though it would be a new, noteworthy path toward manifestation.

He needed to know more.

"What woke you, Doris?"

The next step: repeatedly use the name. By their names they are pinned.

She wept. "I don't know. At first, I almost wanted to go with . . . with . . ."

"With what, Doris?"

"But Tom isn't here. I'm alone. Everyone leaves you, in the end."

Next: increase the anguish. A painful but necessary prelude to the end. Still, he hoped he could get more out of her before they were done here. Such a vague, reluctant wraith. Hardly here at all. Some spirits were more alert than others. Some knew, were aware of nothing at all.

"They all leave, yes, Doris."

"They all leave," she repeated.

"Yes. Can you tell me what woke you?"

"I don't remember anything."

The unaware wraith. "Are you certain, Doris?"

"I don't know."

"Would you like to go back to sleep, Doris?"

The hollow eyes begged. "But will it hurt?"

"Much less than this."

"Then I want to go back."

The final step. The ghost choosing him, and what he offered, over eternity.

He could still appreciate the simplicity and power of such a moment. His embrace being chosen over the arms of immortality. In the beginning, years ago, he had marveled at, had wondered if—why—he needed that power. Later he knew. He was simply human.

"Close your eyes, Doris."

"Yes."

Ash, in a flash.

He had done his best for her.

And though the wraith was uncertain, he was not.

Something had thrown the stone down and woken her.

The desert was becoming ever more unexpected, Pratt thought. And invigorating.

He heard Hogan stirring uneasily behind him.

"I hope that wasn't your first time," he turned and said.

She was looking down at the coated earth. "No. Not my first rodeo. But I'm always glad when it's—over." She looked up. "Are you?"

"Of course."

The truth: once a cleaning was finished, something, for Pratt, a sense of momentum, seemed to go out of the world. It was like climbing a high peak and then running back down again to flat, ordinary, still land. Dull life.

"We have a lot we need to discuss," he said, back to business.

"I'd say."

"And I don't know about you"—he pulled his sleeve down— "but I could use something to eat." This was something else that happened afterward. He grew ravenous. "Up for an early dinner? If you'd care to join me somewhere? Is there someplace we can go?"

She said, surprised, "Shouldn't we wait and see if there are any more like Doris showing up here?"

"No. The field is empty now." Any ghost, seeing what he had done to Doris, wouldn't be close by. The next step lay somewhere else.

But first, living mattered. The need to taste, feel, eat, be alive.

"Then I guess I'll take you into Huff—that's more of a real town," Hogan explained, "where I'm headquartered. We'll grab a bite to eat and get—organized."

She was businesslike, too, making it obvious she was taking the day in stride, as they headed back to their vehicles.

Although something about her, it was obvious to Pratt, stayed uncomfortable. It was in the quick twist of her uniformed shoulder away from him. In the shortness of her steps. Her face losing its dread but keeping its tension. It was that mixture of gratitude and revulsion often inspired by the work, isolating even the best hunter from those unlike him. There was little that could be done about it.

He took one look back at the fallen headstones instead, focusing only on one thing: how had the old woman been awakened? By what mechanism had the fallen stone aroused her? Was it the weight? The sound? The anger it was flung down with? And where would that anger lead now, now that it had failed to call a poor wraith toward it?

Poor woman, Pratt thought. Sad soul. Finding itself, without wanting to, asking, *How did I get here, how on earth did I get to this lonely point?*

5

The hamlet of Huff, if not exactly thriving, at least looked like a healthier outpost than any Pratt had seen so far in Canyon Country. Hogan said it was because there was still water in the wells, along with enough recreation to attract a few tourists, plus the advertised relic of an old log fort to give the place a kind of museum appeal. She relayed all this as they sat down in a low-ceilinged trading post cluttered with Kachina dolls and polished stones and fossils decorating a diner-style restaurant. Her grandmother had worked here for a time, she added. Her grandmother had been a tough one, living most of her life off the grid on the nearby reservation, raising cattle and doing her weaving, making sure to leave a spirit line in her rugs so that nothing was caged inside them.

"The beef here is good," she said as they studied their menus. "And the rugs and jewelry are good quality, too, if you're interested."

He was starving. "Would you recommend a steak?"

"Pretty much everything's good here. The *pozole*. The Navajo tacos. Big portions. You'll be filled up for a week. You could use a few pounds, if you ask me." She seemed more relaxed now, comfortable, back on her own turf. "Skinny people blow away around here, you know, if they aren't careful."

He'd missed a few meals recently, it was true. But it was good to know work was returning his appetite to him. A heavyset woman with the name CALLIE stitched on her work shirt took their orders and brought cool drinks. Pratt said to the sheriff that the air was chilled yet almost damp in the trading post.

"Swamp coolers. Evaporative cooling. Regular AC out here would dry you out like parchment. But they use water, so that's a negative."

"What are your water sources here?" he asked, making conversation until their food came. So much conversation now was about what was running out.

"Aquifers. What's left of the Chute River runs near here, but the town can't draw from it. No water rights to it."

One of the oddities, he understood, of the desert. Rivers passed through, but their nourishment was committed to other places. Casinos clinging to a dying Las Vegas. The withered boroughs of Los Angeles. "But this town is generally healthy," he said politely, trying for a compliment.

"We manage. The future isn't super clear. But then I suppose it isn't in most places. We do what we can with what we have. We try to conserve. We hope for rain, though there's less and less. Do you know what ghost rain is?"

"I've heard of it."

"Storms, rains that fall but dry up before they hit the ground. We get more and more of that here."

"And then you said there have been ordinary ghosts, previously." Like ghost rain, arriving without purpose.

She nodded and said, after draining her iced tea, "Yep. But we do regular checkings and cleanings in Huff now, to put the businesses and tourists at ease. The fort across the street there"—she pointed through the window at the clump of log buildings—"was cleared out a long time ago. There was an RV park with an issue back in the day—and one of the motels, now that I think about it. But these days things are quiet. Maybe even more quiet than we like. We used to have a couple of nice little festivals down here before it got too hot and dry. Kind of like Burning Man, you know, but smaller. We had a ghost that showed up to that once, by the way. It was attracted by the light, the hunter who did the job said. Like a moth."

Always interesting to hear about others in the field. "Who handled that one?"

"Young guy out of Albuquerque. It was a bit . . . messy. And too public. So we didn't want to use him again. That's why we called you. You're known for discretion."

"I'm sorry to hear the work didn't meet your expectations." Pratt suspected they'd gotten exactly the experience and work they'd paid for. Some things couldn't be handled on the cheap. Though the "public" part couldn't always be helped.

Their food arrived. His steak was red and savory. Pratt began to feel less gnawed at. As they dug in, he started again on his notes, the puzzle that lay before them. A strange house occupied, then left vacant. A human shape made out of birds. Toppled cemetery stones. A frail ghost stirred against her will.

"No word yet on the names attached to the downed monuments?" he asked.

She checked her phone as she chewed. "Nope. Not yet. But we'll get them, I promise. Tomorrow at the latest. So you're thinking everything is connected? Everything we've seen so far?"

"You said it, sheriff: you don't get many calls or much action out here, so what are the odds these matters are unconnected?"

"Slim to none. So, if connected, then why do you figure the Poston house was left so clean and neat, while the cemetery was wrecked?"

"Because there was anger at the gravesites and none at the house. Still two sides of the same coin. You always have to remember that haunting is half anger and half trying to control anger." It had to be exhausting, he'd considered more than once. And finally, impossible. Rage finds, always, a place to land.

"So you're saying the cemetery was anger loosed and the house was anger contained."

"Precisely."

"Can you give me other examples of that kind of—distinction?" She tilted her hatless head, her dark hair compressed with sweat. "I mean, as far as you can share anything while respecting client privacy. I like to learn as much as I can from the people I team up with."

They were a team then. That was good news. The little awkwardness at the cemetery now behind them. "Certainly. Do you remember the ghosts we used to call poltergeists?"

"They like to move things around."

"Right. To be more precise, they manifest by pushing things around in the opposite direction of whatever state they find them in. So, for example, I've had clients with messy houses come home to find everything perfectly arranged, and I've had clients with neat houses wake up to find their belongings scattered far and wide. Why? Because ghosts can't make the world the way they want it; all they can do is to make it other than how they find it."

"Because they're angry at the world?"

"Right. Because the world as they know it left them dead. I always find it helpful to think of a haunting as an attempt at unmaking. It's the desire among the dead to upend what brought the dead to their end."

"Well, that's nicely put," she agreed. "But I should point out: I'm alive." She looked at him squarely. "And I often want to upend things, frankly. I don't see that as a purview just of the dead. I mean I'm pretty sick of the whole world as it is right now. I have moments of hope now and then. I see good things going on. I know good things are happening, people trying their best, at least some people. But I'm also sick of having a front row seat to all the trying and failing."

"Yet you signed up to be an officer of the law," he said. He wasn't sure what she was asking for, if she was asking anything at all. Was it encouragement? Sympathy? "You don't upend, sheriff—you keep order. Order matters. You know that. It does. It actually matters. Especially now."

"Some days I know it." She shrugged and looked out the window at the primitive log cabins. "On other days, honestly, I'm fairly certain I'm just fooling myself and what I'm really after is any kind of access to some kind of power I don't really have. Like, I'm a *mestiza* in the middle of nowhere, right? I'm Navajo and Scottish and Mexican and Polish and a woman, and I get spit on from all directions, but other than that I know how far from the center of things I am. But then some days it's pretty obvious to me I do have the power to decide which end is up and which is down—like when I called you, for instance. And I have to be careful with that power. Just so you know"—she looked straight across the table at him again—"I'm not sure I'm really on board with all of what you do. Not the getting rid of haunts, that I get, we have to do that, keep the peace. But the way it gets done. I have nothing against settling ghosts. I just don't like that it hurts. We treat dogs at the pound better. And I'll be dead one day. Who knows what will happen? But what I mind even more is being distracted from the tough going being alive is right now. So that's what I get behind. To me it's not always about order. There are different kinds of order. But what there's only one thing of is time. And I don't have enough time for everyone and everything. There are no troops out here behind me." She waves at the empty fort. "It's just me and a couple of deputies for an area as big as some states. It's nuts, basically. Especially if you're a perfectionist, and I am. Once I get a problem put in front of me, I can't stop thinking about it, I don't sleep, I don't let go until it's solved, or at least manageable, or until I call in someone like you, who can manage it. If I get control, I get sleep."

Insomnia. Something they had in common. "So, will you sleep tonight?" he said, finishing his meal and pushing away his plate.

She was pushing her own aside. "I don't know yet. I keep thinking about the Old Poston place. The cemetery—we'll get a bead on those names, if that helps. But that house. The way it was put together. And so clean and swept inside. The clean things hanging in the kitchen. The tools outside. Everything so placed, so neat. You say neatness pushes against its opposite. So, let's say, it's pushing against chaos. But the Poston house didn't *feel* like it was pushing against anything. It just felt . . . empty. Not really chaos and not really order. More like . . . a stage being built. Like a play, or something getting played with. Until it got interrupted. And then the dead saying, *We did this*, before leaving. Why? Why do that? Especially if they didn't build the house? I get that they don't have minds like ours. But give me an example of what exactly you mean by that. I watched Doris Grunn hold still for you. She seemed sad, and tired. The only part that seemed mindless was how blank she looked when she didn't put up any fight at all when you aimed that"—she pointed at his sleeve—"weapon at her, like she didn't really know what was going on. Why are they part mind and part no mind at all?"

Whenever Pratt was asked this question, he chose a sample case from early on in his career—a few months after he'd been certified by the state but before he'd made a name for himself for the skill he'd come to be known for—those heady, strange days when he'd still been getting used to the new technology and how to align it with the internal mechanism that was his intuition. The ghost he remembered most clearly from that time: a woman named Aurelia Wood. After her death from a heart attack, it was discovered that the woman's Los Angeles bungalow was filled floor to ceiling with shoeboxes. Hundreds and hundreds of pairs of shoes, hardly or never worn. She'd been a hoarder, it turned out, since the 1980s. Soon after her funeral the heirs had gotten into the house and emptied it, donating what they could and getting the property ready to sell. It did, quickly; but to the horror of its new residents, night after night the rooms echoed with the sound of shoes: hard heels, soft soles, sharp, muffled, heavy, clicking, pattering, pounding, hour after hour—as though the dead woman were trying desperately to cycle through every pair she had ever owned, too late, and with no place to go.

"But how do you know"—Hogan frowned when Pratt paused—"she wasn't just having a good time? Playing? Celebrating, remembering all those shoes, or reclaiming them, something like that? A lot of women love shoes."

"Can I ask," he said, "do you ever judge a suspect by the way they walk? Notice a body moving a certain way, and make assumptions?"

"I try not to judge based on appearances. But yeah," she admitted. "Sure. Sometimes the way someone's carrying themselves just seems 'off,' one way or another."

"And you've developed an eye for this, over time?"

"I have."

"It's the same thing in my line of work. An eye." And even before that, instinct. "Ghosts rarely jaunt. They don't enjoy. They don't play. They fret." And the most unstable fumed.

"I see. What did you do about the hoarder?"

He had stayed in the bungalow one night until the sounds started. Then he spoke to the invisible ghost, humoring her, asking her to find her favorite pair. The sounds had stopped, immediately. Instinct had driven Pratt's choice of question. His instincts had proved correct. There were too many pairs, in her memory, to select from. She couldn't choose. She couldn't find order. Her shock—a strong, revealing emotion—illuminated her. He saw the terror on her face. She had wanted to wear all the shoes at once. Even as a ghost, without a body, she couldn't.

"The hoarder has no solace," he told Hogan. "No favorite. No special thing to turn to." An insight now stirred in Pratt. An empty, airy house, like the remade Poston house, would be the better move. Not too much in it to torment. A few things. Shelter, but also space.

Hogan objected, leaning forward. "Cat hoarders have favorites. I've seen it. The ones they beg to keep."

"Cats are alive, though, right? Shoes are dead. Death showed Aurelia Wood how dead her collection was. And how dead she was."

"I see."

"And here's how this connects to your earlier questions about the Poston property," he said, getting back to business, their business, together. "Some ghosts try to mimic life by squeezing back into old shoes, so to speak. Others know that fresh space is more congenial, less maddening. The fact that the house is empty doesn't necessarily make it a complex statement, or a stage, as you say. It's still just an attempt at fitting in where you don't belong. An attempt at shelter. Temporary shelter." Brief and pointless.

"A lot of work sure seemed to go into it for something temporary. Good, here we go." She looked abruptly down at her phone. "This is Darrion, one of my deputies. Excuse me while I step out and take this call."

The server, Callie, good at her work, slipped in, bringing dessert, healthy slices of apple pie. Pratt sliced through his crust, watching Hogan outside the window as she leaned against the door of her Bronco. The low buildings of the fort across the street behind her were a hunched backdrop. They must have been cramped and uncomfortable for soldiers in their time, Pratt thought, small cabins meant to hold in check the wildness of a dangerous place.

She was coming back.

"Up for a little ride?" she asked. "That actually wasn't about the names. My deputy says there's been a disturbance just east of here, just called in. He thinks we need to go and check it out."

"At another house?" Pratt wiped his mouth. Appetite returning. Instinct.

"Yep. And like you said, we don't get many calls, so . . . maybe connected. Why don't you drive out there with me, leave your rig here? It's some rough road, off the grid."

"Fine by me. Let's go." He stood. Fueled and ready.

The sheriff turned out to be a steady driver, handily nego-tiating the potholes a bad road threw down. Pratt had the lux-ury of riding along and studying rocky views or else turning to inspect the gray interior of the Bronco. The obligatory locked and stowed rifle. The digital screen and radio. A braid of what looked like horsehair dangled from her rearview mirror. Beside it, on her raised sun visor, was a picture of two toddlers, sealed in clear pro-tective plastic. Children? Relatives?

Late afternoon light came now from behind the truck, the red canyons ahead starting to blaze. The days were still long this late in summer, but not endless. Pratt held onto the vinyl handle above his right shoulder and shifted with the bucking of the chassis.

"Is this a private road?" he asked. The maintenance was so poor.

"It is," she said, concentrating.

"The owners must not be into keeping it up."

"Actually, they don't want to. It's something of a decoy. They don't want strangers to know what's out here. You'll see what I mean when we get there."

"The owners are . . . ?"

"The Halstens. Rich as all get out, is pretty much all I know. We're heading over to the Halsten Ranch. They aren't here much. They have properties all over the place, all around the world. Crazy wicked loaded but you wouldn't necessarily know it. They don't flaunt it in the ways you think they would. Or maybe it's just not safe to do that anymore. Anyway, the ranch has a caretaker by the name of Winn Towhee. Towhee, you know, like the bird. Winn's the one who called in the disturbance and is waiting for us. I should probably tell you, um . . . He and I had a bit of a thing going on for a while, so if you feel some kind of vibe between us, it's only that. It's over now. We're still working through some things."

"Are those your children?" Pratt pointed.

"With Winn? Lord no." She smiled in profile. "They're my gift from my first marriage. The best part of it, actually. I was just a kid. So was he. Bad decision, our getting married. But we're all grown up and mercifully far apart now, and the twins are both grown up and away, in college, studying sustainable agriculture. Soil crusts, temperature impacts, all that. Good, good stuff. My kids want to save us all from blowing away. God"—she shakes her head—"I don't even know if I'd have any more kids. They have to shoulder so much. Their paths are going to be so hard. You have any?"

"No."

"Let me guess. Your work."

"Yes."

"It is hard, managing it all. Where are you from, Mr. Pratt, if you don't mind me asking? Growing up, where'd you go to school and all that? Your online bio doesn't say much."

It wasn't important to the work. "Back East. One of the barrier islands. North Carolina. After that, Southern California."

"You've come a long way."

"I like to keep moving."

The Bronco entered a narrow canyon. The road tightened, the sun filtering in and out. Slowly the steep canyon walls allowed nothing but shade, rising higher and higher on either side of the pitted road, the road itself rising with them. Pratt couldn't see what lay ahead, then at the summit was startled by a flash of green.

"Surprise," Hogan said.

The walls began to sink and recede, like a red wave falling to earth. The unexpected burst of green widened and spread out below them into a miraculously long, wide, watered valley. It was uncanny—like a postcard from another country. Pratt could make out carefully arranged roofs, glassy black with solar tiles, glinting. Gold-tinted cliffs closed in around the valley, feathered at their bases with shivering cottonwood trees. The blue sky seemed paler here, almost white, for the impossibly green carpet below it.

"Ever wonder where all the H2O is," Hogan said, nodding, "it's right here."

Oasis. That was the word that came to Pratt's quickening mind. And along with it, a feeling of unsatisfied thirst, although he had a water bottle with him from the trading post and the air was cool in the generously vented truck.

"Don't think there's been a disturbance out here before," the sheriff was saying. "The Halsten Ranch is like an entire place that's the reverse of a disturbance. Unless, of course, you count what was disturbed to make it," she added dryly. "To me it always looks like a kind of mirage. Or what should be a mirage."

Another word for ghost, Pratt made a note. *For that which shouldn't be, but is.*

6

The ranch was somehow both modest and incredibly beautiful. This long reach of green, Pratt listened to the sheriff explain,
was called Pastor Valley, for the thin sandstone formation—"Way
over there," she directed Pratt's eye toward the southern end of
the valley—standing tall like a preacher lecturing the flat bulk of
mesa at his feet. In the beginning, Hogan said, the ranch hadn't
been all that much, just a collection of dilapidated buildings and
abandoned corrals, a place all but played out, subject to rockfalls
and flash floods. It had belonged to an older family that had slowly
died off and drifted away from the desert. But the land came with
water rights, and when the last of the original stakeholders finally
gave in and put it up for sale for three times what it was worth,
the new owners, the Halstens, snapped it up. They transformed it,
she said, constructing solar arrays, adding new drainage, clearing
washes, irrigating, planting alfalfa and building a new main house
as well as the caretaker's house, then later adding outbuildings,
greenhouses, and the airstrip they were now paralleling as they
drove, passing a humped metal hangar.

The runway was smooth and clean, a ribbon of straight, pounded earth, Pratt saw. As they reached the end of it, Hogan turned and crossed it. They rode on, past acre after acre of blooming crop.

"The alfalfa is all to get their agriculture exemption," she said. "No horses out here right now. They just bale it and sell it. Or rather, Winn bales and sells it for them."

Beyond the vaguely purple haze of the flowering clover, the main house rose like a small castle. It looked, Pratt thought, like nothing so much as an Aspen chalet, all pale stone and cut logs, a new structure designed to look old as though it had always been there, even if the metal framing around the large windows screamed contemporary, and the solar roof. They pulled into a semicircular drive lined with pots filled with spiny yucca, dotted in between with subtle hoods for evening lighting, unlit crumbs leading toward a stone porch.

"I know." Hogan grimaced and parked. "Total fantasy, this place. Kind of a misleading one, too. Nothing *too* grandiose, notice? It's trying to look very Utah. But nothing native about it. Not even the house stones. Those came from Colorado. Winn's house is over there"—she pointed in the distance toward a miniature version of the owners' chalet. "And over that way," she shifted, "is the Chute River, though it's hard to see from here. Over by those cottonwoods. They have shares in the river as well as the groundwater. Huh. Those irrigators are new." She squinted out at some long trusses, left in the fields like giant wheeled toys. "Well. They pretty much get whatever Winn asks for and tells them he needs." She opened her door.

"How did the Halstens make their money?" Pratt asked as his feet crunched fine, pearl-shaped gravel.

"Cosmetics. Global company."

71

"And you said they're not here much." He could feel it. The place was beautiful yet hollow, like an arena without cheers.

"They're hardly ever here. They prefer all their various city digs, apparently. But Winn says they have ranch-type hideouts all over the world, in case things go south one day. He told me he'd be here waiting for us at the main house."

They climbed the sparkling, mica-laced porch steps to stand between four huge posts carved to suggest trees upside down, as if their roots were holding up the sky. The wide-planked door was already opening. A tall, longhaired man filled it.

Pratt watched as he and the sheriff acknowledged each other quickly and with a smile comfortable and awkward at the same time, in the way of people who share a history. There was still something there between them, Pratt thought, the outline of a passion their bodies no longer fit into but that hung around, on notice.

"Winn, this is Philip Pratt. Mr. Pratt, Winn Towhee."

Pratt found himself having to stare up at the strong-looking man as they shook hands, stoutly. A sun-blasted face. Loose, long-sleeved, plaid cowboy shirt, silvered belt and jeans, scuffed boots. A man who in spite of his heavy work clothes seemed comfortable in the porch's heat, used to it.

"Nice to meet you, Mr. Pratt." Towhee's voice was as loose and casual as his collar. "Thanks for coming so fast. Let's get you into the cool. The AC's giving me trouble at my place," he turned to Hogan. "That's why we're meeting here."

"*Vato*." She made a face. "Why do I think you just didn't want to tidy your place up for us?"

"Because you're always thinking."

Pratt followed them in, strolling into the expensively furnished foyer and great room with its deep-silled windows. The highly refrigerated air was bracing. They stood surrounded by several leather couches, glowing amber lampshades, deep, furred rugs perversely warming the polished and refrigerated floor. A magnificent stone fireplace was mounted with an intricately woven, bone-colored dream catcher. The ceiling was high and beamed. Ceiling fans stirred the cold air.

"Lovely piece, the dream catcher," he complimented their absent hosts.

Hogan was shaking her head. "I always think this all looks like a magazine spread. I half expect to see Mrs. Halsten posing in that chair by the fire, and Mr. Halsten standing behind her, with his arm resting over her shoulders, all nonchalant. With a brandy in his other hand."

"Nice people, your employers?" Pratt turned politely to Towhee.

"I wouldn't know. We don't have that kind of relationship. They pay me fairly." He said all of this matter-of-factly, in that loose voice, without a trace of either gratitude or criticism.

"How often do you see them?"

"Maybe once a year. Over a weekend, usually. I mostly deal with their assistants."

"Do your employers know that you've called us out here today?"

He shook his long hair in the negative. "They prefer not to know anything they don't need to know. If I think I can handle something on my own, I just handle it. I wasn't even going to call you," he said, turning to Hogan.

"What do you mean by that?" She frowned.

"I mean it might be nothing to get too bothered about. It's not even in the house. But Callie at the trading post told me you were out on a spirit hunt."

Pratt exchanged a glance with the sheriff. So word was out.

"Callie just served us at the post," Hogan said smoothly. "What were you doing talking to her?"

"She wanted to know if I needed any lamb chops."

"Callie and her sheep. Gotcha."

"Why don't you take us to the site of the disturbance," Pratt said, sensing some tension he didn't understand, "and we'll see what you're dealing with?"

"This way," Towhee said, also smooth. "It's been going—the apparition went on and off, so to speak. Thought I was imagining things at first. It gets so empty here, sometimes, you start to think you're seeing things in the heat. But usually it's easy to figure what's what. Step outside"—he led them to a pair of French doors and out to a massive, shaded stone veranda with views of the cliffs and a hint of river in the distance—"and just start walking toward the east field, there. Just stand right at the edge while I turn on the irrigation. I'll be right with you."

Together Pratt and the sheriff crossed a perfect stretch of green lawn toward a low, geometric split-wood fence holding back an expanse of blooming clover.

"Winn, dude, this is past ready to be baled," Hogan leaned on the fence and called behind her as he walked away, her mind seeming to have abandoned the reason they had come, caught on some separate splinter.

Pratt surveyed the field, the flowers, and the long, wheeled, watering system. So much irrigation this must take...

Winn was jogging back in his boots. "Takes a second for the well pump to catch up. When you see the spray starting"—his voice was different now, urgent—"look over there, a little toward the right. That's where I've been seeing it."

At first, all the water did was dribble from several valves along the stretched piping. But then, finding pressure, the mechanism seemed to stiffen, and sputtered, and then water began shooting in healthy arcs, spraying prisms into the still light sky. It was a pretty sight, Pratt thought, against the backdrop of the red cliffs. The water continued to spout, glistening with rainbows. A smell of rain came across the field, tangy as it struck plants and earth. Following Winn Towhee's pointing finger, Pratt looked to the right, away from the red cliffs, through a fan of falling drops. There the apparition stood.

He took a step forward and was caught at his waist by the fence. He stared. It couldn't be. He'd only caught glimpses of her—once—twice.

"You do see that, right?" Towhee said next to him.

Pratt nodded, inhaling.

The one that got away. Incredible. Unmistakable.

The Finnis ghost. The ghost of his two years of wandering.

Here? In this place?

"I see it." Hogan breathed out, excited. "Damn."

He hadn't, Pratt realized now, been startled when he saw the woman's shape in the magpie-filled tree.

He'd been looking. He was always looking.

He'd been ready, somehow.

"Stay where you are," he said, evenly.

Carefully, Pratt moved along the fence, away from the two others. Disturbingly, when he lost the angle of water and light, the ghost disappeared. When he moved back toward Hogan and Towhee, she appeared again. A relief.

"She's only in the water," Towhee called, unaware of the whirling, the calculations in Pratt's head. "Turn the water off, she's gone. I'm just glad you're seeing it, too."

"Do you recognize her, Winn?" Hogan said.

"Nope. Never seen her before in my life. Looks like some sort of pioneer. That long skirt. The white shirt. The weird hair with the old-fashioned ribbon."

"She's almost beautiful," Hogan said.

No. Not beautiful.

And no pioneer.

The rough-hewn clothes. Early twentieth century. The First World War. A time of invention. And death.

Pratt's mind was leaping. Ascending.

Her name was Emma Rose Finnis, he knew, triumphant.

The botched, unfinished haunting.

His unfinished obsession.

The figure stared through him, unmoving. It stared through all of them, unmoved.

Now he understood, from Towhee, why he must hold in one direction, one place—so that he would not lose sight of her, never, ever again.

Pratt had time to think, *What was she doing here? So far from her origin, on the coast?* This time he would get closer . . . Behind this fence was too far to confront her accurately.

"Leave the water on," he said under his breath to Towhee, who had come closer. "Stay here."

Pratt lunged over the top rail, the wound from when they'd first met no longer objecting. He found sure footing in the wet field and moved forward, almost in range, crushing the purple blossoms underneath him.

This time she didn't try to escape. She must be worn down, at last. As they all were in the end. She must have needed attention, but now found there was never enough. She stared past him, toward the house, not flinching. That pale face. The sharp, cleft chin. The long neck in its tall, white collar.

Close enough. The spray was striking him, cool. Yes, she was giving up now. She must be ready. Perhaps she had even sought him out, to put an end to her eternity.

He should be getting overwhelming readings now. His heart should be bursting out of his chest.

But nothing.

Ignoring this, Pratt took one step deeper into the spraying water. He slid and tripped forward but righted himself quickly, then realized he had come so far, he should have been standing at her feet. Yet he saw nothing, he felt nothing of the ghoul dead since 1915. No vibration, no pressure. He was getting soaked, but otherwise no sensation shook him.

From the corner of his eye he saw Winn running to turn the water off, and Hogan clambering over the fence, perhaps thinking he was in some trouble.

He was simply wet. And alone.

Hogan reached him, taking his arm as though to make sure he was steady. "What just happened? Are you okay?"

The irrigation system was off now, the machine losing its energy. The last of the spray, dying, fell to earth.

Winn hopped the fence and was running up to join them. "You were right there!"

Pratt's primary, centering thought was to stay businesslike, authoritative. Not betray any confusion.

"What did you see from your vantage?" he said calmly.

"You passed right into her. She was still there when you got right here. Till I cut off the water. She looked like she was right on top of you. You didn't see her?"

Pratt shook his head. There was nothing to do but find some fresh footing in this field. "The image was here, yes"—he looked around—"but there was no reading. Nothing was here. Nothing."

"What does that mean?" Hogan stared.

A sharp sunset was already beginning to dry him. It made it easier to think.

"All I can tell you"—he shook himself off—"is that this couldn't have been a normal manifestation. It was, it had to be a . . ." He was reaching for the right analysis, the correct feeling, or rather the absence of feeling, still with him. *She was here but not here.* And with this understanding, a new idea, a fresh instinct, yes, came to him, the insight that separated his work from that of others, that clients paid handsomely for, his gift, his trademark, coalescing around him and inside him. There. He had it. He had something, now.

A ghost that wasn't there. They loved to play tricks.

"I believe this was a projection of some kind," he announced to them, casually, wiping himself off. It was a trick. Like other tricks. A false performance. Like a ventriloquist throwing a voice. Nothing real in itself. But it could, would, lead to something real. The hunt was only beginning, or rather, this was a hunt that still had to come to its end. "It was nothing, nothing real or meaningful. We need to go back inside. It was looking right at the house."

"And you're sure you're all right?" Hogan said, appearing anxious beside him.

A younger woman expressing concern for an older man's body, Pratt realized. But he shook the concern, and its implications, off, and started back across the field.

7

Pratt took readings in every inch of the Halsten chalet. In its staged, overpillowed bedrooms. In its Zen bathrooms. In a library full of uncracked books. In its mini-theater.

He ended in the spotless, marbled kitchen. Feeling some impatience, even concern rising. He suppressed a familiar sense of frustration, forcing himself to remember his eagerness and delight in discovery when he'd first encountered the Finnis ghost—a crafty spirit, from the beginning. One well worth the hunt, after all.

The sheriff and the caretaker Towhee were watching him closely. He went again through the great room, passing the unlit fireplace. He passed again through the dining room and reached the French doors and looked through them, out across the veranda to where the image had been, adjusting his position until he thought, he was certain he stood where she had been looking, staring into the house. Still covetous, perhaps, of space and shelter.

And still he could catch no whiff, no charge, nothing electric in the air around him. His heart was nothing more than the ordinary brick it was at ordinary moments.

"Come on, you look exhausted," Hogan said, kindly. "You do know you've been going all day, ever since you left Salt Lake."

"Let's all sit down," Winn Towhee urged. "I'm thirsty. I'm making us all drinks."

"Just water for me," Pratt said. He'd been drinking when he'd tangled with the Finnis problem before, two years ago.

But if he was patient, this time . . . If he didn't lose his head . . . If he remembered a ghost showing itself was simply a ghost asking for sleep . . . then eventually there would be rest. For everyone.

"Not that kind of drink," Towhee reassured him. "Just beverages. Ice in your water?"

"Ice, yes, please," Pratt agreed, and sank onto one of the couches.

"Tell me what you're thinking," Hogan said, sitting across from him, leaning forward, her holster and gun tipped slightly.

"I'm thinking I should tell you both that I know that . . . thing, we saw out there."

Hogan's face stayed a blank mask of professionalism, but he could tell she was alert.

"Really? How?"

"On other assignments. Two of them. I first encountered it, the Finnis remnant—her name was Emma Rose Finnis in life—a few years ago, north of San Francisco. She was haunting an estate along the coast. It was a complex case. There were multiple deaths." He hurried on, it was wiser not to say too much, turn down corners it would be pointless to revisit. "The remnant is early twentieth century. A ghost from the logging era in that part of the world. A rough period in history. It produced a fair number of incidents, or used to. That part of the country is quiet now. In the end, she escaped the area." Nor was there any point sharing that he'd been widely disbelieved when he'd reported the startling tricks of this fugitive, a ghost on the run. "It took some time, but I tracked her to the mountains, the Sierras, and found her there." And that should have been the end of it. Was nearly the end of it. "This was in a town near the Nevada border. A group haunting," he nodded at the sheriff. "She escaped again, in a subsequent pursuit, across state lines. At that point I left the matter to . . ." What best to say here? *To overcome an obsession? To prove to myself that I could?* "I left the matter to other jurisdictions to settle. I assumed it had been settled." But of course it wasn't.

"Ghosts can escape?" Hogan asked him, surprised.

"Rarely, yes. For a time. That's all."

"But"—he watched her quick mind working again—"what would she be doing out here? You're saying she's part of our local problem now?"

"Your water." Towhee handed him a tall glass.

"Thank you." The cold liquid traveled down his throat and through his gut, then immediately warmed inside him. The advantage of being alive, of having a body. It could adapt. Reset.

"Your local problem, yes," he went on. "You can now consider the Finnis problem as a part of it." Now that she had woven herself into another beautiful, serene place, the way evil tended to do. "I should tell you, we are now dealing with a highly capable and ugly remnant. Clever. Dangerous. Imaginative." In fact, ghosts were nothing but imagination, conjuring themselves past death. Imaginative in a way that was no compliment. "Resourceful."

If there was, Pratt sat back and decided, any spirit who might be able to project herself, throw her image onto a field of clover, it would be the Finnis ghost. Like a carnival ventriloquist, yes.

Now that he was warm inside and out again, Pratt felt his body lean, challenged. It might turn out he had even needed this. After the blow of Praveena Ayer, so bitter, unnecessary, unexpected.

"Refill." The caretaker handed him another glass of icy water and sat down with his own. "So," Towhee said simply, "I guess it was a good thing I called this in."

"Absolutely. And I want to reassure you both: a ghost is still a ghost, friends. They're all susceptible to the same influence. Some hauntings take longer, are more complex than others. But they're all subject to the same outcome."

The caretaker pointed at Pratt's sleeve. "With that."

"Yes."

"Can I see it? Never have seen one of those braces, up close."

Pratt leaned forward. They both leaned in.

"That's welded on," Hogan explained to Towhee.

"So you . . ." Towhee studied the engraved marks. Each cuff was different. A unique license and piece. "You live in it?"

"And with it. And I'll probably die in it."

"That's a tall order," the tall man said, sitting back. "A big commitment. And responsibility." The caretaker seemed to want to know more, now that he knew what haunted his alfalfa was unusual and would take a while. "How'd you get into this line of work?"

Hogan looked on intently as if she'd wanted to ask the same thing but had been too polite.

He could tell again, if he wanted to—as he had shared with Praveena Ayer only a few days ago—the story of the ghost of his grandfather, the old man who came and pulled the covers away from a child's crib. And he could say even more, more than he had trusted himself to confide in her: that the blankets had been snatched away from his own bed, too, night after night, and thrown to the ground. That night after night, he'd lain exposed, afraid, too afraid, at first, to speak, too threatened by the dark and by the ghost's naked anger—*If you tell your mother I will burn this house down around you all*—too ashamed of his own fear to do anything about it. Until one night he could bear it no more, didn't care what would happen. He'd trusted his instincts and fought back, standing up to the ghoul and to fear, as he would to any and every fear that had come after that, whether it came out from under his own bed or someone else's.

"I got into this line of work," was all he said, "because as a boy I was fascinated by time and place. Where the dead come from, and where they should be going." He pulled out his phone and tapped it until a map came up.

"If you look here, you'll see what I mean. I'll show you where the Finnis remnant started, and how it's been moving." He'd kept his notes. Something was only an obsession until you found a way to end it. "She's been moving very nearly in a straight line. Due east." As if she felt compelled to move in one direction. Which would fit what was inescapably true of all ghosts. They were pitiable automatons, no matter how strong they seemed, compelled by loss.

Why the eastward trajectory? That he didn't know. In the end it didn't matter—apart from the fact that knowing might bring him closer to identifying her strongest, most vulnerable emotion, the thing that would hold her still and let him shoot. Either way he had a compass. He simply had to figure out how to use it again.

Winn Towhee said suddenly in his loose, undramatic, ranch-er's way, "You know it struck me when I was looking at her the first time, before you came, that there was something funny about her eyes. First I thought she was staring right at me. But it didn't seem like she was looking at my level at all. Like she was looking over me. Like there was some serious direction to it."

"Toward the house," Hogan said, nodding. "But we've already checked out the house."

"You said it was a projection." The caretaker gave this some thought. "But what if it wasn't? What if it was more . . . a reflec-tion? You say she's fixated on the east. But that—mirage—or whatever it was—was, I can tell you, facing due *west*. Facing this way, this house, is facing west. So what if she was, I don't know, facing east, say, somewhere near here, but safe, and the water was only picking up the reflection of that."

Trust a man to know his own land—Pratt nodded, impressed—or at least the land it was the man's job to work.

"So if she wasn't facing the house . . ." Hogan said.

"She was facing away from it," Pratt finished. It could be. He studied the caretaker more closely. Yes, if there was anything any man knew, it was where he lived. He would have a feel for it, for what was happening on it, different and more refined than any vis-itor would. A good ghost hunter read the living as well as the dead.

Hogan stood suddenly and went toward the veranda. "So, if the reflection was about there . . ."

Pratt rose and went with her. The sky was going twilit now, but beyond the manicured lawn the alfalfa fields were still visible in the graying light.

"If I'm a ghost facing that way," Hogan said, "and I'm facing due east, what am I looking straight at, Winn?"

"Let me turn a few lights on," he said, "grab some flashlights, and I'll show you."

The hooded lamps accenting the perimeter of the house pooled light onto the ground in closely spaced footfalls. The caretaker's flashlight showed the way to the far edge of the lawn, where they reached an opening in the fence and a fine, graveled path between darkening shrubs. Winn Towhee then led them through a stretch of field. The sound of running water came gently across the cooling desert. A soft murmur, nothing urgent. Pratt's light caught the gnarled bases of tree trunks, the glimpse of a moving river, but well before its border Towhee turned and suddenly sank. Pratt quickened his pace to catch up and saw the man was pointing down a long set of steps leading underground.

"They have a bunker they keep ready," was all the caretaker said, gesturing to them to follow. They descended between two deep, narrow concrete walls, hidden discreetly below the level of the earth.

"I call it the bunker, anyway," Towhee said at the bottom. "They call it the annex. It's a doomsday fallback. Part of my job is to check it regularly, make sure it's always in order and ready to go."

"You never told me this was here," Hogan said, as if unhappy.

"It's a private bunker. For emergencies. End of the world scenarios."

"In a desert where the water is running out? Right."

"Last place anyone would look," Pratt said.

"The entrance is down this tunnel."

Now they were in funneled concrete, dark and cool.

"Feel anything?" Hogan asked Pratt, her gun drawing closer to him.

"Not yet."

"The entrance is sealed and airtight," Towhee said ahead of a metal door. "It can only be opened with a code that changes monthly. It—" He raised his flashlight. His confusion was obvious.

"It's already unlocked," Pratt said, anticipating.

"That isn't possible."

"It is. A remnant has no body. It isn't corporeal. It can fit itself even inside a small mechanism and understand how to turn it."

"I guess that's why hiding in the basement never works," Hogan said uneasily.

"Should I go in first?" Towhee asked.

"Allow me. Stay close by. Where are the lights?"

"Automatic once you're inside."

Pratt pushed the thick metal door inward. It glided open with three soft, echoing clicks, like a bank vault. Lights flickered to life as he passed through another inner door, and at once a fully furnished yacht came into view—that was the only way to think of it.

They were in a ship underground, all bright white and tucked, durable cushions, white walls, white screens, white, sleek tables, white reclining chairs. Beyond these, a gleamingly white galley kitchen. Farther on, open doors to rooms half seen, glimpses of metallic exercise equipment, a bank of unlit computers. Overhead, the ceiling was architecturally traced with elegant silver ducting disguised as artwork. The whirring of an air conditioning system already on, kicked as if into a higher gear. The temperature already felt perfect.

A faint scent hung in the air, like lilies, pumped, Pratt realized, from flowers sculpted and set into the ceiling.

"It's a frickin' spa," Hogan whispered, amazed. "Winn, I can't believe you never showed me this before."

"No excuse till now."

"How big is it?" Pratt asked, gauging.

"Five thousand square feet. Everything you see now, plus media room, bedroom, two baths, and storage for unperishable food and hydroponic seed. Recycled air and gray water. Solar charge from arrays on the cliff, hard to get to, hard to see. Rechargeable batteries, energy turned by anything and everything that moves in the house. Everything enough to last who knows how long. My understanding is my employers have these all over the world, not just in the desert. You never know where you'll be when the lights go out."

Pratt watched as Hogan, unnerved, came nearer her former partner. "Is there a place for you down here, Winn?"

"Nope. Not sustainable for more than two."

"So you take care of it but you get no part of it. Why didn't you ever tell me?"

"Not interested in holes in the ground. To me this would be living in some ginned-up coffin."

"When was the last time you were here?" Pratt asked.

"About three weeks ago. I check it once a month. Change the code I'm given."

"Anything disturbed?"

"Not that I can see from here. Are you getting something?"

"Yes. Something is or has been here." A flutter in his chest. The quiver in his fingertips. "There's a charge."

He moved forward slowly, setting the flashlight down on a polished ivory buffet. Towhee and Hogan followed close behind. What humming energy there was appeared to be in the center of this living—or maybe it was more accurate to think of it as a surviving—room.

If he moved to the left or the right, the charge diminished, that side of his body sagging. The charge was strongest here, at the long white dining table with its high-end steel chairs drawn in at either end.

"Wait, there is something disturbed." Winn pointed over Pratt's shoulder and down.

White on white, it took a moment for Pratt to see it. Then he ran his finger over the surface of the table, picking up the coarse, white grains.

"The dust?" Hogan asked.

"No." Pratt tasted it but was already certain. "This is sea salt."

"That wasn't there when I came last time," Towhee said.

"But they keep salt down here."

"Sure. Loads of their favorite. Carry it with them, too, when they travel."

"Seriously," Hogan said, disgusted.

Pratt moved away from the table and the spilled salt, and the trail went cold. He came back to it, and the charge hummed. There was only this salt. Left deliberately, perhaps. Like the reflection.

What are you up to now, ghoul? he thought, concentrating. *What are you trying to signal with this? "We dead did this"? Is it "we" really? Or just you?*

He wiped his hands free of the brine.

"Salt is a sign," he thought aloud. "A symbol."

They seemed to be waiting for him to say more, as they all stood in the center of this phantom house, pumped full of its artificial air.

He looked at the sheriff. Curious to see if her mind had jumped with his.

Hogan said, "So we brainstorm us some salt."

"Go on."

"A woman was turned to salt for not obeying," she tried out.

Good start.

"Salt of the earth," the caretaker added quickly.

"Salt is life."

"You have to have it to live."

They went on, the two of them trading ideas competitively. It was some old pattern, habit, game, Pratt saw, between them.

"It's used for preservation. For bodies. Flesh."

"It's taste. It's savor."

"It's an imitation of life. Blood," she said.

"It's from the sea."

"It's life but not alive."

"It's an additive."

"Tears."

"It comes to life with something else, something comes to life with it."

"It's a trail. It's a trap," Towhee said. "A salt lick. Those with noses come to it."

"A lure."

"A trap," Pratt repeated. "That's interesting."

They each turned and looked the long distance to the vault entrance, the open door.

"There's no way, Winn," Hogan asked suddenly, "we could get locked in?"

"There shouldn't be. I have the code."

"I told you," Pratt said, "it can get inside things. Change them. We're going. Now." He held his arm out, directing them.

He wouldn't allow himself to be cornered. Not this time.

Safely in the tunnel, they each looked back through the still open door, lightly panting.

"Okay, I need to say something," Hogan said, swallowing.

Towhee closed the bunker, tapped a code.

"All right," Pratt said. Deliberately calm.

"That just messed me up. Same for you, right? Did you feel it? Did you see it?"

"The ghost?" Towhee asked.

"No. I'm talking about that . . . house, hole, I don't know what to call it. Jesus. It was like standing there and staring straight into . . . the end. The future."

They were each silent, squeezed into the narrow tunnel with their flashlights.

But the immediate future was all that required attention right now, Pratt decided.

"Up and out," he said, "Next steps."

8

Above ground, in the night air, Pratt thought: *Salt rubbed into a wound.*

The experience in the bunker had been too familiar. He had fallen, before, hunting the Finnis remnant. Ending up down, down, down in the ground.

Was the ghost taunting him? But why? Why, when it would only lead him to hunt her with even more determination?

Yet every manifestation, he reminded himself, every gesture, every provocation, each wave of anger or spite a spirit succumbed to was, fortunately, a clue. Whether it intended to or not, the ghost was giving some of itself away.

Perhaps it was willing to lose a certain amount of itself in order to go on.

No, that was giving the dead too much credit. It was the wrong idea. A ghost was like scattered salt. Disordered, incapable of logic. It would soon make a mistake. There were always mistakes. He had made them himself. The Finnis ghost had made them, too, but had been quick enough, lucky enough, to outrun them.

But luck, like life, didn't last forever. Pratt stretched and breathed above ground.

A golden buckle of moon had risen and shed soft light into the valley.

Winn Towhee had paused at the top of the bunker steps.

"Mr. Pratt, I don't know what you're planning for your next move, but if you'll look over to the left there, you'll see my lodging. That cabin, there."

The shelter of a cabin sounded pleasant. "Inviting us in for the night?"

"Well, I think I should. Because you see that one light at the window? I don't think I left it on. I might have. But I don't think so."

There had to be a limit even to the Finnis ghost's cockiness.

"It's probably nothing," Hogan said. "I better warn you, Mr. Pratt. Household details and neatness aren't exactly Winn's strong suit." She said this jokingly, as if now that they were above ground again walking a gravel path in a hint of moonlight toward the caretaker's cottage, things had gone back to normal.

"That's right," Towhee said. "I spend all my energy keeping other people's details straight."

"You probably did leave that light on. You leave stuff in all sorts of condition," she said.

"We'll check it out anyway," Pratt tried refereeing.

"Or maybe it's poltergeist action." Hogan nudged her former partner. "You could use someone to clean your place, all right."

They arrived at the smaller version of the main house. Towhee's long legs took the three porch steps in a single go.

Pratt stopped him before he could open the door. "What do you say I go in first again, just in case?"

"I'm absolutely fine with that. It's always unlocked, by the way. Nothing unusual about it."

By the light of the one lamp, Pratt entered a modest room littered with flung-aside clothes, cowboy hats, caps, sandals, worn sheepskin slippers, books, and papers. Every flat surface appeared to be covered with something: empty bottles, aluminum cans. A map was spread out on a buff sofa. The small kitchen alone looked tidy, as if the tide of Towhee's disorganization fell short of overwhelming his meals. The air smelled of beer and sweat.

And there was, again, a charge.

"You want more lights on?" Towhee asked.

"Please," Pratt said, listening.

A quick visit, the charge told him. The remnant had been here briefly and gone.

He was being led on a mocking dance. So be it. He had grown more patient in two years. She would glide until she stumbled.

He turned to the caretaker. "Something's been here too and gone," he said simply.

"Has it just moved right on into the ranch? Everyone make yourself at home, I guess." He seemed tired, more irritated now than disturbed. Hogan was watching him closely.

"Just a few quick questions," Pratt said. "You're not a tidy man, but my hunch is you're a careful one."

"Sure. What makes you say so?"

"You're fastidious about your kitchen."

"Old cowboy habit."

"The dishes are all clean. There are clean pots on the stove. Your spices are all arranged. You're organized where it matters."

"You could say that."

"Can you tell me if anything seems disordered right now . . . inside your own disorder? If anything's, say, been moved?"

"Could you even tell?" Hogan asked.

"I'm not sure. Huh," Towhee said, after looking around.

"What is it?"

"Back up. Right there. On the couch. I was studying that map lying on it this morning. It's upside down now. I mean it's backside front. I know because I was looking at farm roads, and the front is where the farm roads are. I was thinking about going out to Callie's to pick up the lamb and maybe doing a hike out that way I hadn't tried before. The backside is up. That's the backcountry. Trails and UTV roads. Not where Callie's sheep are."

"May I?" Pratt asked, pointing.

"I'm sitting down," Hogan said, also sounding tired. "And parched."

"I'll get the hard lemonade you like," Towhee answered her. "This is all starting to make me feel dry inside, too."

"Thanks," Hogan said.

Pratt picked up the map and sat down on the couch next to her.

"Can you help me understand what I'm looking at?"

"It's the back country, like Winn said." She wiped one eye. Yes, she was tired, like Towhee. They weren't used to the absurdity of ghosts, of the hunt. "Some of it is multiuse land. Old drilling sites. Mountain bike trails. Jeep roads. Open country. No towns. Pretty much a lot of big hot empty. A lot of it hard to get to, if you don't know what you're doing. Hole in the Wall country."

Outlaw lands.

"Any shelter?" he continued. "Dwellings? Structures?"

"I'm thinking. I remember you said they want some kind of rooms or roost. There might be a few caves out this way . . . but what I'm mostly thinking about is this spot, right here." She stabbed the map. "That's called Needlestick. There's what's left of an old fort there. See this little icon, marking it as a structure? That's a kind of roost. Historic site, but not a place many people get to. No services, hard terrain. There was a battle there, about a hundred and fifty years ago or so. Now it's a place, honestly, people pretty much stay away from."

"Why is that?" And how far was it, he leapt ahead, from their present location?

"Winn can tell you. It was his tribe involved. It was Ute land."

Towhee was coming back with the cans. "We're not fond of the Needlestick." He dropped down in an armchair draped with a striped blanket.

"Was there"—Pratt, hesitated, out of deference, but remembering history—"a massacre at the battle there?"

"Depends on who you ask." Towhee shrugged. "So-called Outlaw Indians stole some government horses in the 1880s. Stole them *back*, actually. Everything about taking livestock was a capital offense back then, including Indians stealing their own horses, so when they were cornered the Ute band fought. They figured they were going to die anyway. Two dozen Indian bodies fell from their horses at Needlestick. A couple of white bodies, too, but they got taken away and buried. My ancestors, my brothers, they were left for the animals, along with the dead horses. Then it was turned into a fort. Though not for long. We don't go there now. I had a girlfriend once who called it bad *juju*. I call it just another Friday in the United States of America."

He drank his lemonade.

"What you," Towhee went on, "want to know, Mr. Pratt, is what's there now. If there's anything out there for the dead. Sure there is. There's probably still the ruins of the fort. There might be ghosts in it already. This desert, it likes to dry and jerky and preserve things. It tends to decide the outcome of matters, in its own way, in its own time."

Pratt waited for the caretaker to say more, as it was clear he was going to.

"I don't care much about the old history, Mr. Pratt," he said, setting his lemonade aside. "My job, as I see it, is right now. My job is to keep death back, here. With water drying up everywhere out there"—he pointed through the windows, out into the dark night—"and the river getting lower every year, it's a losing battle, as it is in most places. But they," he gestured in the direction of the main house, "don't want to hear that. They figure, you get what you can, while you can, for as long as you can, anywhere, any way you can. You want to ask me who the ghosts are, where they might be, the ones who think they can outrun the clock? Go right ahead, ask. But they're not just going, maybe, to a fort due east of here. They've got airstrips all over the world. All kinds of ghosts, Mr. Pratt, I'm starting to think. All kinds of things trying to last."

Pratt saw Hogan nod slightly, affectionately, to Towhee, as if telling him to rest now.

"For what it's worth," she said as she turned back, looking down again at the map, "Needlestick is due east of here, like Winn says. Two hours' drive from here, not because it's all that far, but because it's off-road, into a box canyon. Only one way in and out. But that's assuming you think this ghost is going to keep moving that way. Why would she do that? And why, really, leave a light on and a map to show us the way?"

"I'm pretty sure I left the light on," Towhee said, "now that I think about it."

"But the map is a mistake," Pratt said, seeing it now. "She made a mistake, leaving it backward." That reflection she'd left in the water, that salt in the bunker—that was merely to keep them busy while she was busy at something else. The random pieces of the puzzle were starting to come together. The ghost thought her taunts, her antics, would distract him—the writing at the Poston house, vandalizing the cemetery—but all she was doing was revealing her own, one-directional obsession. East. East. But if he met her where she didn't expect him; that would give him the advantage.

"You're going to want to go to the fort," Hogan made out.

"Yes. In the morning."

Pratt saw her link eyes with Towhee again. "Winn won't take you there. But I can, if you think that's where the trail leads. It's still in Masters County. My jurisdiction. You won't be able to find it by yourself, anyway. But before we get too decided on all this, Mr. Pratt, I have to ask: do you really think a ghost would be this obvious? Make this kind of mistake?"

There was nothing perfect about the dead. They trusted too much, lacked self-awareness, made *grave* errors. And an error on the part of the Finnis ghost was due. But even if it wasn't a mistake—what if it were a dare, instead?—a gambit?—a bid to draw him into a box canyon, only one way in, one way out; *come and get me*, the Finnis ghost could be saying, *come and get me if you dare, I have led you on wild goose chases before, and you have lost your way, embarrassed, defeated; let's play that game again*—he could win such an encounter. This time. In close quarters. That would be her mistake.

97

"I say we go check it out in the morning," he said to Hogan, "and come back here if there's nothing to it. Tonight, if I may make a suggestion, I think it's best we all stay together. Would it be better here," he asked Towhee, politely, since he was their host, "or back at the main house?"

"I don't sleep in that house. It's not mine. AC's out here but it's not really necessary at night. If you're fine on that couch, I say we stay put here."

"I'll be perfectly fine."

"Winn and I will sleep in the back room," Hogan said.

Towhee nodded. "I'll wake everyone up and make breakfast in the morning."

"I appreciate that," Pratt thanked him. "And just so you know—it's going to be all right," he reassured them both. "We're right on its heels. And remember they all want to be finished. In the end."

They exchanged good nights as Hogan and Towhee headed to what Pratt assumed would be a messy, in more ways than one, bedroom. What arrangements were made there he couldn't hear; it was none of his business. The feeling of a warm back to lie against must be soothing, at least, to Hogan, an insomniac like him.

He closed his eyes and listened most of the night for whispers, laughter, any sign of a ghost still lingering.

Nothing broke the gentle quiet of the hidden valley. At last, as morning neared, he slept.

9

As Winn Towhee rummaged in the kitchen, already dressed in his cowboy gear, closing cabinets and organizing coffee, granola, oranges, Pratt woke.

"OJ or coffee, Mr. Pratt?"

"Coffee, thanks."

Hogan emerged in her sheriff's uniform, immaculate. Law enforcement careful to represent order while it kept order.

"Sleep at all, Mr. Pratt?"

"Not really," he answered her. "You?"

"Nope. But some good news." She held up her phone. "Heard back from Darrion about the cemetery names."

"Your deputies," Towhee said without turning, "must be having to hold the whole county down without you."

"They're doing all right. Darrion's a good kid. He texted me the names and some info about the five graves that were vandalized. In addition to Doris Grunn, according to the records we're looking at"—she sat next to Pratt at the kitchen's bar and showed him the names—"there's this man who died in a motorcycle accident twenty years ago; this boy, a teenager who died in 2021; another man who died of old age in the 1990s; and a nurse who died in the Second World War. The grave markers are getting put back up later today, unless you have any objection. My second deputy is getting some equipment out there as quick as he can for the families that are still around."

"Yes, please help them out," Pratt said, thinking back to the jaundiced ghost of Doris Grunn and the hollowness he'd felt under the other fallen stones. The old woman had been awakened. The remaining graves had suggested a deep nothingness.

"Does the Finnis ghost," he mused aloud, "want us to think she's alone when she isn't?"

"'We dead did this.' It could still be a group haunting," Hogan said. "With her drawing flak, like a leader, and the others somewhere else."

Except: in his experience, the dead didn't follow leaders. The world of the dead was self-absorbed, segregated. Each, ultimately, tormented in its own cell.

He studied the map again; the topographic horseshoe of the box canyon called Needlestick.

"Why do they call it that?" he pointed at the spot and asked Hogan.

"There's what we call a big hoodoo right there. It's a stone formation, tall and spindly. I can't remember now what the fort was called, but definitely not Needlestick. Probably something trying to make it sound bigger than it was, like 'Fort Resilience' or 'Fort Capture' or something. Winn, you remember?"

"Fort Intrepid."

"That's it. You know, something else came to me during the night," she said, finished with breakfast and standing and adjusting her holster, "about why this Emma Finnis might be obvious about where she's headed. Some perps just love to think they're teaching you a lesson. They're the ones that leave notes, write the newspaper, post online. The standard way of thinking, and I do get it"—she acknowledged Pratt—"is they want to be caught. But what I think they want more is to look smart. Like they're lecturing us dumb rocks. Smart makes them feel powerful. That's how they get caught—not because they *want* to, but because they need to show off or they won't show up as anything at all. So my thinking is, how do you get one to show off when you want it to? How do you create that opportunity? By playing dumb. So let's go do that, Mr. Pratt. Chase her around and act like fools. A duel is only foolish if you don't bring a gun." She pointed at his wrist, then put her hat on. "What do you say?"

"Damn straight."

He drained his coffee and thanked Towhee for the hospitality. "No problem."

"And you'll be all right out here alone?"

"Same as I was before. You have enough food and water in the truck? And you do know there's no cell service out there?" To Hogan he said: "I'll be repairing fence line most of the day. How long before I call you overdue?"

She looked at Pratt.

In uncertain places, Pratt knew, slow moves were best. As in a deep shaft, once, where he'd cornered a poor miner; or when he'd found himself clinging, two years ago, feet dangling, to the edge of a lighthouse.

"Make it thirty-six hours," he said.

"Day-night-day," Hogan agreed. "I'll tell my deputies."

The canyon country grew more inhospitable as they drove. Hogan pointed out the geology was different here—the gray-green, gypsum upthrusts, barren, the blunt, sometimes ugly fins of sandstone. Higher altitude, too, meant different foliage, she said, still some rabbitbrush but less paperflower, more pinyon pine as well as juniper. They cut through outcroppings smoothed by wind and time, mesas that looked like rounded red irons, red and white-banded beehives of rock, headless tortoises of stone. The buttes grew more and more strange in form as the miles passed.

They tracked at first along a paved road with strident No Services warnings. Then Hogan veered onto dirt tracks, hard-packed, narrow. Periodically, Pratt leapt out and rolled back barbed wire cattle barriers while she drove the Bronco between bleached posts. For all the signs of range, he had seen no cattle, nothing living at all, though she assured him this part of the desert was full of life, just not the kind you saw at midday. Lizards and rabbits and snakes were in hiding; hawks, bellies full, were resting.

She cut off the AC as the Bronco worked harder over unrelenting slickrock mounds. The air with the windows rolled down came in like a stove against Pratt's cheek. Another wire barrier rose up, this one marked with a sign: NON-POTABLE SPRING, 500 FT.

As he climbed back into the truck, Hogan told him the groundwater was laced with uranium here. Or used to be, when there was water.

"We're basically absorbing low-level radiation all the time out here. Nothing to worry about. Most of it is occurring naturally. I've been sucking it up since I was a kid, and I'm fine."

"Have you ever lived outside this area?" Pratt asked. "Or traveled anywhere else?" It was hard to imagine her anywhere else.

"On vacations, sure, especially when my kids were young. We loved Disney, back when it was still open. But this is home. Nowhere else I want to be. My kids say it'll be unlivable one day, too hot. I figure, though, I'll be gone by then. You see that skinny tower in the distance, looks like a bony finger? That's the Needlestick. We're getting closer."

They descended into a dry yellow wash, then rose out of it, turned, and entered a rocky, boulder-strewn canyon.

"Almost there now. A few more turns."

"You really do know your way around this outback."

"Actually, I haven't had to come out here in a long, long while, but I sort of have a picture of the whole district in my head. We have to do rescue missions sometimes, along with our friends in the Bureau of Land Management. Or, sadly, body recovery. People get lost in the desert. Their ORVs break down. They don't see any lights or buildings or movement, and they don't know which way to walk, so they go around in circles and dehydrate and drink and eat things they shouldn't. It doesn't take long to stroke out from the heat."

"But it must feel good when you do a successful rescue." Surely not everyone perished.

"To me that's one of the better parts of the job. Saving people. That's a good day. A day worth living. Okay, we're headed into the box canyon now. There's a little flat we drive up here, and then you'll see the archeological site, what's left of Fort Intrepid."

They topped a short rise, and then Pratt could see a half-moon of stained cliffs, with a needle balanced above it. Below, a cluster of small log cabins, similar to the fort he'd seen in Huff.

Hogan stared.

"Someone's restored the fort," she said quietly, setting her brake.

"What do you mean?"

She continued looking down into the empty encampment. "It might not look like much, from here, but somebody's been at work. The roofs on those huts used to be totally cratered. They've been retimbered and shingled. And the logs chinked, too, looks like."

The still-primitive structures were centered around a blackened fire pit. It was shelter of the most basic kind, still a ruin. But the sheriff would know the difference.

"Why on earth would anyone put a fort here?" Pratt found himself asking. "It's indefensible."

"Well, there was probably water here back then, a functioning spring, would be my guess. And you get shade second half of the day. Easier to survive." She lifted up the sun visor with the picture of her children on it. "Or maybe it was more hideout than fort. The kind of place you spring an ambush from. A hole in the wall. Well. What do you say? Ready?"

They'd discussed their plan as they drove. They'd been reactive, up to now. It was time to take charge, create favorable conditions. To bait, rather than take the bait.

"Would you say," she said as they started down on foot, "these renovations remind you of what we saw at the Poston house?"

"They do."

"Last time I was here, I'm telling you, this was nothing but a ring of waist-high logs."

He bared his wrist.

"Be careful on these loose rocks."

It was oddly cool at the base of the cliffs. They landed at the focal point, the fire pit at the center of the ring of huts, black, cold, the stones around it smeared.

Pratt twisted until his eyes had taken in each cabin. Yes, someone had been busy. The hinges on the heavy, old-style doors looked fresh.

Beyond the fort, the canyon's streaked walls formed a kind of painted canvas. Lifeless. Inhuman. Except in one, startling place.

He stepped forward, mesmerized.

"Pictographs," Hogan said. "They were painted with red and black dyes, probably thousands of years ago. They're pretty damaged. Probably by the soldiers at first. See the old bullet holes? And those fresher shots there also. Later assholes. But they're still beautiful, aren't they? I'd forgotten how much was still left. I always wanted to ask Winn if maybe that started the battle in the first place, not just the stolen horses. Taking over a sacred site. I think that's what the soldiers were really here to do. And that's why they set up in what you call an indefensible spot."

Pratt drew closer to the pigments.

"Winn's tribe?"

"No. These are much older. We call them the ones who came before."

The figures on the wall were vaporous in shape, painted in small nicks. Pixilated bodies. They appeared to be made partly out of air, out of the places that weren't colored. Large, square bodies. Saucer-shaped eyes. They looked like nothing Pratt had ever seen, these elongated images that had lingered through time in the only way it was truly valid to do: as history.

Now, how can we use them? he calculated.

The Finnis remnant had watched from the tree at the Poston house. Perhaps she was clinging to the Needle itself, above them. He wouldn't wait this time for his heart to climb like mercury inside him. It was time to call out the dead, not chase it. Could the remnant be goaded into seeing these ghostly figures as an image of the dead like her? Were they not a writing on the wall, *We dead did this*, just as she had written? What if he attacked, or threatened to attack, the images himself? It was time to prod and kick and tempt and wound until the dead were stilled by their own vanity and pain and hope and longing. Be there many of them, here. Or only one.

Which was it going to be?

He heard in answer only a soft, strangled cry, and in the next moment he was gone.

Part Two

THE HUNTED

10

I've been a ghost long enough to know: Death is no less surprising than life.

Surprised I was, when I was dragged to the bottom of the sea and drowned more than a century ago.

Surprised because I thought the wild Pacific Coast was my home. I was wrong.

Surprised I was because I thought the sea would be my friend—until it set its heavy boots on my shoulders.

Astonished I was when, after I'd drowned, I discovered I wasn't yet over. I found I could crawl out of the sunlit waves, onto the sand, and with my red ribbon still in my hair and my long black skirt now strangely dry, and still wearing, underneath my shirtwaist, the slip of my soul, I stood, and greeted the day.

I found I could walk and look around, and having gone as far west, it seems, as any poor Irish servant in America can go, I was only facing east.

You begin an afterlife by keeping mum. That is how a ghost best survives. Anger, words, strong emotion of any kind, you learn, gives the ghost away. So you stay cold and let yourself feel nothing, for if you do, you are finished. If you can agree to do that, to remain invisible, then you'll last in the shadows and sun for one more day. Until one day, you ask yourself: *How is this any different, really, than how they all expected me to live?*

And what's the point of an afterlife, after all, if you don't do anything fresh with it?

I've been dead long enough that I've had to freshen my ideas about ghosting again and again—or else be truly dead. Even though I've had no one to help me see with new eyes, and nothing, no map, to show me the way, I've persisted. Even when I was alive, I always had to cut my own path. I was nothing but a poor immigrant's daughter, and an orphan, too. I lost my mother, and then my father, my entire family, when I was very young. Then I died and lost every friend I'd ever had. I hid for a hundred years in a fine mansion by the sea, while I watched those I haunted die off as well. Until one day a new family tried to buy that house, buy my hiding place, and I decided I'd had enough of both the place and the hiding. A ghost hunter named Philip Pratt was hired to come and clean me out. They call themselves that, cleaners, as though a dead servant girl might be too dirty for a house she once scrubbed spotless. I got away from Pratt, away to the mountains where at last I found others like myself. When the hunter returned, not all of us made it out. More friends left behind. Hunting is a dirty business, and a mathematical one. The living want the dead reduced to nothing. We, the dead, we want to last, to be added to those that matter, and so we're willing to do what we must, so that some of us, in the end, will be counted.

It was just a smattering of us, schoolchildren and grownups, young and old and in between, who made it out of the mountains and down onto the plains. The earth turned hard and white with salt in places. Some of us already knew what a desert was, having crossed it before.

But I—I'd never seen the like of it. So barren yet beautiful a place.

The gnarled, half leafless trees. The bones scattered, not only of once living things but of machines and towns and fenceposts and windmills, fallen on their backs, of riverbeds dried and the earth rumpled into heaps. Sometimes the view was as bare as the logged hills of my childhood, at other times stubbled with spiny bushes that would have pricked and hurt us if we felt things in the ordinary way, instead of with our sight—the sense we ghosts are left to feel and shape and stroke the remembered world with. We settled onto the dry ground and walked on, as the more open and strange it became, this land streaked with bright colors under a white-blue sky, while the sun poured down, surely hot even if the heat didn't trouble us, and so wide it spread flat on the ground like an egg cracked open. Underneath my skirt and boots the crust of the earth held what looked like tiny, hardy mosses in its grasp. There are living things here, I thought. But they're low and careful, like us. And not so many living people.

What luck.

A desert is a place where a band of ghosts can walk for mile upon mile and let ourselves be visible in our happiness and joy, without fear of being seen, and stretch our souls and limbs and hearts and marvel, while the children chase after tumbling weeds, their schoolmaster minding them—*now don't get too far ahead*—while the loving couple that joined us at the last ravine,

111

crawling out from their rusted car accident, hold hands and sigh with pleasure, and the blackbirds follow us all at a distance, high, circling, confused that we don't drop down in our tracks and make a tasty meal for them.

Our numbers have been growing. Even before the couple holding hands came upon us. A family of four joined us after telling us they'd been swept away in a flash flood when they hid in an *arroyo* from a gang of outlaws at the turn of the century before this one. They had come from Mexico and hoped for *tan mucho*—so much, the schoolmaster translated. We welcomed them and folded them in. Three strapping blond brothers came from the south, from behind a mesa. They had been carpenters in life, they said, hired to build a kind of ghost town, the buildings all furnished but empty of real people, so that a great bomb being tested could blow it to pieces. But why would anyone want to do that? the couple from the crashed automobile wanted to know. It was all about beating the enemy, one of them said, and looked around at the mounded desert in front of us, at the blue mountains in the distance, and seemed uncertain. Where was that enemy now?

For a time, a small band of Indians walked and rode at a distance beside us. They left all at once when antelope appeared with the rising sun. Only one of the young men looked back, his shoulders as bare as mine were covered, but soon kicked his pony and was gone.

Last of all an old mule runner joined us, William Briscoe. He came up to us on bow legs, his flop hat well over his brow, eyes sharp, with wide, deep wrinkles. He didn't say much at first, unless he was playing spry games with the children. Then he'd tease them, prodding:

"Git up, now. Hop along. No one likes a lazy gait."

Later he told us he'd been a slave back east; but that out here he'd been paid, once upon a time, to move things on the backs of good animals, none better. A mule is a bank you keep with you, he said.

We grew easy, all of us together, as time passed and we walked, because there was no one to threaten us as we allowed ourselves to see and feel and show our shapes freely to each other. And I suppose it was also because we had—we have—none of the quarrels the living do. There's no worry to be had over food, or water, or rest, or whose bank is the largest. None of us has any more sun on our plate than any other. None of us is stronger or weaker, of more or less value. We are all dead. We can all walk day and night and never grow tired. The sun and wind, and the whirling dust devils, move through us, and we're neither scratched nor scarred. Or, at least, no more than we had been before.

I often walked at the head of our little band, studying and thinking. This desert world that's hard for the living, it's perfect for us, I've decided. A great adventure. And perhaps when the living have drained the whole world dry, which some say they are bound to do in the end, it's we, the dead, who'll inherit it, being better suited to the climate, as it were.

There was only one problem, as we made our slow, steady way east. And it was—it is—that though the desert is wide and full of possibility, still the endless openness of it has a way of wearing upon the spirit hour after hour. It's as though we're traveling through a great arch and have yet to come to the other side, to some place of arrival and certainty. I wonder if our human souls—and maybe animals' souls, too, like the Indians' horses?—can't help it: we look, after a time, for a home, a kind of pause, a moment of shelter, some sand that is firm, some smaller space inside this great domed place in which we find ourselves. Some way, perhaps, to feel a bit of muslin curtain at our sides, at the window glass, for just a little while, to hold off all the silence of the sky and stars above in that space larger even than death itself.

I can't say precisely when we began to feel restless; but I've learned to see and read the souls around me, as best I can, and in most ways carry the burden of being the leader of this band, as I've been since the mountains. So, at one high noon, I looked back and asked the others if they felt it was time we stopped and haunted, for a spell.

They all nodded, eagerly.

Haunting is lingering to enjoy a place.

Haunting is also to leave a mark, so you know you haven't vanished.

We had just come upon a set of ruined railroad tracks, so there was good reason to believe and agree they might lead someplace useful. William Briscoe said he knew where they went, for this was the railroad that had once nearly, though never quite, put him out of work. We followed him and their buried ladder to an empty town. If there were any there still living in it, they were clinging to collapsing stoops. The storefronts were all boarded. The faces of the squat houses were cracked and peeling. Briscoe the mule runner said we should keep going to the outskirts, because, though the heart of a thing might be dried out, it's always the rind that's hardest and goes last. And so we followed him down a pitted and graveled road, and there we found a fair, solid house, its roof only beginning to sag, on a wild, quiet piece of land that surely had been left in peace for a long time. The weeds and brush seemed to be running unchecked across it, like a herd ahead of a storm.

"How," I asked Briscoe, "did you know about this place?"

"The family that owned it goes a ways back. I knew the way-backs. Rail managers."

"Where are they now?"

"It's a bust here now. They've gone looking for cover."

"And won't return."

"I've been here a while. I know an empty trough when I see it. It's good."

"Yes, it's good," the schoolmaster seconded.

I agreed. It looked a nice haunt. And we could get a bit of practice in making and freshening, together.

So many of the living think all we ghosts can manage with our spirits is to moan and complain and drag noisy chains. But we're nothing like that. Not most of us. We're . . . seekers. We're lookers and watchers and doers, even if many of us don't know, yet, fully, all that it is we can do. We do, and make do, with what we come across.

We borrow from the living when they aren't looking. Some-times the living will pass a playground, a deserted park, and notice one leather seat from a children's swing set is missing, the chains hanging loose, the long arms dangling with nothing to cradle. They don't know we've passed by, too, and had need of some sturdy material. After a great storm, the living will remark how strange it is that wind has ravaged one house but left the one beside it untouched entirely—and never imagine it was a ghost that wanted that pair of wooden shutters, a few good slats from the fence. A dog suddenly can't find her favorite toy, though she looks every-where for it. The wheeled grocery basket rolls far from its shop. A tool that should have been in the garage isn't there anymore. While down the street, the yard around an abandoned house looks more tended than it did a week ago. Surely whoever owns the lot had the weeds cut, hoping to entice new owners?

The three blond carpenter brothers stood beside Briscoe and the schoolmaster and me, and together we studied the simple house at the edge of the simple, empty town the mule runner had led us to.

"How did you know any of this was here?" I asked him.

"They named the town after me, after I died."

What a surprising thing to hear. The living don't generally honor ghosts. We're the weeds they want to keep down.

"I wasn't a ghost, so far as they knew."

"So why did they do it, Mr. Briscoe? Name the town after you?"

"Guess it's easier to make a person a place than ask about the person."

He doesn't like to talk much about his life and death, other than about his beloved mules. His mules, he said, had once been his family.

"Two stories we'll build for all of us," the carpenter brothers announced.

The children grew excited. They bounced and floated, their pinafores whistling and scuffed boots chirring like grasshoppers in the sun. One of the younger ones asked, "Might we have a banister to slide down?"

"If you are good, and you help," the schoolmaster said.

The parents whose family drowned in the flood looked around carefully for any dry wash that might suddenly fill. There was none.

The loving couple from the car crash said that though this wasn't the heaven they dreamed of, it would be all right to stop for a while.

The brothers were already pointing, and making plans.

There is no heaven, I thought. There's only waiting for what's owed you, for fairness, or asking for it, or building it, or planning on going forever without it.

We stood among the sage and pieces of tar and shingle blown from the sagging roof, and I thought I should say something, since they were again all looking at me. It's important, I've learned, to keep a company happy and moving in the right direction . . . but then, I'm also fond of getting my own way, and making things go as I want them to.

For my name is Emma Rose Finnis, and like all Finnises, I'm Irish born and Irish stubborn, raised to be staunch in the face of wounds.

And I want to stop here for a while and play.

"Would we all like to start tonight?" I ask them.

The carpenters throw their caps in the air for an answer, and the older children make a game of catching them on their own, bare heads.

The most surprising thing, being dead, is that you can still laugh.

Even while you look over your shoulder and wonder if the hunter is still after you.

11

It's out in front of the house that I'm standing, admiring how the blond brothers have cut the peaked, finished roof against the sky, with the abandoned tools they found all around the town, sawing and hammering and nailing in the way of ghosts by seeing and remembering what it is to hold a thing you love and then lifting it with all that love and memory and reaching—it's a blue sky above us again, high over the roof, like the sea if you could hold it there and not drown—when I first hear, and then see the workaday truck and the living man coming in a plume of dust toward us.

Such pleasant days we have had here. Each of us making a part of the house in some way we wanted it.

And now this.

The others have heard the sound, too. The women on the porch tell the children to stop their games and go cold and invisible. All of the men step forward, disappearing, only the ripple of their coldness inside the heat of the day throwing off tiny shimmers like the glints from the nails left on the ground.

They stand shoulder to shoulder, at the property gate.

If a ghost doesn't want you to enter a place, she will find a way to tell you.

So peaceful it's been, for so many days now, haunting this house. So many ideas we've had for how to remake it, each one of us saying what we would like, so that each might feel at home in it, for a little while. It isn't so much a house, the schoolmaster had said to me, as it is a meeting place.

We'd only just begun finishing the window frames with scrolls and fancifulness. No one had stopped to trouble us. No one cares, one way or the other, if a thing improves if the bettered thing holds no meaning for them, if they don't want it. It's only when someone starts to want the abandoned thing you've bettered with love that all the jealousy starts.

"I'm all for stuffing him under the cattle guard if need be," the oldest carpenter brother whispers.

"Give him a chance," William Briscoe says. "Let's see what else we can do."

"I don't like to cage a man any more than anyone else," the youngest brother says. "Unless it's necessary."

"And it's always someone, somewhere," the old mule runner whispers, "who'll think it's necessary."

The intruder has halted his truck before the gate and is hopping down from it. He's a smallish sort of man, a little stooped, as though he's been looking at the dry ground more than he's been noticing the ocean of the sky.

We can allow him a moment to make up his own mind.

A moment. That's all.

He walks slowly, raising his eyes to look at the house. His bearded jaw hangs a little, amazed at what he sees. He straightens a bit, feeling at something behind him, a gun sagging in his back pocket. His look grows more certain, stiff, the lifted chin of a dog in front of a dry bone.

Soon he'll be close enough to feel our cold.

Sometimes the living, meeting us this way, turn away, understanding and wanting nothing more to do with dead marrow.

You go on now, I think. *Leave us be.*

But his is the look, I see, of a man lost in the wilderness who won't admit it. He thrusts his boot forward. Our wall of men throws him back. He staggers, like a drunk, balancing on one leg, pitifully.

Then he's foolish enough to try again.

The children have had enough and giggle.

I turn to scold them, but they say, plaintive:

He looks so funny now, Miss. Doesn't he?

But every frightened soul looks foolish, and we must be careful now, I tell them, and see what he does next.

The poor man, understanding, blinks unhappily. His shoulders droop. His eyes go hollow and sad.

Ah, so this is a man who's seen death up close, and not so long ago.

Let us give him a moment more.

A man, knowing death, is sometimes more charitable around it.

He turns away all at once, muttering. Perhaps he's had enough. It's only when we see the anger curling back into his body, the gun in his pocket glinting, the way he glares back at the house for a moment, then turns again, his boots pumping, leaping back into his truck, that we know that our little time in this house will soon, when his bitterness returns to him, be at an end.

"How long would you say we have," Briscoe asks me, "by the look of that?"

"I suppose we can let the children romp for a little while longer. He'll be alone out here. There's no one quick at hand."

"True. But we should be ready."

"Yes."

Our wall of spirits comes apart. The children, their laughter quieted, grow solemn. Peace has been stripped from the air. Any encounter with the living can do that, and quickly. Seeing, and even more, touching, pushing against a live body—it feels like pressing your hand against a cushion that sinks into you rather than giving way. It brings back all the knowing and lusting, because no matter how hard you try not to remember, when you see a living body like that again, up close, when you see and feel it, living, remembered skin, and see what life there is in it, such glowing, even in the angry, gray-stubbled skin of a tired, old man—it all comes back to you, the memory of sweat and heat and shivering, the taste of your own tongue, swallowing, the feeling of biting wind and stinging salt on your neck—and suddenly, there it is, you're a proud young girl again, standing alone above a spray-blasted cove, freezing around the ears yet hot at the chest under a thick woolen sweater. In your pockets your fingers are red furnaces, thick with callus but cold, just come from scrubbing a floor, along with another servant girl. On her knees, sweating, she'd asked you, *What is it you want most in all the world, Emma Rose?* And hungry orphan lass that I was, I'd answered, I want not to be alone all my life, and I also want to be free. And she'd stopped and thrown her brush in the bucket and knitted her damp hand into mine, and we'd vowed that we would be free, and though life had cast us in a hard place, we would be both loved and free, somehow. We would find a way. We would.

Yet now as I flit back into this high-roofed house made out of our memories and the bones of the desert, I see each one among

121

us, though trying to take comfort in what is still loved, is not yet free. The Mexican family carried away by the flood sits in their corner, their heads bowed, softly praying. The loving couple that crawled from the Edsel automobile have floated to the rafters and roosted there like turtledoves, neck on neck. The schoolmaster and his students sit on the unfinished stairs and are making a game of sums out of the half-spindled rail. We were once quite close, the schoolroom ghosts and I, but as time has gone by, they've retreated into each other, recovered their own little family. The carpenter brothers stand in front of the unlit hearth, brooding, for when will they build a shelter that won't be blasted, blown away?

Briscoe comes to the window where I stand guard ahead of the night. Like me he has no one with him. He had, he told me, died long ago, on a moonlit night, taking the wrong step at the edge of a canyon. No one troubled to find out why he had disappeared. People leave the desert all the time, he said. No one asks where you've gone. They named the town Briscoe because he was the first man who wasn't an Indian to survive there. He was a pinhole on a map. He was a time, a place.

"Penny for your thoughts," he says to me now.

"Today was unlucky."

"It was. Poor man."

"We'll be a splinter under his skin now," I say. Once the living get the feel of us, they have to work us out, one way or the other. If only more of them understood the deep woods we come from, and where they're bound, too.

"The children won't be happy to leave," I say.

"I know."

"We were just getting settled."

"Might take a while finding the right spot for a longer spell. Mind you, it's not perfect here. We never meant to stay."

"No." But something so brief couldn't be called a proper haunting. "Maybe farther east."

"Could be."

"How far will you go with us? This is your country."

"Wouldn't call it that. Haven't decided how far. How far will you?"

I've always fancied travel. I never went anyplace until I died. I feel the wanderlust coming back to me that's in me all the time. We never meant to stay. Not here. Maybe somewhere else.

"I don't mind moving," I say.

"That's because moving's a magical thing. Me, I used to love moving around on the back of a mule. Riding along, the feel of that spine bobbing, my spine, too. It's like life. Especially if you're not doing it alone."

Yes. If you're not alone in the air, bobbing up and down.

As I knew I would be again, as soon as Briscoe wandered away.

12

We all glided together at dawn. The light in the east was turning pink, then yellow, like a rose, brightening. The flat mountains in the distance looked blue and bruised with the sunrise hitting behind them.

Out that-a-way, Briscoe had explained to me, was a place called Castle Mesa. Not much to speak of, but a good rendezvous point. There would be a cemetery. It would be easy for me to find, butted up against the red mesa.

"Sure you want to stay behind?" he asks me again.

I'd decided during the long night that someone should wait to see if we hadn't needed to run away at all. Maybe the intruder wanted to think no more of us. It was more likely someone would be sent. But it would be good to know about that, too.

"We have to know who's coming," I say, "and get the children out of the way." The schoolmaster's pupils were already moping about having to leave the house, but the promise of a cemetery had cheered them. Boneyards make them feel alive. *Those people are truly dead*, the little ones will point at the headstones, earnestly. *We're not truly!* They liked to dance and play on the graves and feel themselves silly and giddy, not burned corpses.

Me, I'd also been feeling a pressure coming on, since the wee hours of the morning. As though something were coming upon me from behind. Spend enough time running from what wants to get close to you, and you'll start to feel a strange, connecting fiber. They say love is like that. That you can feel a person, even when they aren't near.

"I've started to feel the hunters before I see them," I tell Briscoe.

"Don't let anyone feel you or see you, Emma Rose."

"I won't." I'm careful. A good, practiced ghost.

Remnants, they call us now. Leftover bits. Pieces of nothing. The living, they're always calling us by some new name, as if it excites them to keep us fresh that way. But what I say is, they don't want to admit what they truly think of us, so they come up with new words when the old ones—*hant, specter, spook, pest*—start to sound too naked on the tongue.

The hunters call themselves *cleaners* or *removers*. But they're all shameful. Some are crueller, maybe, than others. No matter. What they all seek is a world without us.

I turn to Briscoe. "You'll get everyone there safely."

"It's what I do."

"I'm staying," I turn and say again to them all, "until I know what's behind us, and if it's anything, throw it off our path. If I haven't come to you after a day . . . well . . ."

"We'll wait," the schoolmaster says, certainly.

Briscoe touches his flop hat as he turns his bow legs to the east. "We'll git along now."

125

They move away from me, flowing, walking clear and straight and beautiful, like water pouring over ruts and grasses, a river free of its bank. Strange that I've never thought to be proud of being a ghost. Yet I am. I don't know why it is that some souls survive and manage to flow in this way and others can't. I only know that those who manage it are brave, in our way.

A haunted house, when the ghosts all leave, feels like a kettle with the lid left off. There's still some steam, but it's melting into the curtains and floorboards.

It was a tall place we built. I look up, admiring. The hem of my skirt glides along the banister rail. How the children had loved to slide down it. The scavenged rafters are sturdy above me—the carpenter brothers had so been happy to find the wood. Such a shame, they said, to see good timber going to waste. Some things just have to do what they're meant to do. You don't see an elephant's legs lying by the side of a road. They're meant to bear weight.

And then we want to leave our mark, too, I know. It's all we can do.

Wherever we've been, but especially in a haunted house, hunters, if they come, can pick up the trail of our passing. If we haven't stayed cold and invisible at every moment—if we feel a spark, our own fire—we leave a sign. There's no getting around it.

It would be safer, of course, to be blank always. But no one wants that.

The best thing, I think, as I travel up and down the house, is to try and think as hunters do and fool them with their own eagerness. Most want to earn their money easily and make a quick killing—as they say. Most of them are fond of telling themselves, and others, that ghosts yearn for sleep, and that we walk weary through our afterlives, tied to a place, tired and sick of it after a while—as if a fledged bird were forever leashed to her nest. They don't imagine—or most don't, in any case—that we might be able, when the time is right, to leave by the very door they came in by. They can't imagine we have free wills. They see a shadow, rub their hands, fire their weapons and say a house is safe. Some ghosts, it's true, won't be parted from their haunts. But there's no cause to believe every soul is alike in death any more than we are alike in life. There are those who will try to make the shoe fit. And others of us who've never yet found the size of a thing that's right for us.

I've come to stand in front of the hearth, and the wooden mantel the brothers have so proudly made above it; and it seems to me that if it is indeed the pressure of a hunter I feel at my back, coming, from somewhere, this way, my way—and if hunters can always find the trail where feeling ghosts have been—then why shouldn't we claim it, proudly? Why do we always pretend, hunter and hunted, that we don't know exactly what game we're playing?

We're not invisible to each other, I think, not really.

I don't show myself plainly to the living because you think I have no right to be seen. While the living, you imagine you're unseen by me, because you can't see me watching you.

"And in that case neither of us is free," I say to the pretty shelf and the whitewashed board behind it.

The brothers have left a pot of black paint, a color they'd meant to spread on the window frames. I see and dip my finger into it, and oh, it feels like wet earth sinking into the root of me, and isn't it as sweet as child's play.

We dead did this.

I step back from my lettering. A pretty hand was a thing I learned in school, before life tossed me out of schoolrooms to serve those who write daintily on papers with their names already stamped at the top in gold. I've done something now, I see. Not only to tease the hunters. For if any other ghosts should pass this way, crossing this desert, and think to stop here, at this house with its turned posts and fine gables, they might come in and see my words, and then they'll know:

I am not alone. I'm not nothing. We are not nothing. Look what we can do. Look how fanciful we are, how queer and strong and brave and clever. Who made this house out of odds and ends. Out of what others had thought there was no use for. Remnants.

When night comes, the pressing feeling behind me grows stronger. Somewhere, some decision has been made for me, the way it always seems to be for every one of us who doesn't write with gold.

I float to the ceiling and gaze out a high window. Were anyone outside the house, now, they would see my glowing shape. My dark hair. My cleft Finnis chin. My memory of myself. At any moment I can go cold so that I disappear. What I don't like is feeling I should do this even when I'm alone. How is it now that the world makes some of us feel like we're hiding, even when no one's looking?

The very idea makes my soul burn so brightly I shine like a lighthouse into the empty night, my hands tightening with such anger I might shove any living person who came to this door into a hole as big as the sea and care nothing at all while doing it. So much anger and injustice I feel, even now. So wrong it was that I died so young, all alone, with no one to miss me, sinking tangled under the waves with my hair wrapped around my neck and my skirt floating up to cover my face as I fought, fought, fought so hard *not to breathe*.

The nights are long when you're dead. A ghost doesn't sleep or dream. But sometimes, dull in the darkness, I do fade away, turn cold and invisible and go away from myself, wandering, hunting in a kind of blankness. The thing I most wish I could find in this great wide nothingness and see, and that even a ghost can't, is the future. If I could just see what was going to happen next, then I wouldn't be a soul hunted. Hunting needs a kind of blindness, from moment to moment. The truth for all of us, living and dead, is that we can't see what's coming. If we could, I suppose we wouldn't end up in the holes we do.

13

Philip Pratt, facedown in darkness, chest, stomach, knees pressed against what felt like warm, sliding earth, struggled, and found he couldn't see.

His head was enclosed in a sheath.

I can't move my hands, he realized. *I can't breathe. I can't see. What's happening?*

This is my turn. The next thought came. *This is death.*

So narrow. So suffocating.

His lungs fought against the earth. Or tried. His legs kicked. His heart struck like a fist against a wall, as sweat rimed his neck below the ears. Next he would grow cold, that was what would happen, the light would go out, as he'd seen it go out of kind eyes as she'd lain folded over her own lap, *but not face down, at least not face down,* Pratt thought as he wheeled on his back and understood from the sudden, searing pain that he'd been struck on the back of his head, it wasn't sweat but likely blood on his neck, though his hands, tied behind him, couldn't reach up to be certain. He lay still and could make out vague voices whispering.

Mocking. The distant, whispering voices seemed to be mocking him.

Who else was with him in this darkness?

Was he alone?

At night?

What would be his last memory, before he joined, as he must by law and rights, the sleeping dead?

He winced with pain. A thousand needles at the back of his skull. That was it. The Needlestick. Above. He had been standing below it, looking at images on a wall. Painted bodies with great round eyes. He'd heard a cry. He hadn't been alone, then. Hogan had been with him. Had she fallen, too? It had happened before. A bystander taken down by his work.

Everything, it seemed, would be swallowed by the work, in the end. Years, decades, a lifetime, the work had taken and taken and he had given and given to it, shedding family, friends, companionship, all to fight the best fight, the battle against what wants to ensnare and encircle what is bright, real life, and choke it all with regret and memory. That was why so few, whether they believed in God or Allah or pagan stones or like him nothing at all, complained when a ghost hunter arrived to burn away unreal, greedy hands. Life stalked by death would never be life. It would be the future taken hostage.

Long ago an old man had grabbed the sheets away from him at night, hoping to cover up a nakedness, his weakness, his wizened body, his shriveled genitals, his stooped shoulders and angry, quivering chin, with a boy's living warmth and cover.

I fought back then, and I'll fight now, Pratt willed himself. *Fight. Fight.*

He thrashed and writhed.

It was like trying to be born again, to crawl out of a place small and tight.

14

I have some of the Irish darkness in me. And some Finnis hard-
ness, too.

But I've an Irish optimism as well.

In daylight, when I've come back from my not-sleep, from my
blank wanderings, and there's still no sign of any hunters coming
to the house, the pressing feeling weighing on me, like a chain
hanging down my back, begins to grow lighter—as though some
slack's been let into it.

Perhaps I'd been wrong about our foes coming. It could be. A
hunch can turn out to be nothing at all. Everyone makes mistakes.
No one's more perfect in death than in life. Life, and even afterlife,
can be lucky, after all.

Still, better to walk around the yard, I decide, with my guard
up and my skirt fluttering. It's just past midday as the air begins
to cloud. Not the sky, but the road below it. I hear the churning
before I see it. I rise a little off the ground, and spy two bright
glints, two flashing roofs above silver wheels driving with some

distance between them, as though one is leading and the other following without coming too close to the dirty wake.

So much for luck, then.

I flit back inside and hover at a window and turn as cold as a frozen tap.

They stop outside the cattle grate. Dusty doors open. The first figure that stretches a leg out is a short, strong-looking woman, brown from her hat to her hair to the points of her boots. I don't know her, though it seems somehow I should.

The second is— All the slack in the air vanishes. A length of tailored pantleg stretches out and finds the ground.

One minute, your future isn't here. And then it is.

It's Philip Pratt.

Never, never, never cry out in frustration and knowing and surprise and no surprise at all. For that's what he wants, this predator, this stalker who lives for nothing more than to hear a ghost's cry before he lashes out at it and drowns it.

My foe straightens and squints at the house. He follows the woman forward. He walks no more with a limp, I see. I suppose he's shaken me off like mud.

I stay numb at the window, perfectly still. The woman weaves comfortably between the brush and sage, she's so easy in her own skin, and with the land. Pratt is slower and more careful and leaner than when I saw him last, and he's lost some of his color. I've had my hands in dishwater with better tint.

But I can't laugh at him. I can take no chances. He wears on his wrist a circlet so evil they've welded it to him so that he must carry the burden night and day.

They open the door and come inside the airy space of the house. I rise cold up into the rafters, watching. The short woman takes off her hat. She's an officer of some kind, and telling Pratt she's been here before. I don't understand. I've never seen her. Had she come while I was away in my blankness?

"I assume all this inside was salvaged, too," she's saying, pointing at the banister rail, the smooth spindles. "Or stolen, according to Tom. But over here is what you'll really want to see. Check this out."

They cross to the mantelpiece with my painted writing above it.

"Well now," Pratt says. He lifts a lean hand, stroking the black against the white.

We dead did this.

My little stand, for all of us.

His face is white and open all at once, like a mist I can see through. He's keen but uncaring.

The woman officer says earnestly, watching him, "*We.* That's why I thought: group haunting. With this and what Tom told me about the voices. But please tell me I'm wrong. I'd like to be. Or I'd like to think they're gone. We've never had a bunch of them all at once around here. Just loners, now and then. And not for a long while now, not since people left town. I've never seen anything like this. Have you?"

We've exchanged messages before, Pratt and I, haven't we? Whole books, in a way, have passed between us. Yet he still thinks no more of ghosts than he does of moths smashed against a glass. He's making his notes and taking his photographs. We're just jots in his ledger. We're all one sum to him.

But he doesn't know yet who he's found, I think. *How can he?*

For why would *she* be out here, far away in the desert, so far from where she started? The ghost that keeps always ahead of him. No matter how close we've come.

The woman, meanwhile, is watching Pratt closely. When his eyes are on her, her face is steady and helpful. When he looks away, her gaze turns hard and measuring. *Well now, here's someone*, I think, *ready to kill the canary if she needs the meat.*

"Let me," Pratt tells her, "take a few readings around this room."

I follow high and cold above the hunter. Tall ceilings make it harder for the living, even his kind, to sense us, so we favor and look for height. He strokes the walls and the window sills. The salvaged curtains the women brought. He's certainly picking up the charge we've left behind. He lifts his hand to his chest in that evil way he does, as if his heart were a trap laid for someone else.

All at once he stops and peers out the front windows, as though he's forgotten something somewhere behind him, tugging. Then he turns, quickly, as though whatever it was has stung him and he wishes he hadn't looked after all.

So, Mr. Pratt's been dragging some chain behind him? I wonder whose name is on it.

"There have been ghosts here. Or perhaps one pretending to be more than one. Pretending to have done all this."

"Pretending to have done all what?"

"The renovations. Laying claim to something belonging to the living."

"So you don't think a ghost or ghosts 'did' this?"

"There is no ghost," he says, "that can design, plan, build on this scale."

Why does he keep underestimating me, us? Does he imagine because we're dead we're lazy and have no work we like?

He's so certain of himself. Look at him. Still. It's almost a thing to be envied. His face has lost none of its conviction, even though there's the little matter of my having escaped him, twice. His words come so smoothly, causing him no trouble.

He says, "They simply don't have the capacity for it. They don't have the mind for it, the way we do. Their forte is small tricks. They play games, like children. And destroy things. Because they can't make their way out of what has happened to them. They don't plot on a grand scale. So something else has been at work here. Someone could have built this and then left it, or been chased off, as you suggest. Or else someone could have been assisting this haunting. Aiding and abetting it."

He can't imagine we can organize ourselves, help each other.

"In any case, a ghost or ghosts has definitely been here." He nods, pleased.

The hunter loving his hunt.

"But are any here right now?" The woman touches her hip. She carries a gun there. Her badge says she's a sheriff. It must make her feel safe.

"No. I don't feel anything at all. Not in this room. Let's keep going."

She points again at my writing on the wall. "But what about that? What does it mean?"

What, really now, could be clearer, I ask you? Shall I paint a picture? Haven't I done it?

"I don't know yet," Pratt says. "It could be a trick. Or a taunt."

"You think so?" The woman frowns, sharp. "To me it feels more like . . . pride. Like, 'look what we did.' That cursive's like something you'd see on a plaque. Or a marker. But that's just my gut. Whatever you say I'll go with. There's another room, this way."

He's got himself a smarter one this time, Pratt does. But what happens to all of them, in the end? Sadness. While he keeps on going.

The kitchen's too small a space for me to follow them into. I slip out through a crack under the window and perch outside, listening from a twisted gray tree. It's clear, as they move back and forth in front of the window, that Pratt's excited by our haunting. He wants to know all about Briscoe's harness, a piece of the mule runner's life. It's an odd thing about possessions from our former days—they're more strange than useful. What are we supposed to do with reins we don't need? We see such things and they're fond as a photograph, that's all. Briscoe didn't mind having it nearby. But he hadn't mourned to leave it, either.

"There are no bedrooms in this house," I hear Pratt saying through the window. "Nor does there seem to be any intent to build any. There are no bathrooms. There's nothing to sit on in this kitchen, dine on, eat with. There are no living comforts here. It's only the dead who need no rest, no bath, no nourishment."

He's a smart one, too. I've never denied it. A man who can be tricked now and then. But not every time.

That's my worry.

It isn't only me, now, that I have to worry about. There are all the others. I feel a shackle, a weight different than before. We've been careful, all of us—but we're none of us perfect. The children, especially, have made mistakes as they did when they laughed at the man who came to this house and gave away our hiding place. We might be leaving too many signs too close together, cutting a deeper rut than we should through this dry place.

The door at the rear of the house opens. Pratt and the sheriff come into the white light. I should go now, tell the others, we must push farther on.

Only something there is in me, all at once, that balks at running.

Running yet again.

Why is it that I must race all the time, as if *I* have no time? When mine's the soul who has all the time there is in the world? When time is all the payment any ghost has ever received for losing flesh, blood, and bone? I've had my strong body and my youth taken away from me. And with no feet, I still must scamper?

I'm sick, sick, sick of it, I tell you. I want to do more than write on a wall and run away to hide in a tree. Let the birds have the trees. I lift my chin to the sky and whistle. The magpies like the game of it. They land all around me. Perhaps they like my coldness, too, this midday. I rise, leaving them, and look toward where Briscoe has told me he and the others are waiting for me. I must go to them and tell them we must find a way to stop and stay.

The last I see of Pratt he's running toward the tree, scattering the magpies. He's stumbling. Falling. I watch him land in the dirt. He's seen something then. Let him. He lifts his face from the earth. I could smile but I don't, because when you see a thing you badly want, like a man you hate fallen down so that he knows what it feels like to be that way, it's like looking into a mirror that's already been your own.

Pratt doesn't understand, yet. The fear of being nothing. Not yet. Not really. Nor has he learned you don't manage your fear by raising your hand and pointing a weapon at it and blasting away. There's always more fear behind the last one. All you can do is kick faster than the fear can chase you, and climb toward the light.

I don't often fly. We're not creatures of air. The birds are. We're souls of the earth, and so flight feels like distance and losing something, somehow, especially when we must stay cold at the same time so as not to be seen as we flee. Strange, that when you travel fast, you feel the heaviest. Somehow the soul knows it isn't in command, and drags.

I see a cluster of houses that look little better than the abandoned homesteads of Briscoe. Then the cemetery below, away from the roofs with tires on top of them, as if they could be blown away at any moment.

The graveyard is a yellow patch in the shadow of a red cliff, its own tall headstone.

The children are climbing on the monuments and obelisks. The others sense me and turn.

It means something, truly, to see the happiness in their faces.

"You're safe. And," Briscoe says, smartly, "you've found out something."

"Yes."

I tell them a hunter has indeed come—*but I can't bring myself to say his name, not yet*, I think. It will make for harsh memories for some.

"Just one hunter," I say, "and the local constable, helping him out. He knows the house was visited, though he doesn't think ghosts can have built it." I smile as I say this, to put the others at ease. The children go on playing on the tall gravestones.

The carpenter brothers seem piqued by Pratt's lack of faith in their skill.

"Given what you've seen, Emma," the schoolmaster says, "what do you think will happen next?"

"He's like all of them," I say to everyone. "He's a vulture, and now he's got the whiff of us, he won't stop until he's sitting on top of us."

"That won't happen," one brother says.

"Because we'll keep moving," says another.

We can move, I think. But I want to stop fleeing.

"Or we could do something we haven't before," I say. "Find a good place and dig in. Take a stand. For the little ones." I point at the children. "For ourselves."

For a moment their faces are all as blank as sheets.

Then their voices chime in.

"That won't work!"

"They'll put us down."

"Once they know where we are, we're finished."

"Or take the place itself down. Brick by brick."

"*Es imposible. En serio.*"

"That's if we could even"—the woman from the car accident shakes her head—"find a place that would make everyone happy. I'd want a heaven. Nothing less. If I can't have it, I'd rather keep moving."

A great silence now.

"Well, what would heaven look like?" I ask.

"It would be easy," says one.

"And beautiful," says another.

"And peaceful."

"I wouldn't mind a garden."

"Room to move."

"Buildings to manage."

"Safe. Very safe."

"Out of the way."

"Room for the children."

"A place for them to be loud and happy."

"*Un santuario.*"

"Happens I like water," Briscoe says. "The pleasing sound of water."

They've all stepped forward, closer together, wondering.

We fall silent.

The children are giddy and playful, growing louder as they hop and crawl on the headstones, impatient in the way they often are when we're paying no attention to them. The schoolmaster and others turn to soothe them.

Briscoe says to me, in a low voice, "Happens there is such a place."

"I know it." I've seen them in my life. Beautiful places where the happy and comfortable live, with copper gutters and a kitchen the size of a dance hall and a marble fireplace in every room.

"I mean fairly close by. Good sort of place. Not exactly to my taste. I'm partial to what's wilder. But if I told you about it, where it is—what would you do?"

The mule runner is asking me: will it matter? Whatever we can find can be found out, too.

That's the trouble, isn't it? If you found a heaven, how would you keep it? How far would you be willing to go?

Plenty far, maybe.

"I'd first have to see it for myself," I say.

142

"But not risk everyone all at once," he says, nodding. "It's not unguarded, there's someone there. One person only, but well . . . You could go, I reckon. Do the reconnaissance." A man's fine word. Briscoe had been in a war. "Report back."

"And the others?"

"We won't stay here. I'll get them somewhere. Ask them to wait. We could make camp on that tableland, up there." He lifts his wrinkled eyes toward the cliff. "Can see everything coming on you from that high. Let's say you get to Pastor Valley—what the place is called—and you find it fit. What then?"

"Then we make the hunter come." That would be the trick.

"But why on earth," he stares at me from under his hat, "would we want that, Emma Rose?"

"To make it safe for us."

I can see it all at once. We make him think we were there but have passed through, have moved on. As we did from the last house. As we've always done.

"And then send him to . . . another destination." It could be managed. Maybe.

But this time it would need to be different. A permanent direction.

"His name is Philip Pratt, Mr. Briscoe. He's seen me before. He won't want me to get away from him again. And I must let him think I fear seeing him, too." In truth, I still do. But I'm so weary of this weight and dread, so weary and sick of being hunted, I'll take my chances. "I need to send him on a search for me. So that," I say, "he'll never think to turn around and go where I've already been. Because I'll lead him on." He must taste blood and want to hound me. And with luck, when he

143

goes, when I'm done with him, this desert will be safe for the rest of us.

"You mean you're gonna turn yourself into a salt lick, girl. That's what you're saying."

"There's still plenty of salt in me."

His old face is worried.

"So this hunter, how'd he find you here?"

"I don't know. An accident?" Though I don't believe there are such things. Chance is just what you call a partner you didn't know you'd dance with.

"Pratt," Briscoe says, "is his name?"

"Yes. Philip Pratt."

"Pratt?" the schoolmaster says turning, shocked.

I've spoken too loudly. Before preparing anyone for—

It's too late. The schoolchildren have heard the name. They wail and swear. Their outlines grow hotter, bright as fire, they shake with mourning and rage, they pull, they tug, fiercely, at the headstones they've perched on, heaving them to and fro, rocking them like cribs they've been left forlorn in.

"No, Willie!" the schoolmaster calls. "Addie! Jack! No! Be still!"

The first tall stone falls. Then another. And another. Each making a thick sound like a clogged bell hitting the earth as the children leap away.

The smallest among them, Willie, runs to hide behind his teacher.

"Mr. Longhurst!" he whimpers. "Look!"

Out of the tiniest crack in the soil, a pale finger reaches up and feels for some firmness.

15

My Irish Catholic lumberjack father used to say: there are many ways to rise.

I rose from the sea.

The children rose from ashes.

Others among us dug out from under heavy mud.

I've seen ghosts trying to break free of earth—nightcrawlers, they're called—tangled in the ground, twisting and turning.

Some of us aren't allowed to break free for some reason. Others are.

A single finger claws out of the ground, feeling around it for anything solid, not feeling the way it used to. Having to understand. It becomes a curled hand.

"There, over there, too!" the schoolmaster, with the children behind him, shouts as he points to another grave.

Another pair of hands pushes the dry earth aside, groping.

Beside it, another.

Not every stone the children threw down is raising a spirit. I count only three.

To rise is a lonely thing, and frightening. Your legs underneath you feel as weak as broken stems. Your eyes feel peeled, and your skin seems sloughed away, and your heart feels naked and floating, like a cut bud in a glass.

The schoolmaster keeps his pupils back behind him. The others hold still. It's hard, this moment, seeing a resurrection. When you see another ghost, all your own dying comes back to you, and all your life before it. It's like looking into a glass, bright and terrible. Surely, this is not what happened to me. Surely, that's not what I've become. It's not how I feel. Not so alone and stripped. Am I?

Only the wife who died in the car accident, finding comfort in her husband's eyes, steps forward in her creased pants.

"Don't be afraid," she says, smiling at the newcomers. "We're friends, here. We're just like you. Welcome. What's happened? How did you wake up?"

She means: *We all rose soon after our hearts stopped. But not you. How have you done it?*

I have never seen the like before.

A young, thin man, not much more than a boy, finds his dead boy's voice.

"I—I was in a hospital," he says, wide-eyed. "They said my case was too far gone. That was it. Then someone threw my name down on top of me, just now. It hit me, hard. My own name. So big and heavy. I had to get up."

"Does he mean his headstone?" the schoolmaster wonders.

"It was the same for me." A middle-aged woman steps away from her plot, stroking her green uniform, as if from habit. "I went for the war effort. They needed nurses. I heard the shell. I never felt it land. Till now. Something landed right on top of me. But I managed to get out from under this time."

There is one more—an old woman, so wan and shrinking she seems to be trying to hide from us. I come closer to her. She's unhappy. She seems to need some encouragement.

"I want no part of you," she croaks at us.

"It's all right," I tell her, kindly.

"It isn't. I want no part of this, I tell you."

"I understand. You don't have to come with us. But you can, if you wish. We're friends."

I step to one side, so she can see the boy and the nurse joining our band, coming to stand with us, nodding and shaking our hands.

"You're not my friends." The old woman lowers her head, looking down at her yellowed shins. "I don't know you. I had him. My Tom. And he's not here. I won't go with you. It isn't right. It isn't the law. But that doesn't matter. I won't go."

I've never seen a soul, granted a chance, not take it. I have seen terrible ghosts. As evil as any living soul can be. Others as sweet as the children. I know there's no reason we should all be friends, nor ought we necessarily trust another soul, just because she's been fed through the same dark ringer. It would be a fine thing if death would bring us all together, but it doesn't, and it's because of the anger, the knowing, the feeling that you'd murder the world, if you could, for what it's done to you, for what it's taken from you. Why the children threw the stones over when they heard Pratt named. Because he wants us to lose the world all over again.

This woman. She doesn't want to be moved.

The others are waiting.

"Leave me alone," she says.

"Are you sure you won't come with us?" I ask.

"He's not here. He loved me. We said goodbye. I let him go. I loved him. But that's what you have to do. Not be a burden, afterward."

I feel a flicker of anger. Why is it a woman will forever fret over being burdensome? When it's she who's had so much to lift and carry?

But it isn't really that, Emma Rose, is it? I think. *It's that she had someone to say goodbye to. And who said goodbye to her.*

Such a thing it is, it must be, to love and be loved.

"Please come with us," I try a last time. "If you stay here, if you don't join us, something terrible could happen. There's a man, a hunter, not far from here. He might already be on his way." My heart tightens, imagining what might come. How can we leave her here to face what might be done to her? "Do you understand?"

"It doesn't matter."

"It's worse than you know." I put my hand out. "What he does."

"What you offer is worse. *You* are worse."

Another stab of anger cuts through me.

What is this foolish old woman saying? That we don't deserve to be what we are? That our lasting is terrible, worse than a grave?

"You know nothing about me," I say.

"I know you're strong," she whimpers suddenly. "I can see it. I'm not strong. Not anymore. Sometimes the strongest last the longest. Sometimes not. In the end, we all go. Everyone leaves us. Abandons us."

"It doesn't have to be that way."

"Go away."

The others have seen and heard. They beckon to me. I slowly go to join them.

Briscoe sees the anger still rippling through me.

"Get on to Pastor Valley," he says. "Just go. Search it out, see what you think. Leave this to me."

"How do I get there?"

"Head for that ridge in the distance. It looks like nothing from here. But you'll see. You'll see when you get there."

He's consoling me for something; he doesn't know what.

"And you?" I ask.

"I'll stay a bit longer and try to convince this one. But I don't think she'll budge. We'll go up to the tableland and wait. In case she changes her mind."

"Try."

"You can't save everyone, Emma Rose. Sometimes you have to let go. Come back and let us know if you think we have a stand in the valley. Keep safe. Sometimes you have to sacrifice one of the line to keep going. It's a pity, but there it is."

I nod. It is pity I feel now, not anger. At least not at the old woman.

But imagine what we could do with all our anger, I think, if we aimed it at the right place.

16

Something was in the struggling darkness with Pratt. He felt it crawling near.

Hands were laid on him. Feeling. Groping. Moving over him.

His name was being said. Two hands crossed over his back. A woman's hands. So strange to feel them. The groping continued and reached his neck. Fingers pulled at his hair, lifting. His head was pulled back. Was she going to snap it?

All at once he was free.

"Breathe," Sheriff Hogan said. "Deep. I got the hood off. Let me get the rope off your hands."

He was breathing deeply now. It was still dark, but not as dark as it was.

Blood surged back into his wrists. He felt carefully for his weapon.

He hadn't understood until now how he was bound.

Released, he raised his hands to where his face should be.

There I am. Not dead. Not yet.

He swore with gratitude, then with a fierce sense of victory.

Not yet.

He heard her soft panting beside him.

"So you're all right?" Hogan said.

He could hardly see her. But that was her even cadence.

"I'm fine. Thanks for the save. What's happened?"

"As near as I can tell, we were hit with rocks on the back of our heads."

He felt for the blood. Sticky, drying. His skull still throbbing. Some dizziness.

"Where are we?"

"I think one of Fort Intrepid's huts. I've been feeling around. The ceiling is low. Don't stand yet. Not till you've got your head back. We've been unconscious for a while."

He could feel, smell, now that he'd had the cloth sack taken from his head, they were in a wooden box. The air smelled of tar.

"Do we have our phones with us?"

"Nope. Taken. Wouldn't matter anyway out here. And my gun is gone. Don't know if they cared about your weapon."

His senses were coming back. Needlestick. They hadn't planned on this.

"We were tied up pretty good. But they put my hands in front—guess they didn't think this little lady looked strong—and forgot about my belt buckle. That's how I cut us out."

Resourceful. "What time is it, do you think?"

"This dark. must be late at night."

"We have to get out of here." His throat was parched. His voice croaked. "Do you have any water?"

"No. And we're not going to last without it. Can you stand up now? Feel around, feel what we're dealing with?"

He got to his knees, then his feet, the dizziness ebbing. Wooden crossbeams loomed overhead. He traced along one with his finger and reached a wall. He felt for cracks, for any openings.

"It's chinked pretty tight," Hogan said. "Recently, like I thought."

He put his cheek to logs. They were cool. Almost fresh.

The desert, he remembered, lost its heat at night.

"We have to stay focused," Hogan ordered, standing in the darkness. "Listen. You hear that?"

Indistinct murmuring at a distance. Neither whispers nor shouts.

"I make it three individuals," she said. "Three men."

He would take her at her word. His own ears seemed dulled.

"And do you smell something?" she asked.

He came closer to her. He could smell her uniform, her skin, her blood.

Along with a whiff of smoke, seeping in.

"That's a fire being started."

Crackling outside their wooden box.

17

When I was a little girl, I imagined that when you arrived in Heaven, you would be walking on clouds that were like the softest pillows, and it wouldn't matter if your shoes were worn. You wouldn't need any shoes at all, nor a woolen coat, either.

When I was older, Heaven looked more to me like a fine, tall mansion with wide-sashed windows and a columned porch and a widow's walk edged with scalloped shingles and copper gutters that poured like money down to the ground.

When I died, I saw neither the roof nor the foot of any heaven. I thought I was done with it, and it done with me. I taught myself to rise like a cloud and hurry across a landscape as though there were a wind behind me.

So when I first saw the place Briscoe had pointed me to, as fine and green as an emerald floating in an emerald sea, I thought that it wasn't Heaven but Éireann, where Noah himself told the Irish to go to keep safe from the coming flood.

This valley, I stare at it in wonder, *it must be a dream.*

I trace along the high ridge, looking down at it. It's nestled between sheer, dry, high red rocks like the richest blanket. A green ribbon of water cuts along one edge of it, below the cliffs, where lush trees lean across, their leaves jingling like coins. Away from the water the land is being farmed, and I see field after field of green and lavender, with good fencing in between, and where the fences end there are solid buildings, some large, some small, covered in shingles that gleam like mirrors, as though the roofs were made of water, too.

All of this hidden, with no sign of it at all until you come upon it.

For the living, I see, there is only one way in or out of the valley, the narrowest of cuts through one of the cliff faces. And perhaps by the river itself.

For a ghost there is any way you like.

I drop to my knees on the cliff where I'm standing, for it makes me want to weep, all at once. A homestead of this size, and as Briscoe tells it, not but one person below? A valley so grand there could be a whole village in it—yet there's only a house or two?

Why, it's a crime.

I come to rest on the bottom land. Here is the green, green, green dampness. It sinks into my soul. I feel every leaf of it, so sweet after our long walks through the dirt and sand. The scent sinks into me, too, because I let it, it's how a ghost smells, by letting the world in that won't let you come to it another way.

I want for all the world to lie down, on my back, and take my ease, to lounge and stare up at the sun feeding this valley and not burning it because the ground has been soaked in this wet perfume. I want to stop and linger, but I can't. I might have all the time in the world—but I have none of it to waste. The others are waiting.

Here is a place to be safe, I think, as I walk through the fine, healthy clover, and safe perhaps from all hunters, not just one. A place so hidden away and easy to keep watch from, along one of its ridges. A closed valley it would be natural to defend. And if such a place happened to look like the home you never had, a memory of a place your ancestors planted until they were driven out by famine and sickness and want . . . call it some Irish luck that's been long, long overdue.

There's this luck about it, too, peculiarly and particularly: when you see something like this so fine and hidden, so tucked out of the way and with no sign leading to it, you can be fairly certain whoever's hiding it doesn't want it to be seen or found or spoken of, on other people's tongues or in the news, no matter what trouble comes. What is secret doesn't want any attention.

A ghost knows that. Whosoever land this is, I think, whoever it is, they're afraid, too. There's something behind this valley, I sense, as I stroll toward the gleaming buildings, trailing my skirt through the clover. This is a place that doesn't want to be mapped. The road then is open to us. Perhaps.

How will I describe it to the others?

There's pasture as wide as your legs could want. It's a place that's ready for animals, but there are no animals as yet to see. There's hay ready to be baled and laid down. There are greenhouses, in pretty domes like cups turned over. There are good buildings. Shelter. And in every direction you cast your eye, loveliness, not only the fine green fields but cliffs and stones in fantastical shapes, like bodies standing up and pointing, and the sun moves across the long blanket of the valley and finds shade to draw out of the furrows and rows. It's quiet here, but not dead. The water moves and the crops bow, and there are bees, and here is a garden and lawn and here a beautiful, grand house of stone, nothing falling down about it, as sturdy as can be, and I'll wager behind it are people who aren't accustomed to sharing it with anything less grand than they are, but well, you shouldn't ask for good manners, should you, from what you won't shake hands with.

I've haunted the houses of the rich. I know them. There's a light about such places. It's different from other lights. It must be because the windows are wide and grand, and when you slip in under the great front door, notice that every corner where there can be a lamp, there is a lamp, and every lamp there is so beautiful that electric current seems a mere excuse for it, and the floor is so polished, reflecting the light, you could have a supper of eggs on it, then wipe your hands on the fine rugs as colorful as feathers.

What else makes the light, in a house like this, I'm certain, is that there's nothing crowded around it. Every bit of wood and stitch of leather has its own acre. Every pretty thing hanging on the wall is like its own sun, with plenty of sky around it.

For a ghost, such a house is a delight. There's no worry you'll bump anything in the night unless you mean to. And for some of us who lived with so little, while we were alive, to have what we didn't have in life is a sweetness all the stronger because we must taste it with our eyes, and swallow it with our hearts.

The grand house is so still I thought I was completely alone in it at first. But now I hear a sound—it's to be expected, if as Briscoe says someone is here—and go as cold as stone and follow its tapping to a great, white kitchen.

A tall man is there, making himself a tall sandwich.

I nestle against the white-tiled wall, watching. This must be the lone guard Briscoe had warned me of. Whoever he might be, he doesn't look like a man that belongs to all the peacocking rugs. He's too tall for the stone counters; this house wasn't fitted for him. His shirt is thin and cool but rough. His black hair is combed behind his ears with sweat. He's making himself, I think, a midday meal. He's done some work already this day, outside, before I arrived, and now he's come in to where the air is cool and the light softened.

He moves around the kitchen, the cupboards also too low, and his body is lean and alive and comfortable, and his face is calm, his skin glowing from his work.

My soul does something strange while watching him. I haven't moved, yet it seems for a long moment as though I were falling backward in time, until I'm being caught by waiting arms, and every inch of my body is pressed against another man's body again. Skin that once leapt at a touch. An ache, that wanted more, and more, and more, but that didn't dare to take it.

A servant girl in trouble, in those days, was branded a hussy. You could be sure there'd be no work for you after play. You could be sure every promise would be broken and you'd be left like a rag by the side of the road.

But once you're dead, there's surely no harm in lying in remembered arms and feeling again what it was like to be a body that wants another body.

I feel myself warming. Careful, now.

A hot soul can be seen.

The tall man is lifting his fine, blunt chin, forgetting his meal, tilting his head, as if alert.

Go cold, cold, cold, Emma. Even if you hate it.

He turns back to his meal and finishes it in a few quick bites. When he's done, he takes a glass of water and goes to sit on one end of a long leather sofa. When I'm sure I'm perfectly cold and invisible, I go and sit with him at the other end, perched on the sofa's rounded and tacked arm. He's staring at something hanging over the grand stone fireplace. A netted hoop. It reminds me of the fishing nets I saw in the seaside village where I died, where they were hung alongside the floats and buoys.

"How much longer," he suddenly asks, "am I just going to sit here?"

I don't know. He sits for some time. I don't move, myself. I'm careful. It's strange, but pleasant for a change, sitting and not moving with a living soul.

Finally, he finishes his glass of water and sets it on the carved table in front of him. He closes his eyes. A few minutes more of rest, his shoulders seem to say.

I suppose it's the warmest part of the day. He might be waiting for it to pass. He doesn't appear to be sleeping. His sunned hands cup evenly and awake on his thighs. His chin is neither raised nor lowered.

He looks nothing like any man I've ever known, truly, dead or alive. His seems a body stiff and apart. His breath is even, as though he were being careful to make it that way. His body looks peaceful. But I don't feel peace around him. That isn't peace hanging in the air.

Haunting is studying. We study the living when they don't know they're being watched, when they give themselves away like a piece of laundry fallen from a line.

Still, somehow, this man, sleeping or not, doesn't really give himself away. I wait and watch, for I must decide what to do next, what to do with him. If we dead want a place in the world, then we must rid ourselves of the troublesome living. It can be done. But it takes some doing.

At last a telephone device rings in his shirt pocket. He opens his eyes and pulls it out, and speaks.

"Hey there, Callie."

His voice is steady, with only a bit of yawn in it.

"Yeah. Been working. Yep. Repairing the new irrigation out here. I know. There's nothing pricey enough that it doesn't want to break and then be babied, right? No, I'm fine. It's lonely, but I like it." He makes a quick face, pushing his sharp cheeks up to his eyes and then lowering them, as if clearing his thoughts. "You what? You got lamb out there? Yeah, fresh lamb does sound good. I'll pick it up on my next trip out of here. Can you hold it in your freezer till then? Thanks. Where are you right now? At the trading post? How long is your break? How've you been feeling? How's the arthritis? You get Big John to give you longer breaks. I'm serious. You make him do it. What else is going on? Oh, is she? No, don't bother her if she's sheriffing. Yeah. Yeah. We've been doing all right, I guess. Yeah, we're better apart than together. She likes it out there, I like it out here. Life is good the way it is. Yeah. The owners keep me busy, I mean I keep myself busy. Nah, they never come. You know how it is. They just want to know they have it and it's taken care of. I send them some video, time to time. It's nice and pretty here. No, just me. Might as well be mine. Hold on, you're breaking up, it's the satellite. All right. Get back to work. Thanks for the lamb. All right. See ya."

He sets the device down on the cushion beside him. He rubs his face. To me it looks as though he's rubbing some feeling back into it. It's been a long time since I've done it, but I do remember when you're alive your skin can grow stiff from making a pleasant face, and then you have to knead and start the yeast of your true self again.

He leans forward and puts his device into his hip pocket, and stands, stretching. How long has he been alive? I wonder. He seems neither old nor young. His back looks strong, as mine was. He clears his throat, coughs a little, crosses the room with a few long strides of his boots and leaves the house at the rear by a glassy door.

I'm alone now indoors and can see if the house will suit.

I go floating through it, upstairs and down. Large rooms, uncluttered. High ceilings with thick log beams, places to move and tuck into and hide. But also places to play in, and things to admire and enjoy, pretty objects, crystal balls, collections of arrow-heads, wooden carvings. In one room there's nothing but velvet chairs in rows, like a moving picture hall. Another room is filled with nothing but wines, and no one to drink them. And from many rooms there are wide, picture-pretty views of the green fields with the red stone and cliffs behind them, so that the house feels safe but open.

But what to do with the tall, sober caretaker? For a caretaker he is, I'm certain of it—a housekeeper, as I had been. Trained to do hard work yet be invisible. It's good practice for being dead. It's not so pleasant while you're alive. The caretaker likes his loneliness, he said—though I'm not sure I believe him. You can't always trust the words of the living, especially while they're talking to each other. They hide all sorts of dirty brooms inside their closets.

So I won't trust this caretaker, though he says he's content. If he truly is, then he'll want to be careful to be seen as a good guardian. If he isn't, then I'll look for some sign of it, that he craves something more than serving his masters. And I'll feed on that.

I float out of the house now and find him busy at the edge of the nearest field. He's bent over the wheeled foot of a great watering arm swung out across the clover—it looks to me like a wheeled skeleton—and is working at it with some tools. I fly up to the mirrored roof of the house to watch. He might do something that will tell me how it is we can manage to take this place from him. I stand and look down.

He straightens and walks away from the task he's just set his muscle to and goes to the other end of the arm. There he turns a valve, and after that hops a fence and begins walking back along its posts, never taking his eyes from the metal pipes shaking a little now, sputtering at their seams with mist. Then the water comes on fine and strong—what a thing it is to see against the dry cliffs in the distance, strange and beautiful all at once, the water hissing and spraying in clouds to the earth.

His back stays turned to me. He watches the drenching from a spot on the lawn where he stops and stands, seemingly satisfied. Then he reaches into his back pocket and pulls out his device again, and with it this time a long white ribbon with a pearl at each end of it. He puts a pearl in each ear. It's how the living listen to music now. They let it sink inside them. As we do, in a way.

161

Slowly, holding his device in one hand, he begins to move. Well now, you don't expect a thing like this. He's dancing. One long leg slides right, the point of his left boot trailing along the grass. His arms lift and arc like a seagull's wing at the elbows. He rocks back on his heels then forward on his toes, as if he's trying to lift himself from the earth itself. His hips sway, he leans, his shoulders relax, he's found some rhythm, and the rhythm has found his body, and it's a waltz, a waltz, I can tell, I can see it, hear it, feel it, rippling through him, rising and falling. He's tucked his device into his shirt pocket now, and with both hands free he taps his fingers as if on piano keys in the air. He thinks no one is watching as he strokes and then folds the air into him and lets it go, folds it in again and lets it go, his whole body alive and awake, from his toes to the center part in his long dark hair. He's waltzing, as I did once, long ago, in love with the flow.

Time is nothing, all at once. I'm eighteen years old again. A music hall's parquet floor is filled with boys and girls and tables banked with bunting and topped with punch bowls and glasses, and the air is warm, the windows all open but draped like the tables with flags in red, white, and blue. It's 1914, and the boy I loved is in my arms and we're whirling, twirling, with all the prudes staring at us. We shouldn't be so close, but we are, because it's 1914 and the men in this room haven't yet gone off to war. And now the band is taking a rest, and a barbershop quartet is coming onto the dais and still we sway, we sway, we won't be stopped, because the music and the air has taken us and it's all inside us now, whispering as close as lips can come, singing:

> *Candlelights gleaming on the silent shore;*
> *Lonely nights, dreaming till we meet once more.*
> *Far apart, her heart is yearning,*

With a sigh for my returning,
With the light of love still burning,
As in days of yore.

It was so warm, then, and I wasn't dead yet, at this the last moment I was happy while I was still alive. Happy and free, and hot, every inch of me, on fire, and glad to be with that boy, glad. Let them all shake their heads, disgusted at me. Aren't our eyes meant to shine at night, and our hearts meant to boil over, and our feet meant to dance?

I look down now. The man below me has suddenly stopped moving. His legs stand wide, frozen, as he looks across the field at a girl in a long black skirt and with white shirtsleeves staring back at him from the water fountaining there.

No.

I've made a terrible mistake.

I've forgotten myself.

I've lit up.

That's my body upright in the water. My hot reflection is in the spray, shining from the mirrored roof.

Quick, quick, I darken my spirit, turn it to ice. I drop to my knees, dead cold.

But the ghost of my ghost in the water doesn't flinch. She doesn't kneel. Or fade. She stays. I don't understand.

Please, heavens, let him think he's imagining me, that he's closed his eyes and with the swaying of the music and the hot sun beating down hard on him he has opened them too quickly and can only be blinking at a bright fancy.

He's turned and is going, running now, to the water valve. He shuts it off and hurries back again, pulling the music from his ears.

The sight of me has disappeared with the dying of the water. Thanks be—

He runs back and turns the valve again.

And there I am.

I don't understand it. This can't be happening. I'm afraid. How can this be happening? I've gone invisible and cold and turned myself into nothing on this mirrored roof. I know I have. There should be no more of my standing form to be reflected. I'm crouching down.

Yet still she stands tall, the girl of 1914. And he stares at her. Neither moving.

I want to rage, *Is this some new torment? Some unjust punishment? Why? All because I dared to let myself feel alive and hot and full of longing again for just one moment, and so this is my reward, that some bright steam I let out of my soul will now burn me?*

It takes all my will and strength not to howl like a banshee at my reflection, at the green wet field, at the sky. I want to scream, yet I must stay calm, calm, and sort out what to do. The caretaker turns the water on and off again, to be certain. Finally, he shuts the machine down, panting from all his running to and fro. He turns and goes toward the house and I follow, quickly, cold behind him. His dampened back shivers and twitches without his knowing why.

In the house, he closes the glass door and looks back. The field is empty of me. He takes out his device. He's going to call someone. If I'm going to stop him, I must do it now. Strike fast. Now.

But when I'm cold, I think very clearly and always ahead.

His seeing me as he did was all much sooner than I'd imagined—but it was always the plan, and had to be after all. There is no need now, I tell myself, for hastiness or panic or any cause for dread. Let this caretaker do as he likes. He doesn't even know I'm perched at his shoulder, like a bird. He feels another cold twitch coming on and only thinks himself tired from wonder, all that running back and forth.

"Deputy Darrion, that you? Yeah, it's Winn Towhee."

So now I have a name for him. Always more polite.

"Listen, hate to do this to you, but I need to call in a disturbance. No, not that kind. The other kind. Out here at the Halsten place. Maybe you could come out and—Yeah, heard about that, I heard Sherry's at the trading post with someone. But I figured maybe you could come out and—Sure. Fine. Yeah. No, it's not an issue. Just let her know. Tell her to come on out. I'm here, not going anywhere. I don't know, maybe it's connected to whatever they're doing, I have no idea." He wipes some sweat from his neck and seems irritated, the wonder turning into an impatient sigh. "What did it look like? Female. Young. I don't know, I wouldn't say modern. Out in the alfalfa. Yeah, you could've knocked me down with a feather. We don't tend to have problems like that out here. Yeah, we'd better. The Halstens want everything kept neat. Great. I appreciate it. All right. Still plenty of daylight left for them to come out. You tell her to drive careful on the Halstens' road, I know she knows, but—All right. You take care now, too."

The man named Winn Towhee puts away his device and goes to look out the glass door again. His chest rises and falls, though more slowly now. His eyes are still half bright, as if recalling what's just happened.

Maybe I had meant to do it this way, all along. Or some part of me did. Dance in the water for a dancing stranger. The soul is a mysterious thing. If you knew every inch of yourself, Emma Rose Finnis, how dull eternity would be.

He sits on the leather sofa again, perhaps to wait for the sheriff and Pratt. For I know they're coming now, or soon. And we'll each have to get ready. He takes a breath and lets all the air out of him, like a man who knows he's found trouble, or it's found him, and now he'll have to live with it—at least for a little while. And I'll have to live with him and it, too, this man who waltzed on green clover in a desert and tricked me back to my own salad days.

I don't know how it is that my own eyes grow heavy with his. I don't, I can't flag; there's too much to fight for. But once upon a time I rested, before my soul was left to balance, delicate as a bird on a wire.

18

I used to sleep and dream when I was alive. I don't think about it much now. If I dream while awake, I suppose it is mostly about somehow being safe without being dull or small. It was a small life I had, when I was alive. I cleaned others' pots and polished their brass and beat their rugs. I carried out their waste. I stood by the side of the road and waited for their deliveries and toted the packages in and untied and unwrapped the brown paper, and saw the silks inside. I mended blouses and darned socks and cleaned out the coal grate and cooked meals over hot stoves, sweating inside my shirtwaist, and brought cakes to tables I never dined at, and in the evening if I went out I dodged sailors who wanted a piece of me, and often I had to fight off grabby hands even if I didn't go out at all. Once, a man I worked for tried to browbeat me into being a morsel for his hungry fingers. I hit him over the head with a wrench. It had to be done. Then I had to leave. When you're made to live small, if you do something big you're the one who pays grandly for it.

If I dream while awake, it's that I won't forever pay. That I'll have some chance to see that the dead are recompensed for having been hunted for no reason; that the dead I know will have a place that makes them safe and happy, while I send everything that wants to hurt us to the devil and dance a jig while I do it.

If I dream, it's that kindness won't arrive too late for all who need it and justice will be served on those whose thoughtless, careless lives are exactly what they mean them to be. From what I know of the world, what you do isn't always what you mean to do. But when it is, your name is stamped on it. And those like Philip Pratt who think that when they die they'll be at peace with their lives and their name will be cherished, perhaps they should come to know what it's like on the other side, where your name is turned against you and hunters call it out only to taunt you into their laps.

How long a time have we been sitting like this, the caretaker and I, on this sofa?

A great span of time? None at all?

Winn Towhee suddenly stands. The grating sound of wheels has come, drawing up outside this house in the desert.

I rise too and stand on the stone mantelpiece.

The caretaker goes to the door, and his tall frame fills it. I can half see the hunter on the other side of him. Pratt is like a tilted shadow with the light behind him. He's having to look up at the caretaker, and the stretching of his neck makes the older man look younger, stronger, and more pleasing all at once, his skin pulled taut and his head tipped that way.

How he likes to charm them, those troubled by haunted houses.

"Winn, this is Philip Pratt," the woman sheriff says, pleasant, too, as if they haven't all gathered this fine evening to do murder.

"Nice to meet you, Mr. Pratt." Towhee shakes his hand, and quickly lets go. "Thanks for coming so fast. Let's get you into the cool." He turns to the sheriff and says in a low, smooth voice, the kind you save for someone that knows you and that you've whispered to alone in private places, "The AC's giving me trouble at my place. That's why we're meeting here."

"*Vato*, why do I think you just didn't want to tidy up for us?" she teases easily.

"Because you're always thinking," he teases back. But not so easy, I think. There's been trouble between them. They pretend to walk comfortably side by side, but the air is full of some private tune between them that hasn't died, and it sinks into me and makes the cold I stand in above the hearth, in front of the woven, bone-colored net, lonelier.

Pratt, for his part, seems comfortable, strutting around the fine room. He likes his work.

"Lovely piece, the dream catcher," he says, pointing in my direction without knowing it.

"I always think this place looks like a magazine spread," the sheriff says, taking her hat into her hands as though she's honoring something she can't see. Her dark hair is thick and heavy. Like mine was. The fan stirring at the ceiling can't lift it. "I half expect," she goes on, "to see Mrs. Halsten posing in that chair by the fire, and Mr. Halsten standing behind her, with his arm resting over her shoulders, all nonchalant. With a brandy in his other hand."

You imagine the rich, I want to say, *and not the poor.*

"Nice people, your employers?" Pratt asks the caretaker.

"I wouldn't know." He shrugs. It doesn't matter to him. I understand that much. "We don't have that kind of relationship. They pay me fairly."

"How often do you see them?"

"Maybe once a year? Over a weekend. I mostly deal with their assistants."

It all grows more perfect. Once a year only they come. And it doesn't matter to the rich how their gardens are tended. As long as the chore is managed.

"Do your employers know that you've called us out here today?"

"They prefer not to know anything they don't need to know. If I think I can handle something on my own, I just handle it. I wasn't even going to call you," he tells the sheriff. He wants to remind her he called someone else first. I saw it. I see it now. He didn't want her to come. He didn't want to have to ask her for anything. That's how it is, I know, when the net is tangled and you're trying to get clear. *Once I wanted to be with you. But now I'm trying to see past you. I'm drowning, but it's not you I want to save me.*

"I mean it might be nothing to get too bothered about," he says suddenly, surprisingly. "It's not even in the house."

Could it be, I wonder, if a man doesn't really want the company he finds in this room, he might change his tune about a dead girl doing nothing more frightening than standing in clover in water?

"But Callie at the trading post told me you were out on a spirit hunt," he finishes.

"Callie just served us at the post," the sheriff says, nodding. "What were you doing talking to her?"

"She wanted to know if I needed any lamb chops."

"Callie and her sheep. Gotcha." She says this easily again but doesn't seem so.

"Why don't you take us to the site of the disturbance," Pratt says, as if he cares little about the secrets of the living, "and we'll see what you're dealing with."

"This way. It's been going—the apparition went on and off, so to speak. Thought I was imagining things at first. It gets so empty here, sometimes, you start to think you're seeing things in the heat. But usually it's easy to figure what's what. Step outside, and just start walking toward the east field, there." He's brought them out the glass door, into the lowering sun, where the cliffs are glowing, smoldering where it beats against them. The clover in the field shimmers.

"Just stand right at the edge while I turn on the irrigation. I'll be right with you."

I follow them as they cross the lawn, keeping my distance. Pratt squints and stares as if impressed by all he views. The woman named Hogan goes to lean against the fence, one boot propped on it, comfortably. She must know it well.

"Winn, dude, this is all past ready to be baled," she calls after him. She wants, I'd say, to act concerned, but not seriously so.

Coming back the caretaker says only, "Takes a second for the well pump to catch up. When you see the spray starting, look over there, a little toward the right. That's where I've been seeing it."

It's almost comforting, seeing my pale reflection appear again. Isn't that strange. How the soul can leap with fresh wonder at the same time as familiar dread. Look at that. Look at me. *Why, what a pretty girl I was.* I didn't know it then. Now I see I was as fine as fivepence, even in my ordinary clothes. That's a nice long neck and shapely hands. Hands that might have held a companion warmly after a long day. True, good hands. When you're dead and alone, it's sometimes hard to hold fast to the idea that you're real outside your own thoughts. That's why it's good to have company, other ghosts around you, so that you know you're not mad, not really trapped in a wooden box somewhere, blind and coffined, six feet under, and everything you think and feel and want is just you inside a box.

They stare at the ghost of my ghost. I really do frighten the living.

Pratt jumps forward, as he had at the last house, toward the fence in front of him. I see the breath go out of him as all the while wonder fills his eyes, along with pain.

There she is, his look says. *I've found her. Again.*

"You do see that, right?" the caretaker whispers.

Pratt nods. He can barely move.

Hogan sputters, "I see it. Damn."

"Stay where you are," Pratt orders. He won't give away his eagerness. He'll grow calm now, settle into the moment.

I must be very careful.

He's no fool. Always a truth to remember. He won't act quickly. He studies from the fence, as if circling prey, taking the measure of the mirror in front of him.

The caretaker says quietly, "She's only in the water. Turn the water off, she's gone. I'm just glad you're seeing it, too."

Hogan comes close to him. "Do you recognize her, Winn?"

"Nope. Never seen her before in my life. Looks like some sort of pioneer. That long skirt. The white shirt. The weird hair with the old-fashioned ribbon."

I fly to the roof of the house and there stand and watch and listen.

It doesn't matter what they say. I was fine as fivepence.

I hear the woman below saying, surprised. "She's almost beautiful."

Pratt ignores this. Of course. He calls, hissing, "Leave the water on. Stay here."

He clambers over the fence now. His feet sink in between the green stalks. He puts his hand to his chest, in that motion I know so well, that pretense at having a heart. He begins walking toward the glow of me, my twin brimming in the spray in front of him. He grows more damp, the mist hitting him the closer he comes.

But are you feeling anything below your hand, Mr. Pratt? No. Because your heart isn't there. And neither is mine. I don't know how that is; I suppose we're all a puzzle to ourselves. There in front of you is the picture of a girl who was at a dance more than a hundred years ago. A photograph that no one took, a name no one remembers, or thought about when she was gone.

Pratt walks right through the absent heart of me and freezes. Stiff as a gravestone.

Hogan jumps the fence and hurries toward him, perhaps thinking he's been hurt. The caretaker runs to turn the water off. They both dash toward the hunter, calling, asking if he's all right.

"What did you see," is all Pratt answers, coming to life again, "from your vantage?"

"You passed right into her," the caretaker pants. "She was still there when you got right here. Till I cut off the water. She looked like she was right on top of you. You didn't see her?"

"The image was here, yes, but there was no reading. Nothing was here. Nothing."

"What does that mean?"

I know what it means. It means now he'll try his tricks. He'll bring out his hunter's words. He'll make himself look grand and knowing, to the living and to the dead, too. He'll remind us all who's someone and who is nothing, hoping to lure a ghost to him, in anger or in sadness or because she wants to prove him wrong. I've heard what comes next, before. *You are nothing, spirit. You are nothing but pain and misery. You bring nothing to the world, nothing that matters. Nothing you want will ever come to you. You don't even really want. You only imagine you do. You are finished. The past. Already passed through. Did you see me passing through you? Let me end such terrible sights for you. End your pointless wanting. Don't you want to rest, at last?*

"This couldn't have been a normal manifestation. It was a, it had to be a . . . a projection of some kind. It was nothing, nothing real or meaningful. We need to go back inside. It was looking right at the house."

I shut my ears and back away.

The most dangerous thing about a hunter is the peace he'll try to use as bait.

I must be very clever now.

Pratt is searching the house. He's having trouble. I'm not the easiest of ghosts, am I, any more than he's a careless hunter. Soon he'll be telling the caretaker and the woman following him that some ghosts like to lead the living on an unexpected dance, but not to worry, a puzzle isn't clever for being difficult, it's nothing but pieces pretending not to be broken, and also, a ghost is forever giving herself away even if she doesn't mean to, because forever is a terrible, terrible place, unbearable, and the only cure for it is release, and so on and so on and so on.

But who can say forever is unbearable, Mr. Pratt? Who's even tried it all yet?

It's growing dark outside. I must take the next step in this dance. I stand outside the glass door, listening. Pratt is finding no charge because I've been coldly careful not to leave one. He's the one growing heated, thirsty.

"Come on, you look exhausted," the sheriff is saying to him. "You do know you've been going all day, ever since you left Salt Lake."

"Let's all sit down," adds the caretaker. "I'm thirsty. I'm making us all drinks."

The living can only cool themselves with some help. That's a problem for them here.

"I'm thinking," Pratt says after he's drained his glass, "I should tell you both that I know that . . . thing, we saw out there."

Now he's come to it. *Go on, Mr. Pratt. Introduce me. It's only proper.*

"I first encountered it, the Finnis remnant—her name was Emma Rose Finnis, in life—a few years ago, north of San Francisco. She was haunting an estate along the coast. It was a complex case. There were multiple deaths."

That's all he ever says about it. As if he hadn't been in the middle of it.

"The remnant is early twentieth century. A ghost from the logging era in that part of the world. A rough period in history. It produced a fair number of incidents, or used to. That part of the country is quiet now. In the end, she escaped the area. It took some time, but I tracked her to the mountains, the Sierras, and found her there. This was in a town near the Nevada border. A group haunting. She escaped again, in a subsequent pursuit, across state lines. At that point I left the matter to . . . I left the matter to other jurisdictions to settle. I assumed it had been settled."

It's never wise, is it, to imagine others will fill the holes we dig? The sheriff looks amazed. "Ghosts can escape?"

He has to admit we can, and that this county is now a haunted place. Now he shows off the abomination clamped on his wrist, that blindfold he wears though not around the eyes.

Doesn't he remember at all? That before he tried to finish me, the first time, we held each other's gaze for a long second, and there was something, not understanding, but seeing, of a kind, between us?

"I should tell you: we are now dealing with a highly capable and ugly remnant. Clever. Dangerous. Imaginative. Resourceful."

If I paid attention every time we were called names, I'd never hear my own thoughts.

He'll come to something useful, surely.

He's showing them his telephone device.

"If you look here, you'll see what I mean. I'll show you where the Finnis remnant started, and how it's been moving. She's been moving in very nearly a straight line. Due east."

There.

There it is. How I'll fool him.

I hurry across the fields. The stars are only beginning to throw their sparks out.

I go east. Due east. What might be handy, here? At the edge of a field close to the valley's shadowy river I find a set of stairs. It leads down into the earth, to an odd dugout, I see, maybe of the kind my Irish ancestors used to burrow into for safety. Its door is heavy metal, sealed tight as a ship's hatch. No matter. A puzzle can break into pieces, fit a tiny sliver in.

I've never been inside a dugout before. What a strange place this is. Here's a house underground, with every fine thing a living person could want—rooms and cupboards and food and games, and only windows lacking. It must be a shelter of some kind, from storm or wind. The living here might find a way to last longer than others. But they all come to an end, in the end, though I suppose already being buried underground will save some trouble.

I leave a trail of heat and dust for Pratt to find. Why not be generous? I'll give him more, too. He likes to goad the dead. But we dead can goad as well. There's a savor, we might both agree, to pulling at what worries and frightens others, and not our own nerves. In the neat underground kitchen, I find a cellar of salt. I came from the sea. He wishes he'd finished me there. I leave salt on the table for him. In memory.

If only I could summon all those I carry in memory. The boy I danced with in 1914, who died far from me on a distant shore. My family, long moldered in their graves. Friends living and friends dead and left behind, as I've made my way forward. Who would a ghost ask to see first, if she could?

No, it's better not to dwell on such things. Forever goes only in one direction. And it takes so much effort.

I hear the hunter and his companions now. He's followed my path to the top of the stairs. But I can't stay where I am. The ceiling is too low in this coffin underground. I'll need to do more than make my soul icy. I must make myself small as a key, and hide in the lock I've left open for them.

"The entrance is sealed and airtight," the caretaker is saying. "It can only be opened with a code that changes monthly. It . . ."

"It's already unlocked," Pratt says calmly.

He knows. We're playing a game.

Towhee stares. "That isn't possible."

"It is. A remnant has no body. It isn't corporeal. It can fit itself even inside a small mechanism and understand how to turn it."

How Pratt likes to turn my cleverness into his own, parade my understanding as his.

"I guess," Hogan tries a laugh, "that's why hiding in a basement never works."

Well, that and it's always the first place we look.

The caretaker pauses. "Should I go in first, Mr. Pratt?"

"Allow me. Stay close by. Where are the lights?"

"Automatic once you're inside."

I watch them from the lock. It's like staring through a spyglass.

"It's a frickin' spa! Winn, I can't believe you never showed me this before."

"No excuse till now."

"How big is this?" Pratt is impressed.

"Five thousand square feet. Everything you see now, plus media room, bedroom, two baths, and storage for unperishable food and hydroponic seed. Recycled air and gray water. Solar charge from arrays on the cliff, hard to get to, hard to see. Rechargeable batteries, energy turned by anything and everything that moves in the house. Everything enough to last who knows how long. My understanding is my employers have these all over the world, not just in the desert. You never know where you'll be when the lights go out."

So very true.

"Is there a place for you down here, Winn?" Hogan asks.

"Nope. Not sustainable for more than two."

Of course not; the servant's job is to tend a place, not take it.

"So you take care of it but get no part of it. Why didn't you ever tell me?"

"Not interested in holes in the ground. To me this would be living in some ginned-up coffin."

That's the spirit. I might be more fond of this caretaker, I think, if only he hadn't called these two hounds on me.

"When was the last time you were here?" Pratt interrupts.

"About three weeks ago. I check once a month. Change the code I'm given."

"Anything disturbed?"

"Not that I can see from here. Are you getting something?"

"Yes. Something is or has been here. There's a charge."

The trail I've left.

They go on following him, circling inside the rooms, while he lays his hand on his chest and closes and opens his eyes as though pressing the air into himself.

"Wait." The caretaker stops. "There is something disturbed."

"The dust?" Hogan looks, eagerly.

"No." Pratt is running his finger over the table, picking up my gift at last, tasting it. "This is sea salt."

"That wasn't there when I came last time."

"But they keep salt down here." Pratt looks around, then down, rubbing his fingers, breaking the grit apart.

"Sure. Loads of their favorite. Carry it with them, too, when they travel."

"Seriously."

Pratt lifts his thumb. "Salt is a sign. A symbol."

"So we brainstorm us some salt."

"Go on," he invites the sheriff. He knows the more the living act against the dead, the more excited they are by his work.

"A woman turned to salt for not obeying," she says.

Not that one, surely.

"Salt of the earth," the caretaker says.

Now it's the Bible they want to bring in? Have they forgotten who doesn't fit through the eye of the needle? How easy it would be to lock them all in. I could see to it they never left, closed forever in with the pretty furniture and no windows.

"Salt is life." The woman nods, excited.

They all chime in, eager as a revival. *You have to have it to live. It's used for preservation. For bodies. Flesh. It's taste. It's savor. It's an imitation of life. Blood. It's from the sea. It's life but not alive. It's an additive. Tears. It comes to life with something else, something comes to life with it. It's a trail. It's a trap. A salt lick. Those with noses come to it. A lure.*

I could bury them all. Easy.

"A trap," Pratt says and closes his eyes. "That's interesting."

When he opens them, he's facing the door.

With me inside it.

They follow his eyes.

They see. It's quite a far way out of this coffin, isn't it?

Hogan asks, "There's no way, Winn, we could get locked in?"

"There shouldn't be. I have the code."

But I have what matters. A reason.

"I told you," Pratt says quickly. "It can get inside things. Change them. We're going. Now."

It wouldn't be quick enough. *The only thing that saves you all is that I want no trouble just now.* No living souls reported missing, no attention, no more hunters.

This beautiful valley must stay peaceful.

I leave them to their scurrying, and fly on ahead of them, a better idea with me.

I want to see how this caretaker lives his life. This man who says he isn't interested in holes in the ground.

Any man who says that might have been down a well and come back.

The kind who might lend a hand without meaning to.

It isn't only Pratt who can invite the living to be useful.

19

The valley is full of darkness now. The path below me is lighted, and the sky starry, but in between is the shade of night, the space left to ghosts, though we care no more for shadows than a living soul does.

Here's a smaller house, and it must be the caretaker's. I lived in a cottage, too, once, on property that wasn't mine. A place I was, in a like manner, expected to tend as though it were my own. But it wasn't. Others had the right to come in whenever they pleased. I was always watched. I was told to keep my lodgings clean and neat. Sometimes I returned after a long day's work and I would find something of mine had been moved, the few belongings I had and kept on a windowsill askew, the curtain rearranged. It might have been the work of a ghost, but it wasn't. It was the right of others to do as they liked with me—even the children. When a house isn't your own, you're forever a guest.

Now I'm the one who can come and go as I please, and there's a certain fitness in that. The caretaker's porch is narrow, the roof steep in the dark, the door nothing at all to open. I slip in and put a light on—so the change will be noticed—and though the lamp is a warm yellow, like the lamps in the grander house, the cottage doesn't seem to be kept by a man who's at all troubled about being watched and judged and scolded. I do like that. The wood floor and rubbed furnishings are strewn with tossed clothing and scattered belongings, papers and books. The small kitchen is clean enough, and the soap's been rinsed before being set on the edge of the sink—it's the kind of thing a soul does who thinks one good deed can make up for all the rest—but the bedroom is a muddle of tangled sheets and worn blankets. The night outside the window makes this small room seem even smaller. There are thin curtains. No need for something thicker, when you're perfectly alone. Or invisible. One or the other.

I think quickly. There won't be much time before, seeing the light, he and the others come. He must help me find a way to send Pratt onward. If the caretaker wants to be alone again, if his life has taught him, as it seems it has, that being alone is best, then he'll be ripe to take a hint and choose the easiest way back to quiet. He can have his valley free of disturbance from ghost and hunter both—or have it seem so.

Yet I can't make it too obvious. Pratt is no fool. He's proven before that he needs the hook set deep. The luck I have on my side, and it's all that needs remembering, is that hunters love the hunt as much as the kill. If the tracks they follow are distant and difficult, it's all the more exciting to them, a sweeter challenge. And more luck still: this caretaker, I see as I look around me, is a soul who likes books and maps, for they're scattered everywhere, though he seems to go nowhere. I do wonder what keeps him so still, here, what's hunted him that knots him in tangled blankets.

I want to send Pratt east. That's the direction. He'll think I can't stop, because he thinks ghosts have no minds, only habits.

On the caretaker's sofa, on a map, I find to the east, in the center of a red-colored space that looks like a waving ocean of stone, a name. Needlestick.

And I say it is easier for a camel to go through the eye of a needle, than for a rich man to enter the kingdom of God.

He thinks he can go anywhere, Philip Pratt. He thinks though a ghost can slide through a keyhole, we're the ones who don't fit anywhere.

When I've left my mark, I leave the cottage and draw into the shadows. The others have arrived and go inside. I can see and hear through the windows.

"You want more lights on?" the caretaker asks.

"Please."

"Something's been here too and gone," Pratt says.

He moves around the room, speaking and touching things. He wants to know about the caretaker's habits. He's prying. The caretaker seems not to care.

"Can you tell me if anything seems disordered right now inside your own disorder? If anything's, say, been moved?"

The woman says something low and quiet.

"I'm not sure," the caretaker answers. "Huh."

"What is it?"

"Back up. Right there. On the couch. I was studying that map lying on it this morning. It's upside down now. I mean it's backside front. I know because I was looking at farm roads, and the front is where the farm roads are. I was thinking about going out to Callie's to pick up the lamb, and maybe doing a hike out that way I hadn't tried before. The backside is up. That's the backcountry. Trails and UTV roads. Not where Callie's sheep are."

Pratt's excited again. I understand. I was a hunter long before he was. A child by the sea, I netted and fished.

"Multiuse land," Hogan is saying. "Old drilling sites. Mountain bike trails. Jeep roads. Open country. No towns. Pretty much a lot of hot empty. A lot of it hard to get to, if you don't know what you're doing. Hole in the Wall country."

"Any shelter? Dwellings? Structures?"

"I'm thinking. I remember you said they want some kind of rooms or roost. There might be a few caves out this way . . . but what I'm mostly thinking about is this spot, right here. That's called Needlestick. There's what's left of an old fort there. See this little icon, marking it as a structure? That's a kind of roost. Historic site, but not a place many people get to. No services, hard terrain. There was a battle there, about a hundred and fifty years ago or so. Now it's a place, honestly, people pretty much stay away from."

Nothing too obvious. You don't circle the place on the map. You don't want the net to have holes too large. You tempt. You hope.

How perfect it all sounds. Better than I imagined.

The caretaker is saying he wants nothing to do with the place. There's been death in it. His own tribe, long ago. Does he know, I wonder, about the ghosts hunting the plain, after the antelope? They walked and rode with us only a little while. If he knows, he says nothing.

They go on with their plotting and planning, drinking heartily, as though they're toasting. The caretaker, it seems, won't go with them in the morning. He's done all he means to do. His shoulders say: it's not his work, this hunt.

"You really think a ghost would be this obvious?" Hogan asks.

"I say," Pratt says and finishes his drink, "we go check it out in the morning and come back here if there is nothing to it. Tonight, if I may make a suggestion, I think it's best we all stay together. Would it be better here or back at the main house?"

"I don't sleep in that house," Towhee answers. "It's not mine. AC's out here but it's not really necessary at night. If you're all right on that couch, I say we stay put here."

"I'll be perfectly fine."

While Pratt sinks down into his bed for the night, I move around the outside of the cottage to where a light has come on in the small bedroom.

Towhee and Hogan are there, talking in low voices.

"You sure you trust this guy, Sherry?"

"He's got a stellar reputation. He knows what he's doing. He put Doris Grunn down at the cemetery earlier today."

My anger wants to rise. The old woman should have come with us. Briscoe would surely have tried to make her see. But in the end Pratt had come, it seems, and blighted her with pain.

Nothing said about other ghosts. It means Briscoe and the others are safe, and waiting for me.

"Doris who?"

"God, you're so buried out here, Winn. Always."

"Because I don't know someone named Doris? Who is she?"

"Was she. A woman from Briscoe. Died last year. We found her at Castle Mesa Cemetery. All the big stones turned over. She was standing by hers as plain as day. She was a sweet old lady, but Pratt took her out like a warrior. Nothing fazes him. You saw him. He walked right into that apparition. He's been picking up ash and salt all day, like it's nothing." She's taking off her buttoned shirt, a white shirt under it wrinkled but clean as a fresh pillowcase. She seems cool and satisfied. "I thought we were dealing with a group of ghosts, now he's zeroing in on one that just happens to be a pretty famous one from a thousand miles away. It's fascinating."

"Is that why you're going to Needlestick with him when it isn't really necessary?"

"It's still in Masters County. And he wouldn't be able to find it on his own."

"But who cares about a ghost out in the middle of nowhere? There's probably plenty of ghosts out there. Let 'em have it. They've probably earned it. I just can't have one here. Now it looks like I don't. Gone off to greener pastures. Great, perfect, case closed."

Exactly. That's the spirit.

"That's fine for you, Winn. I've got a responsibility to—"

"That's *your* way of staying buried."

"Not a fair comparison."

"I couldn't agree more." His own shirt comes off now, nothing underneath it, just bare skin, ribs as lean as wrapped bars. "You're still addicted to the rush. The adrenaline of being a cop. It's your way of keeping your head down while the world fries."

"And you still prefer hanging out on this golf course made of alfalfa. Let's talk about something else. What do you want to do about sleeping arrangements?"

"I'm fine on my side, you stay on yours. How are your kids?"

"They're going to be all right. It's what I keep telling myself. The world'll keep throwing shit at them, but they'll figure out how to fertilize. You gotta admire them. The young people."

"You act like we're old, like we're not smack in it. We're not even forty."

Not old at all. They know nothing about age.

"You said it yourself. We're just hiding out. One way or another."

"Yeah."

"Yeah, well."

"Goodnight."

I've watched people sleep before. Many times. It's the closest we ghosts can get to the living and let ourselves be seen, the only time we can stand in front of them and be safe. I've stood beside other beds, like this one now, and watched the living breathe in and out. The sheriff is tossing away her covers, she's too warm, sleeping in half her uniform. The caretaker draws his sheet more firmly around him, as if in complaint.

Ghosts can enter dreams, if we feel like it, standing close by and whispering. I've done it.

I don't, now. It will only mean lingering, and lingering tonight will, I can feel it, sow a jealousy in me, too painful. It's already on its way . . . it's arrived. Twining around me, braiding me to their shared bed. Look at how they sleep, side by side. The closeness of it, even in spite of their grumbling. The comfort they don't even know they feel, back to back. I've never felt it. I'll never feel it. Not only the touch of a partner; the peace of sleep. A ghost's cheeks never slacken. Our grip on the sheet never lets go. It can't. Sleep is too much like death to come anywhere near it, and yet it's so much also like life, dreaming life—that even now I'm leaving the room, I have to, for the caretaker's breath is so soft, for all that he's a large man, and the woman's faint snoring is a step behind it, and the gentleness of it all is enough to make me lonelier, more alone than I have ever felt in my whole afterlife.

20

I stand guard outside the cottage until morning comes and Pratt and the sheriff are bidding goodbye to the caretaker, standing with his coffee in his hands.

"Thanks again for your hospitality," Pratt says quickly, champing to be off.

"No problem."

"And you'll be all right out here alone?"

"Same as before. You have enough food and water in the truck? And you do know there's no cell service out there? I'll be repairing fence line most of the day. How long before I call you overdue?"

"Make it thirty-six hours."

He won't come back. That's the trick. He never admits defeat. Nor do I. He knows how far I've come, and that I don't like going back either. We don't look behind us. We always go on. A habit we seem to have in common.

And that's where he'll go wrong.

*

The caretaker and I will have some time together alone again now. Enough for me to decide what to do with this man who called the law because he doesn't want a ghost nearby but is also happy enough to send the law away.

He seems pleased, putting on a straw hat against the strong morning sun over his long hair, as he goes out to the clover fields. He leans on a stretch of fence and stares at the color for a long, steady moment.

"Yeah, now that all this is finished you should be cut. But you look too fine today. Won't cut you, not yet."

Instead he sets the long-armed watering machines to raining. He walks the fence line, tightening bolts. I catch him squinting, once, looking to see if the shape of me is still there in the closest field. No. I'm not there. A feeling faded, I suppose. The stamp of my reflection from a moment of remembered happiness hasn't lasted any longer than any happiness does.

He ducks his head under his straw cowboy brim, and turns away.

From there I follow him as he goes to a large, green shed. Out of it he drives a yellow tractor. He passes over the lawn at the rear of the house again and again until the grass is as taut as the velvet kneeler on a church pew. I sit on the roof and study him as he carries out his work in circles, the way I used to scrub floors, round and round and round, careful not to miss a spot. He seems a man of careful and steady routine. Someone it would be easy enough to plan around or against. When he's finished, he drives along the lane of red earth that is the road from the canyon, and then along another red ribbon. He trims the verge there, too, looking to his right and left to keep himself even, though it looks to me as though he's still glancing aside to be sure no one is watching.

He doesn't like intruders. He's made that much clear. If I bring the other ghosts here, and any of them, the children especially, makes some mistake, we'll have tasted paradise only to be forced out of it again. How cruel that would be.

If we stay, then the caretaker must go—yet he can't appear to, or another will be sent in his place.

His place will have to be filled, it seems.

At noon the caretaker puts his engine away. I think he'll turn in my direction next, toward the main house for his midday meal. But no; he walks toward the red cliffs with the twinkling trees quivering below them.

It's to the river he must be going.

I trail him past the last fence, where the ground opens up and turns pebbly, then sandy, like a dune on a beach.

It's red sand, smooth where it isn't stubbled with bits of stone. His feet sink into it in his boots. Then he yawns before looking down and starting to unbutton his plaid shirt. The pearled buttons fall to the side. He sits to take each boot off. The water, a cool, clear green, shimmers just beyond his soles. The trees fan the invisible breeze overhead. There are no trees on the other bank, opposite, only great blocks of stone that have fallen from the cliffs above. The tallest bluffs are stained and streaked in dark colors, bloody, that drip and look as though they should be wet but don't seem to be.

The caretaker is pulling off his socks, tossing them aside. He unbuckles his belt where he sits and then stands to do the rest of his business.

I've seen naked bodies before. I look. I measure. I turn away. Stare for too long and the pain's too deep. I've lived both with a body and without one. With a body you stroke the world and the world strokes you back, and that's a kind of heaven. Yet you're weighted and can be struck down. The spirit, cut from the body, is light as air. She can walk or fly, she has no fear of watery depths, the sharp cut of stones, the fall of a boulder from high above. She has no skin to burn or fret over. But she'll never feel another back sleeping against hers in the night. Or the hot love that comes before sleep.

The caretaker straightens, and his skin is beautiful, too beautiful to bear. It glows. It makes the red sand seem sluggish. A working body, his is, with all the muscles I once had and more, a man's chest and man's luck swinging between his legs. He wades out into the shallow water. He crouches to wash under his arms and to douse his scalp, and his face gleams like a lamp on fire, and I can't, I can't bear it, I tell you, that I can't have this, have both. It's one or the other, it's skin or lightness, it's feet or air, it's the hunter or the hunted, him or me, the green valley or the desert, and what do you do with what you can't bear except bear it, the only thing both the workaday living and the workaday dead know equally well?

I calm myself so he won't see me. I must prove to myself that I'm stronger than this pain, greater than the memory of my body and my drowning and all that I lost because of it. Invisible, I wade into the water with him. The current sinks into and passes through me, like a shadow brushing by, while the glinting all around me is as bright as knives bobbing in the sun.

I'm right beside him, so close I see the beads of water in his hair. He doesn't know it. I'm cold and he's cooled.

He turns his head away, upstream, and shakes aside his wet locks, as though he's seen something through them.

He takes one step deeper and bends at his knees. Something light is floating downstream, and catches in a little eddy at his shoulder.

A pad of wet green leaves, with a white flower in the middle.

Where I come from, we call it primrose.

He lifts it out of the water, straightening.

And swears.

"Something Rose, Emma Rose. Yeah. What was I thinking, calling that in? She wasn't some Mormon land-stealer, I guess. Spirit woman. Should have let her be."

I glide, confused, out of the water. Hearing my name on his tongue, it's bitter, and maybe sweet. Too close we were. I slide into the flicker of the quivering cottonwoods.

Still half in the river, he goes on staring at the wet weed in his palm. Then he turns around and carries the primrose back to the beach, where he sets it down on the sand, and picks up his clothes.

I'm so close to him I could do anything I liked.

I could have sent such a flower. But surely . . . I didn't.

He keeps staring at the poor wet thing.

Does he imagine I'm a poor wet thing?

I'll have to show him.

Once you've seen a man naked, it's curious—you don't see him clothed the same way again.

Some give away who they are no matter their coating—Philip Pratt, and his like.

This one is walking back through the fields, buttoning his shirt over his wet skin. His steps are slow and deliberate, as he looks down between his boots. He's changed, somehow, and not just by my looking at him. The river's changed him.

His name is Winn Towhee.

What sort of name is that?

He's said that he wished he hadn't called Pratt down on me. That's all very well, but it's always much easier to say a thing than actually mean it.

I never meant any harm to that ghost, not really.

I never meant any harm to that caretaker, not really.

Winn Towhee walks back to the grand house he keeps and, inside, fills a glass at the kitchen tap, and gulps it down. He shakes out his hair, already drying. He's shaken himself free, and now he only has his lunch on his mind, I see. I stand behind him.

This time not coldly.

He takes a jar and some bread from a cupboard. He pulls a knife from a drawer and lifts it in front of his eyes. I watch him stiffen.

Our eyes have met in the silver of the blade.

He doesn't move.

He looks.

I don't know how afraid he is or isn't. I don't know this man.

At last he lowers the knife.

He says simply: "I'm going to turn around now."

No need. I swirl in front of him, on the opposite side of the blade.

"Nice." He nods slowly. "Move."

It's been some time since I've spoken to anyone with a heartbeat. It always takes a bit of getting used to. You have to pretend there isn't a knife between you.

"So you're still here," he says.

"I never left, Mr. Towhee."

You can't really see a soul's eyes until you look straight into them and they look into yours. His eyes are the color of the river we just swam in.

"My name is Emma Rose Finnis."

"I've heard. My name is Winn. As I assume you know."

"I do know."

"What else do you know?"

"You live here, but it isn't yours. You care for the place. You work here. It's beautiful here. You like it. I like it, too."

"You plan to interfere with my work?"

"Do you like your work so much?"

"Why does everyone always ask that? It's better for me here than anywhere else."

"But you're here alone," I say. "It's lonely."

"I don't like—distractions."

"I see." I don't say: it's only when you die that you learn what's a distraction and what isn't, what's real and what doesn't matter.

"Emma, if you don't mind my asking, how old are you?"

"I was born in 1896." To a mother who died giving birth to me.

"So not that old, as ghosts go. We've got much older. Out there." He points with the winking knife.

"I'm not so old, I agree." I don't feel the centuries, at the moment. I feel like the Emma Rose he saw reflected in the spraying water, waltzing and then stopping for punch, in a bunting-draped music hall. There's food and drink in this kitchen, and the same high ceiling and long curtains at the windows.

"How old are you, Winn Towhee?"

"I was born in 1989. I'm thirty-eight."

195

Twice my age, then, when I died. It makes me four times older than he is now. Though it feels as if there's no time at all, suddenly. Perhaps the clocks have stopped. Or the sun has slowed in the sky.

"You're a long way from home," he says suddenly. "You're not from here, I understand."

"No. And this isn't your home, either."

"It is and it isn't. Excuse me, mind if I eat my lunch? I'm feeling a little lightheaded. Must be, you know, all this expanded space-time."

I almost laugh. I feel his lightness.

"How do you," he says as he tries to chew his sandwich, "control whether I can see you or not?"

I shake my head. *I can't tell you that.* We've only just met, after all.

"Pratt told me it's anger or strong emotion that gives you away. But you don't look angry at all to me. Are you angry?" He's trying to swallow calmly, but a vein at his forehead is bulging.

"I am, but I spend a good deal of time managing it."

"Makes two of us then. Interesting."

He drinks more water. His throat is dry.

"Emma, what are your—ah—plans, exactly, now that you've clearly fooled the rest of us?"

The rest of us. That little moment of *two* has passed.

I still have to decide, Mr. Towhee, I don't tell him. And not just decide for myself. Almost a full day I've been gone from the others. They're still waiting for me.

"Any way I can encourage you, Emma Rose, to move along?"

"As you say, it's better here than anywhere else."

"For me, I meant. Anyhow, you can't stay, you know. That Pratt guy will come back."

If you say so.

"And Sherry, too. Our sheriff. She's tenacious. It's better," he says, more eager now, "if you keep moving, isn't it?"

Moving's a magical thing, Briscoe says. Like life itself. But then must that mean stillness is death? Isn't there a way to be still and alive, too? Where is balance, justice, for those like me?

I want a stillness that moves.

"It's pretty here," I say. "Like a park with a fountain. Like a picnic."

"Exactly. A picnic spot!" he says, nodding swiftly. "You enjoy it for a while, but you don't stay. Because it isn't yours. How about I show you around the place, you know, really show you? Let you enjoy it, have your picnic. Then you'll have the feeling you visited it and can move on. I can give you a nice break before Pratt gets back. And then you safely go. See?"

A little holiday, he means? Death on vacation.

But what does he imagine he can show me, who's seen so much?

"Emma." And there is the sound of my name in his mouth again, rubbing, humming inside it. "You look like you're wondering why exactly I'd do that for you. I think it's because I want to show you—how the world is, now. When I do, maybe you'll be glad you don't have to be a part of it. I'll show you. We can make a day of it. Until they get back. I'm not against you, I want you to know that." He looks carefully at me. He's trying to gauge if I trust him, if I will trust him. Ah, I've seen that look before, from men especially. *How far will she trust me to take her?*

"I've got nothing against you," he says again. "I feel for you, I do." He's watching me closely. "I really mean that."

You think you can see through me because I'm not solid the way you are.

"A holiday would be nice," I say sweetly and smile. "A little holiday from the ordinary."

"I feel that way, too." And his smile is a mirror of mine. We're both reflections now. Unreal.

21

He holds the glass door open for me. He wants me to leave the house but is clever enough to act the gentleman about it.

I glide past. As I do, I sense some brittleness in him. He's more anxious than he's letting on.

Outside he fits his straw hat back onto his head.

"So you've seen the owners' bunker, I know that much. And my place, I take it? So let's go off that way, just past my cottage. There's something pretty there you might like."

Dear me, does he imagine a girl who's been dead for more than a century and that the whole world wants to put down in the ground only wants for something "pretty"?

I nod, and my black hem skirts the gravel path between us as we walk. He can have no idea, this caretaker, what I want. But we're cozier together than I would have guessed. Well, a holiday is a holiday, even if you hadn't planned it.

"I'm taking you to the greenhouses," he says as he points at the glassy domes up ahead. "They're state of the art." Whatever he means by it. "Both an expression of what life can be and how bad it's gotten."

He goes on saying things I half understand. *The tipping point*, he says more than once. It doesn't matter. He seems distracted by me, by company he can talk to yet imagines won't stay.

"The technology isn't in plain sight when you look at it, but it's something. What we have here is the ability to cultivate with very little water."

Close to hand, the greenhouses remind me of the sunroom in that mansion by the sea I used to haunt—glass all broken into smaller panes, delicate and shimmering.

The dome's panes aren't fogged, he says, they're coated.

He holds open a frosted door, and I obligingly step inside.

"Now, these vertical wires running down from the very top"—they're wrapped like the poles of a merry-go-round—"these can support vines, legumes, as they grow. The dome adjusts to the light, filters to the appropriate level, which is why it's fairly shady in here right now. Success, in the future, is all going to be about managing light and dark."

As it already is, for some of us.

"And dew point, of course." He takes off his hat and scratches the part in his hair, as if doing sums under it. "As well as soil and seed. Below this, underground, for when the time comes, we have the seed and soil stored."

"We?" He seems to forget he's quite alone, apart from me.

"The owners plan to keep me on to manage the farm when the time comes. One person to do all the work. Fewer mouths to feed. The Halstens, they're not particularly handy with tools. What's coming isn't good, and it's going to take practical skills to get through." He puts his hat back on. "Does any of this make sense to you?"

They're all worried they'll have nothing to eat. I'm not worried that way.

"Sense enough," I say.

"What do you think? See what I'm talking about? How life is hard, and is going to get harder?"

"I think it's very pretty," I say. The children will love this greenhouse. All these wires going up and down to play on.

"Everything's on hold in this valley—but it's ready for the worst. The alfalfa, right now, is being sold as feed, but it's really just for show. The owners don't want to give anything away. Not now, not later. They've got guns locked away. A lot of guns. There are plans for how to block the only entrances into this valley. So there'll be no need for things to get out of hand. There are water tanks underground. Plans for protein sources. Are you getting the picture? It's not rosy this side of the grave. It's a barbecue waiting to happen. Would you like to see the animal stalls?" he says as he leads me to the many-paned door again. "I do an inspection of them, too, about this time, every week."

Not such a holiday, after all. Winn Towhee, it seems, is just a man folding me into his daily routine. Well, it was the same when I was a working girl. Every day with its own task. Monday was washing. Tuesday, the floors and beating the rugs. Wednesday was baking. Thursday, polish the silver and crystal. Friday was mending. Saturdays, we served at parties or visiting guests. There was always some lively spree we were meant to see but not enjoy.

We walk toward some wooden buildings beyond the fields. He's close at my side, but not too close, as though something about me might be catching.

"How do you do it?" he asks suddenly. "I can see you right here. Beside me. You look perfectly normal." He seems amazed by how real I am, how present. "How do you go about—I mean Pratt said you can fit into keyholes, said you can change shape. Do you"—he looks down at his scuffed boots, embarrassed—"just decide? Do you—is this—was this how you looked when you were . . . What I'm wondering is, if you can look any way you like, what, who am I looking at now?"

As if the living only ever look one way? As if the living don't ever change their faces and never hide what they are, or sometimes only show themselves truly for an instant, or only show themselves truly to some. It isn't only ghosts who shape and shift. Only the bit about keyholes is eerie, I'll grant you that.

"Do you know," I ask him, while I look straight ahead, "what you look like, without looking?"

"More or less."

"Do you know how to be anyone other than yourself?"

"I've tried. I keep coming back to . . ." He catches himself, surprised.

"Haunt yourself," I say.

"Yes." He laughs, a pleasant laugh. "Though it's not the same thing."

"Maybe not." For to be a ghost is to will yourself, at every moment, into some form. I don't say this to the man beside me. I won't share my secrets. There's no need. It wouldn't be safe, in any case. "Not all of us are the same," I go on, striking out a little ahead of him now. "Most of us want to look as we did just before we died.

Or younger. Some don't know yet how to manage it, so look as they do in their coffins, or before they were burned in a crematory, or wherever they were left to rot." A monstrous thing to behold, a moving corpse. You don't forget it.

If we appear in other ways and forms—a mist, a spider's web in the corner . . . or trail something behind us . . . a chain . . . a flower's petals—it's because we've turned ourselves into crumbs so that we can find our way, not back, but forward.

In truth, no one likes to be as small as a keyhole. It's like being nothing. No one wants to live inside a lock. Especially when that's what the living want for us, to lock us away, so they won't see what's truly behind and in front of them. Death's shadow.

In this valley, it seems to me, the living are trying to stay alive forever—or at least longer than the dead. That's all the answer they can ever manage to come up with, and it's why so few of them ever try to stop what's happening to us, preferring their bunkers and domes and here now the empty animal barn we walk into, with its wooden troughs and its rows of stalls, for all the world like an empty ark, waiting.

The caretaker stops inside the shade of it, and turns to study me.

"So you looked like this right before you died?"

"Yes." This shape is as far as I got. I wanted more. Like all the rest. "What sort of animals," I say quickly to change the subject, "are meant to be in here?"

"The plan is," he says as he slides the door of one stall back, "for minimal stock, for protein, some biodiversity, genetically superior, controls for inbreeding, and for use as basic power, and transportation, if needed."

It looks like a waiting jail cell.

He picks up a broom and sweeps the red dust out of it. If you don't stay on top of dust, I know from being a maid myself, it creeps up on you, and the next thing you know you're buried.

This isn't much of a holiday for either of us, I decide.

"Chickens," he says abruptly. "Chicken would be better. But the Halstens appear to have something against chickens."

"That's foolish of them."

"I couldn't agree more. Compact to house, you get eggs, meat, fertilizer, they'll eat anything, in some ways they're perfect—"

He looks around. I've disappeared.

A holiday has to be fun or else what's the point?

"Here I am. Up in the loft," I say.

A bit of a lark.

"Wow. Nice. Should I come up?"

"I'll wait."

He leaves his straw hat on a peg below before starting up the sturdy ladder. He keeps his eyes up, on me. His hands know the way without looking. He never loses sight of my face.

He twists and sits beside me, dark boots dangling beside mine.

"Must be nice, vanishing and appearing whenever you like."

"It is, once you learn."

"Does—everyone—every ghost—ah—learn?"

"Some not fast enough. They're the ones that Pratt and his like get."

He looks down at the floor of the barn.

"You must hate people like him."

"It's mutual."

"It's unfortunate."

It's more than that. It's damnation.

"How do you go on?" he asks.

"By escaping them. By learning about them, too. And the way they think. He wouldn't do what you're doing, now, you know." Pratt doesn't ask questions. All the answers have been his. Up to now.

"It's pretty clear he wouldn't."

"When I was a little girl, I used to sit in lofts like this. It's so pleasant."

"We can sit for a while, if you like."

"No. I go on by going on." I stand. "Let's keep going."

"I have to go back down the ladder," he says with a laugh.

"Be my guest."

I join him as we pass through the rest of the stalls.

I say politely, "It must be cooler for you in this shade."

"You can't feel it, then?"

"Not at all."

"That must be strange. Are you . . . neutral?" he asks, awkwardly.

A soul can be hot or cold. But it's not the same thing as feeling what's hot or cold. I can only guess, in the end, by looking, at what anyone, what this man beside me might be feeling.

"I'm warm," I say, "now."

"Me too."

We've reached the wooden, bolted door at the end of the barn, and he opens it. The back of the valley appears. I start a bit.

It's heaven.

"I know." He squints under his hat. "It's something, isn't it? That formation in the distance, that hoodoo and that mesa, they call it the Pastor Before His Flock. That's not the Navajo name.

To the Diné, it's *naat'áanii*. That means leader. I'm not Navajo, but I prefer it. You have an accent," he says abruptly. "It sounds Irish. You're really not from here."

I never said I was.

"Maybe I'd like to be, Mr. Towhee."

"Sure. Everybody's always wanted this land. This water. It's been taken and taken, over and over again. Who knows how many people have died here? Who knows who's buried under all of this? Why aren't they all raised up, is what I want to know. Tell me, why isn't everyone a ghost?"

He's angry, all at once. And he thinks I have the answer.

I don't.

"I want to lie down in the clover," I say.

"Why?"

"Because it's beautiful."

"All right then."

He follows, staying clear of my skirt, as though he's distracted and imagines he might trip on it.

I've wanted, since I first came here, to lie down, of my own choice, on the planted earth. On this mat so green and fresh that, even though I have no skin to touch it, it will still sink into me, and at the same time float me, hold me up.

I start to run—he can't stop me—and here throw myself down on it.

He takes off his hat again and seems blinded by the angle of the sun. Or is that me he's blinking down at?

"I guess I'm joining you."

Yes. Let's lay back in a green field for a moment and let nothing matter at all.

He throws his arm over his face to shade his eyes. We needn't see each other.

"Tell me about your life," I ask. "I want to remember life."

"How will that help? Won't it hurt to hear?"

"Only if you've been luckier than I was."

I turn my eyes, my cheek, to face him. His mouth is frowning, under his arm.

"I don't know if I am." He shakes his head, his closed eyes. "Since I don't know you."

22

Life, as the living man named Winn Towhee tells it to me, has for him been mostly quiet.

He was born the youngest of two sons, on rangeland on the far edges of Masters County, he says. He grew up tending sheep and the dogs that tended to the sheep. His father left his mother when he was five years old. She wanted to stay on the land. He wanted schooling, college, to climb. He had little memory of the man, although he knew he later joined the military. His mother had accepted his checks until she died. She was repairing the roof when an earthquake caused by a gas company draining nearby land knocked her off her ladder. She broke her hip.

"My mother had a gift for fixing things. She would go to anyone's house and bang it into shape. She was loved by everybody for that. My father's gift was different. It was sight like an eagle. They loved him in the Air Force, apparently. At least, he never wanted to come home. My take is, he loved that Uncle Sam loved him, and he loved that more than he loved what we did and who we were. Or maybe there was trouble with my mother she never told us about. She said he was moody. My brother—he's an attorney, lives in Phoenix, now—got into a fight with her once, told her a family isn't a mood, you don't leave it for a mood. My brother wanted her to divorce my father. She wouldn't. My mother took the money from the Air Force and when we both wanted to go to college, she made sure we did. Do you know about college? Sorry, I don't know about what you would and wouldn't be up on."

Of course I know. I wanted schooling myself, I remember as I look into the sun overhead. I wanted it so badly. Where I grew up, all the wealthy boys were sent east for knowledge, because the West was thought too wild and uncivilized for modern learning. I used to imagine myself on a train to a different ocean, to whatever secrets lay there that weren't packed in brown paper and sent west. All my life and afterlife, I've wondered about why some places are thought to be keys and others not. If you reach one of the keys, they'll even hang it around your neck, so you can use it. While in other places, you're left to dig in the dirt.

I've had to learn everything by looking over the shoulders of the living. I've done well enough, crawling into the locks of books and opening them. But no one should have to be dead to be knowing.

"So you went to college," I say. "Did you like it?"

The caretaker sits up on his elbows and looks straight ahead.

"School was good. I thought I'd study mechanical engineering. I did for a while. It was fine. I mean there was nothing wrong with engineering or me. I have a good head for how things work, growing up with the kind of mother I did. I liked botany, too." He spreads a hand over the tops of the clover. "I liked a lot of things in Flagstaff. Friendly people. Good mix. I worked nights for a package delivery service. Loading trucks. Graveyard shift. Sorry," he says, "I guess that sounds rude to you."

"It's all right." They call it the dead of night. It's far away, as we loll in the bright day of this field.

"When I was twenty-one, I quit college," he goes on. "Took what little money I had from UPS, bought a used motorcycle. Thought I needed to see the country past the Four Corners. I headed to Texas, Louisiana. From there north, Arkansas, Missouri, Iowa, Wisconsin, Michigan. Beautiful country up there. I didn't realize. I took jobs in every place I went. That's how you learn what a body's worth in the marketplace. Not much these days, just so you know. I met a lot of people who worked hard and then got thrown away. Human beings treated like they were beer gone flat and the world wants to stay drunk. The bigger cities weren't much better. I did like Chicago. Chicago has a few things going for it. Ever been to a big city?"

His eyes are bright. He's remembered something. Is he going to tell me about the East? I've always stayed away from cities. There are too many hunters in them, they're too crowded, and too many people who don't want to share what little space is in them.

"I want to go," I say.

"Seems like a city would be a perfect place for your kind—for you."

So. Now it's clear. His eyes are bright because he's recalled: he wants to get rid of me. And he thinks he's found a way.

"Big cities are exciting. Lots of people. Easier to get lost, hide, not be noticed. Wouldn't that be safer for you?"

You can be schooled and know nothing.

I shrug, still on my back, unmoving. "I like open country."

"Open country." He falls back again. "Me too. That's the trouble, isn't it? I missed all this, when I was traveling." He tilts his chin backward toward the cliffs. "It's why I came back. I got home in time to see my mother buried, patch things up with my brother—he mostly had to take care of my mother and everything himself while I was gone. He asked me if I wanted our family house and land. I said no. Some memories are too hard to go back to. Maybe it's the same for you." He says nothing for a moment. "Anyway. We made a deal with some neighbors, sold it to them. Sometimes just deciding a thing, taking control, feels like property."

Yes. That's true.

"I worked in Huff for a while, tourist jobs, guiding, till that started to dry up. I got into a complicated relationship. Got out of it. I landed this gig in the middle of that. I've been here five years at the ranch. It's perfect for me. I'm perfect for this place. Jack of all trades. I know everything that needs to be known. Agriculture, mechanics, maintenance, construction. I even take care of their Cessna when they fly in on that runway over there. See the hangar? You know anything about airplanes? I mean, you know about them, right?"

"I know." I remember the first one I ever saw. It looked like a metal box inside a paper kite. I thought it was a miracle.

He says, "I guess flying is no big deal to you. You hopped up to that loft like the jump was nothing. If it's not too rude to ask, how high can you go?"

It's easy and not at all, leaving the world. The farther you get from earth, the floor underneath you, this grass, this dirt, the more you don't feel a part of what's happening. The more you might let go. *Careful, Emma Rose, careful.*

"We stay close to the ground," I say. "We keep low."

"I understand. Keep low, and you'll be all right."

He falls silent. There's something more he isn't saying. He stays on his back, his long black hair fanned on the ground. I sit up.

"Why have you stayed low here?" I ask. "You're not flat beer."

"They at least pay me what I'm worth."

"Do they?"

"I like the solitude."

"Do you? You've started talking to a ghost."

"Fair enough. Maybe I'm afraid."

"You don't look it." He doesn't. He looks haunted. There's a difference.

"Trust me, ghost, I am afraid. You don't know what it's like to be alive right now. Here, in this valley, isolated, maybe we'll last a little longer than in other places. When the shit comes down, I hope to last a little longer."

"You're afraid of dying."

"I'm afraid of what's coming."

No, that's not it, or not all. I see it in his face. I know fear well enough. I've felt it often enough. I know how to make others feel it, when necessary. Winn Towhee isn't afraid in the usual ways. There's some other concern stretching his skin.

I say, "You like caring for this place."

"Sure. There's that. I spent a lot of time caring for myself for a number of years. So . . ."

"So now you're caring for something else. Or is it someone else?" I see that much in his eyes. I know that look. I've worn it. *There's someone you think you must care for, though all your senses tell you otherwise. Someone you should have given up caring about, that went away, yet still you haven't given up, or no, you have, but the memory of having cared once haunts you still.*

"I remember the habit of caring," I tell him. I remember everything. Because when you die, everything comes with you—a tail of knots on the kite.

"It's your turn, now," he says quietly.

"Mine?"

"I've told you about my life. I did as you asked. Now I want to hear yours. Before you go."

He still thinks I'm leaving, does he.

He says, "It doesn't happen much, does it? That you get to sum up your life to someone else, a total stranger, and not worry about how it sounds. But you and I can do that. No one's . . . auditioning here. We're not even on the same stage. None of this is real, in a way."

He's wrong. It is real.

We are real. Both of us.

I'm real.

He thinks we're not of the same world, that talking to the dead is whispering to a dream after sleep. He has no idea.

How do I make him see?

My life. My afterlife.

They're too long a tale to tell in one sitting. But if I were to choose one moment, just one moment, from each—to show him that I'm no different than I once was, and no different than he is—and how unjust it is that the world imagines we're simply soul and body, spirit and flesh, one of them meaningless without the other, as though we couldn't be something else entirely besides, something there's no word for—so we settle for *soul* and *body*, but here I am, something more, something besides, and *so are you, here, now, caretaker*—if I could find one moment from my life and one from my afterlife to make myself as real as he is in his own, what would I choose?

"When I was a girl," I say, "I lived in a place where there were cliffs as tall and harsh as these."

I straighten my legs out in front of me—I want him to see how long I reach, how tall I am—and point my cleft chin to the cliffs.

"Instead of looking down on a desert," I go on, "the cliffs I know stood high above an ocean, and all its spray and foam. There's a headland there, covered in mustard seed and sea-thrift blossoms. It's damp nearly all the year round, and salty always, and the ground smells of the air and the air smells of the ground, not one or the other. The fog comes in, and it's neither cloud nor rain. The tide comes in and goes out and comes back again, there's no one level to the water, and some high tides are higher than others, and some lows are lower, and that's the way of things. Have you ever lived by the sea?"

"No." He shakes his head. "I've seen it. But haven't lived by it."

"Do you feel the place where you were born does something to you?"

"I do."

"Even if you leave it? Even if you want to leave it, and have good reason to, it's still in you, isn't that right? You can't see the wind and spray in me. I can. The cliffs and the flowers and the foam. They're in me. And they're there, still, too, along that coast. The sea is there, and it's also here. And I don't mean just as a memory. I mean something else besides. There's the sea, and there's me, and there's the place where me and the sea meet, and it's as real as anything you can touch, and maybe more, because it lasts and can travel farther."

I can't stop. "The sea . . . it drowned me when I was nineteen years old. I don't talk about how it came to happen." It's not a story I want to tell, today, to this man. "The sea by itself is a real thing. I was nineteen, a girl and not the sea. I couldn't breathe in it. I sank to the bottom, and the fish and crab tore me to pieces. But if that's all I had been, meat for the crabs, I couldn't be here now as plain as day beside you. A person isn't their grave. I'm not ground. I'm not air. I'm something else, I think. And I think it's so for others, too." Only why, why, then, when the children tipped the tombstones over at the cemetery, did some rise, and others not?

"I'm everything I ever was, Mr. Towhee, and ever saw. When my father was still alive"—perhaps this will teach him, since he's lost his father, too—"he used to take me to that headland above the sea at night. He'd point out all the stars he could name for me, and say, 'Back home, in Ireland, they're seeing the same stars.' The stars were far away and strange, he said, and you'll never touch them, but you'll share them all the same. That's a thing I remember and still have with me, from when I was a little girl, that night. And something else. We were waiting for the moon to rise, not over the sea, but from behind the cliffs. It was a full moon, and at first it looked huge, egging over the land. Then as it rose it looked smaller and smaller, and I said to him, 'Da, the moon is shrinking.' He said, to me, 'No, dear, it only looks that way. It only looks that way apart from the land. The land beside it, when it's closer, gives it a measure, something to compare it against, and so the moon looks like a giant to us. But floating out in the sky with no measure around it, it looks smaller and less, though it isn't that at all.'"

215

I felt what my father was saying through every part of me that had a measure and that didn't. I felt the moon puffed up when it was close to something and small and shrunken when it was alone. But neither were true, and I knew it, because that was me. When I was close to my father, I felt sturdy, and when he was away in the forest or at the docks, I felt like a wisp. When he died, it took me a long time to believe I was like the moon and that I was there even when no one saw me or saw me the wrong way.

"How did your father die?" Winn Towhee asks.

"He was felled by cut timber."

"And your mother?"

"She died when I was born. I never knew her." Except from photographs, and by how my father hung her in the sky.

"I'm sorry."

I say swiftly, for I won't be pitied, "After I was dead, it was mostly at night I moved. I was afraid of being seen in the day, although once you know how to manage the light"—I look without blinking at the sun—"there's no hour you can't find a way through, one way or the other. I stayed for a long time on the coast. All my family are buried there. I visited their graves at night. I spoke to them and thought maybe I could pull them out of the ground. I couldn't. I kept busy during the day haunting and following the living and learning all about them and what was new, coming into the world." Yet at night a big house goes quiet, everyone's asleep, the laughing and the fighting and the brushing of teeth and the lovemaking are all done, and you can either curl into a ball in the attic, go as gossamer as a spider's web, or you can stroll out under the moon, to the graves where no one stayed.

"Only once did I go to the cemetery and find a ghost there," I go on. This was just as evil men like Philip Pratt, with their hunts, were coming along to empty the night of its ghosts as fast as the sea was being emptied of fish. "The ghost I saw came up from the sea, as I had done. He was a fisherman. A trawler had capsized in a gale. The living had all been talking about it. He was as lost as any man can be, this fisherman. He was from a place farther up the coast. He couldn't recognize at all where he was, or what had happened to him."

I tell the living caretaker breathing next to me that the poor fisherman kept coughing and coughing, as though he could cough the sea out of his lungs. *Hush, hush*, I said, or you'll give us both away. We're in the time of the hunters, remember, and there are more and more of them and fewer and fewer of us who make our way. I asked for the fisherman's name but all he could do was cough and weep. He was far from home and what he loved, I saw. He never meant to sink and end here. If he had a family, they would have nothing of him to bury, unless in a few days his body washed ashore into a tide pool or onto a beach. Though mine never did.

As a new ghost, he knew nothing about disappearing. He stood there, hunched and plain as day. He was a heavyset man. He must have liked his fish battered and fried, as I used to make it for my father. He was in that frightened state before we ghosts learn that, in order not to be discovered, we must vanish like vapor, becoming like air and smoke, like we imagine the soul to be. He was still in that moment when we are most like our living selves. It's only trying and training that teaches you how to disappear and become nothing, invisible, cold, so that you have to remember, and decide again, each time you come back, what you look like, and that you still *are*.

The ghost asked me how far it was to Humboldt Bay. I told him it wasn't so great a distance, but he was in no condition to make the journey. He was freshly dead and innocent and would be caught in a hunter's net. I told him he must grow cold, stuff every warm living feeling down inside him and close the hatch to it, if he hoped to reach a familiar shore.

"I must go cold?" he said. "I don't want to." He'd spent his whole life trying to stay warm, he told me, warm and dry out on the frigid sea.

"I know. But you must manage it. It'll grow easier, I promise."

"I don't like the sound of that."

Death can make the strongest man cry. I was long done by then with tears, but it didn't mean I had forgotten how hard it is at first. I told him I would teach him to vanish. He listened, miserable and amazed, as I helped the candle of him go dark.

"Yes, that's it, that's good. It's like holding your breath when you haven't any left. You'll grow easier with it," I promised. "And with other things, too. There's a lightness, feel it? Hold onto that. And you'll see things you never might've. I promise. And some you won't want to. So you must be careful."

"The hunters," he'd whispered. "Is it payback for everything I killed?"

I didn't know. There's no book or bible, after you die, that pretends to make things plain.

I look now at Winn Towhee. I've told him what I meant to. To make him see. That's all I meant and cared to do.

"Then the man left," I finish. "Weeping as he went."

"Did you ever see him again? Did he end up being . . . hunted?"

"I don't know." When the hunters first appeared, there were fantastical news stories about each of the dead they cleaned. But as time passed, only the most stubborn ghosts warranted any attention.

I was one.

"Thank you for telling me about the fisherman. And your father," he says as he turns his head away from the cliffs. "You didn't want to, I think. But I asked you. Maybe I shouldn't have. Thank you."

There's a kindness in his voice, something new, fresh as a sprig of clover. I wonder if he sees, in my face, that I've heard it.

"Something's changed between us, hasn't it, Emma? It almost seems like you trust me now. When I've given you no real reason to."

I never do things without a reason.

He stands suddenly. "Can I show you something?"

The sun has shifted. Time has moved on. He throws a longer shadow on the field as he beckons me.

I stand and follow.

"This is a runway, as I mentioned." He points to the red earth he's led me onto. "The owners fly in and out on it. You see this dirt?"

"I see it."

He bends to stroke it. "What it is, though you can't tell it now, is worn-down mountains. Mountains that rose up, long ago, mountains that turned to dust again. All of this"—he sweeps his cuffed sleeve, taking in the whole, fine valley—"was a sea three hundred million years ago. To the east there was a mountain range, the Ancestral Rockies. Taller than the Rockies we know now. Time and wind and water acted on them, and their grit broke down and blew away and landed in the shallow sea that was here. More and more bands of sand landed in the water, got compressed. Dinosaurs wandered through the water and mud. They left tracks. More sand was laid down. The tracks got buried. The sea drew back. It came and went. The land started to rise. Everything you see here now, the cliffs and the mesas, *naat'áanii*, the leader, it was all sea floor at some point, it was all under water—and then it wasn't. The land lifted. Again. Now it's being worn down again. Mountains are under our feet. The sea, too. Mountain and seafloor, they're the same thing. Like you. Earth and air and something else." He rubs the dirt between his fingers. "Like all of us."

He walks without saying more to a great humped silver building at the end of the red lane of vanished sea.

"This is the hangar." He approaches it and taps at numbers on a pad on the wall. The metal mouth of the building yawns and rises, opening mechanically, disappearing into itself.

"There's nothing in here right now apart from tools and a cot I keep in here for no reason that will make any sense to you, unless I tell you." He stuffs his hands in his pockets as we go into the shade, as though he's suddenly cool. Though he can't be.

He looks up at the metal roof with no sun coming through it.

"You told me things, Emma. And I lied to you. About why I'm here."

Well, we're both real. That means we can both lie.

"How have you lied to me, Mr. Towhee?"

"Winn, please. I consider it lying if you don't tell the whole story." He keeps looking up, into the metal emptiness. "I told you I'm here because the job pays well. That's true. And because I like tending things. That's also true. And because I have fears. Also true. What I didn't tell you is that my father died not far from here. My father, he killed himself. The way he went, he went looking straight at the thing that killed him. When the Air Force was about to kick him out—he had demons, he was good about keeping them down, apparently, until he wasn't—he climbed into his own twin-engine and flew out over the backcountry, here, out over the canyons and slots, and picked a particularly narrow fissure and pointed his nose straight down and jammed himself right into it. He wasn't found for over a year. He was reported missing, but nobody knew where to look. When another plane, federal, finally did spot the wreckage, there was nothing left to recover. Animals probably dragged off his bones. We never had a service. There was nothing to bury. We could have gotten one of those headstones the military gives veterans' families, but my mother never applied for it. I don't know whether my father wanted to be found and remembered or not. Maybe he just wanted to disappear. His spirit has never shown up here, even though this is the closest human site to where he died. I used to sleep at night out here, just in case the hangar attracted him, the place for a plane. I still sleep here sometimes. It has a cooling system. It's airy. Covered but not confined. Like flying. He didn't know how to be with us, and I'm not sure I know how to be with people. I agree with you: we're always something else besides what people see or think about body and soul. I think about how much of us isn't even us. It's the demons we're made to carry by others. My father wanted to be loved by something that's always been better at not loving people like him. He flew alone, and he never flew alone. It's something I know now. That I live with."

He sits down heavily on the blanketed cot.

I say nothing for a long moment. *I think about how much of us isn't even us.* I'd said, what you can't see can be real. But he's answered: yes, or it can be too real.

"May I sit down with you?" I ask.

"Sure. This cot isn't very—" He blinks and seems to remember. "You weigh nothing, I guess."

I sit. We're as naked to each other as we dare be, I think. Someone looking at us would not be able to say this one has skin and this one doesn't.

"I'm sorry about your father," I say at his ear.

"Thank you."

I stretch out a hand.

He takes it.

What a wonder.

It feels like sand and sea. The sand of him scrapes and swirls against me, and the foam of me, I think, wets the sand of him.

"You don't feel cold or dead," he says.

"I'm not cold."

"You feel like . . . everything." He closes his eyes.

"So do you."

"How do we do this?"

"I couldn't say. It's my first time for anything like this." Anything close to it.

"I think you're beautiful," he says, his voice steady.

"Thank you."

"I'm sorry I called a killer on you."

"We don't have to worry about him."

"I was upset. I wasn't waiting for you. I was waiting for another ghost."

"I wasn't waiting for you either."

"We can wait for the wrong things."

"Yes. I think we can." Waiting gives the devil time. And fear. And doubt. "I want to kiss you," I say, quick, before the devil comes.

"Should we just see what happens?"

*

The first time I was kissed, so long ago, the pressure was so new and strange to me that it stayed on my lips for hours and hours into the night, as though the one who kissed me was still there.

The pressure is still the same, but when we move apart it's gone.

"Come back," I say.

He does.

I don't know where we are for a moment, who is outside or in.

A ghost doesn't undress in the usual way. If I want this to happen, I must decide for it to. I must choose my remembered bareness, forget the clothes I wore when I drowned, as he sheds his own.

I've seen his skin already this day, but he hasn't seen mine until now.

Mine is a fine nakedness. I trust it. I feel every inch of it. I know myself.

I'm no reflection. I'm as he is, everything I carry and feel inside me.

What a wonder it is, the peak, the cry of lovemaking. We make sounds like caught birds as the hangar above us grows dark. No one is there to hear us. No one is here to see our eyes so close, it's as if each of us crosses over to the other.

And then, after a long while, it's drifting sleep, side by side in our narrow bed. I'm drifting away again.

But ghosts don't sleep.

Where do we go, if we do?

23

Flickering light. That was fire.

Pratt, in the dark, swallowing against something tight in his throat, strained to see beyond the log hut's door.

He felt Hogan beside him, struggling in the same way.

There was comfort at least in having her body next to his.

Smoke had begun seeping in around the frame.

"We haven't been set on fire at least," she said, tense. "That's a campfire out there. I wish I could see more than a sliver of what's happening. I wish I knew who was out there gaming us."

All he could make out through an uneven crack were their wavering shadows. Impossible to distinguish any form. Or intent.

"We have *got* to see what we're dealing with." Hogan groped at herself. "Belt buckle. They made that mistake. Take yours. Right now. Go after the chink."

Hogan's was a quick, good mind. He trusted her. Yet when he unthreaded the leather at his waist, he felt stripped.

An unimportant detail. Time was of the essence. *Try. Try,* Pratt urged himself. They nicked and picked as softly as they could and widened a few crumbling gaps. He began making out hunched forms. Whispering. Rocking laughter, pitching, leaning, shoulder against shoulder. Delighted.

Weapons gleaming, resting against the log stumps they sat on.

"I still make it three men. Shit." Hogan stopped and stared. "This isn't good: you don't wear camo out here unless you're hunting. Or like the idea of war."

He could make out the clothing now, too. Earthen. Mottled in the firelight.

"Who are we looking at?" He knew the answer already. Not the dead; those attracted to death.

"Take your pick. Survivalists, off-the-gridders, religious apocalyptic nut types. We see the far, ugly edges in this desert sometimes." Her breath was coming fast now. He could make out her worried profile in a gash of light. "They do tend to have a few things in common, though. They all think the end-times are near, and they hate people like us."

"Us?

"Law enforcement."

Of course. There were always those who didn't like to be told that order was greater than their fantasies.

"Listen. Can you hear what they're saying?"

He couldn't. Was it the blow to his head? Or age, coming on at last?

"They're laughing at us," she said. "They can tell we're awake. From the way they're talking, I think they're a restoration militia. To them, sites like this, old forts, have to be taken back from the federal government, or the tribes, by force. A lot of them got pushed out of their homes when their wells went dry. Now they pretty much hate everyone and everything. They probably shot up the pictographs we saw. They're saying the Needlestick belongs to them, not the—the—I'll spare you what they call the tribes. People like me—badges—they call targets."

She scooted on her pants away from the light, falling silent.

There were protocols, strategies, surely, to fall back on now. "Can we communicate with them?" Pratt asked. "Make them see we're real people, not—badges?"

"Making us real will only whet their appetites. They're already talking about how juicy we are. That they won't even have to open the door, can do it from right where they're sitting. They know we can hear. They want us to be afraid for a while. All part of the fun."

"My God." It felt less like a word, leaving Pratt's body, than a hole.

"What about your weapon?" she asked.

"It can only react to remnants." A safety feature. Technology with only one focus, the only one necessary to it. Pratt had never considered until now its limitations. He'd never felt the need, in his work, to carry a gun with bullets. *I am not a violent man. I have never been a violent man.* He'd always been invited, welcome, wherever he went.

But admit it: not this time. He had followed his gut, a hint on a map, a possible track. That was all. He was, for the first time, in a space, a place he had most emphatically not been invited into. He was off the map. This had all been a mistake, either by design or accident. The trouble he sought hadn't come here. Or rather, there was trouble, only of the wrong kind. The dead weren't here. He was boxed in with the dangerous living. The living dressed for a hunt.

"So we have to think," he said, aloud, "like hunters."

"Yeah? How?"

"Dig in. Dig into the dirt." He knew how to get his hands dirty. He'd dug into graves. Those of others. Maybe now it would be his own—there was no time to speculate, fall back into fear. "We get down. Low. Get through the first volley."

"Enough," she agreed, "to get them to come in and savor their victory. Then we hide behind the door. I feel some good rocks in here. That'll be our only chance. They could also be drunk. That might help us."

"Buckle down," he said, more to himself. "Dig."

The ground was dry and friable. They scraped, frantically. Dust rose and clogged Pratt's throat. Could they really be digging their own graves? Surely this wasn't real, he thought, this wasn't happening.

Laughter still, outside, by the fire. His eyes had adjusted enough that he could see around him, and see Hogan tearing at the earth. Her lips were moving. As if in a prayer. He heard the low words:

> *Grieve for me.*
> *For I would grieve for you.*
> *Grieve for me.*
> *For I would grieve for you.*

"What is that?" he asked, spitting dirt from his mouth.

"It's Navajo. My grandmother, before she died, she said you don't talk about death, not if you're trying to avoid it. Talking about death can bring death. But I figure, if it's already on its way . . ."

Then grieve for me, Pratt thought.

For the work unfinished.

For relatives far away.

For skills gone to waste.

For a gift about to be extinguished.

But not yet?

He wrapped his belt around his hand.

His heart, which had merely been pumping oxygen to his lungs, seized.

There it was.

He was certain of it. Had been so all along.

I knew this was a place of the dead, he thought, triumphant.

A ghost or ghosts were close.

But did the living, outside, in the firelight, know it?

He reached over to stop Hogan's hands.

"Hold on," he said.

The laughter of the militia halted. Their campfire had died. The faint cracks of light through the chink were erased, the world stamped black.

Suddenly the air shook.

"What—" Hogan said.

Pratt leaned forward and pressed his hands, his ear, straining against the wood. At first, nothing else. Then, like a drum, it channeled sound. Pounding. Growing loud. Louder still. Abrupt cocking of weapons. Sudden screams. Running, scrambling feet, followed by thick, muscular blows, guttural falls, then harsher sounds, heavy, inhuman, snorting, whistling, like a wind driving or being driven. Over this, ecstatic howls. Rhythmic circling.

"Those are war cries," Hogan said at his shoulder. "From horseback."

The haunting was a riot, a rout in the dark. Pratt could see nothing, nothing at all, not until there came moving bursts of light, figures, shapes too fast to have any meaning beyond the waves of anger he felt coursing through the walls, his gut.

Then abject oaths of defeat, receding.

"They're going." Hogan stood, excited. "Whatever, whoever it is, they're going!"

At once the door to the cabin swung open, fiercely. The fire was down to embers, sparkling faintly against the circle of stones.

Silence filled the night.

Hogan straightened in the jamb. Pratt stood beside her.

The earth was churned with the militia's departure.

"A party of ghosts," Pratt said, putting his belt on quickly.

"Jesus. Ghosts that chase thugs off? And then unlock the door for us?"

The dead were menaces. But in this case, the menace had been timely.

"Do you hear a motor?" Pratt asked, tucking his shirt back in, his heart still throbbing.

"It sounds like my Bronco being driven away." She was shivering but also seemed to be collecting herself. It was cool as they stepped out into the open, into the fresh air, the smoke dissipating. Safe and cool outside the claustrophobia of their prison.

Pratt felt the blood coming back into his throat and head. There it was. Inside him. Life. Real life.

"More ghosts," Hogan said, bending to touch the barren ground. "Okay then. So you tell me how to thank the dead."

"You don't," Pratt said. He scraped some dirt out of his beard. He'd set himself to rights. He was ready to move on. He peered into the gloom, where the ancient drawings would be. "They weren't here for us. The tribes were called a slur. You said so. These ghosts—their war cries—were provoked. Probably doubly. You said the militia wanted to claim this site. Apparently, they weren't going to be allowed to. It had nothing to do with us."

"Then why open the door for us?"

"Were these ghosts you knew personally?"

"I don't think so."

"Then you can't know it was opened for you, or for us. It doesn't matter." A lucky, advantageous attack on the living was still an attack on the living. There was no forgetting that. He checked his cuff. "Where would they have come from or be likely to go?"

"Jesus," Hogan said. "You're not serious. You're after *them* now?"

"It's my work. My responsibility."

"It isn't, point of fact. We hired you to deal with a specific case. Affecting the county. A very specific case."

"This is a part of your county, yes?"

"This affects no one. You heard Winn. No one comes out here anymore. And now we know why. This is none of our damn business. Not anymore. And this is what's going to happen." She went quickly into the hut and came out again with her belt, whipping it around her. "We're leaving. Right now. We have to, frankly, if we don't want to die. It's a long walk out back to the road where someone might see us. We'll get moonlight soon. It's cool enough at night, and if we don't flatline because we're completely dehydrated, we'll be okay, we'll find help."

She was an officer trained to stay focused. She was showing him that. Fair enough. They could go. He could always return later. He said as much.

"Pratt, do you really not know how to be grateful for a rescue?" The dead were still the dead. "It's nothing for right now," he said, conciliatory. "Right now, I agree, we need to get back to the Halsten Ranch. We've been sidetracked here."

Led astray. Been beguiled. The effort, in the end, had failed, thanks to the history of the Needlestick itself. The Finnis ghost wasn't educated enough to have imagined the vagaries of, as Hogan had put it, *the edges of the desert*. Neither was he, admittedly. But he was still on the case. Or was again. And in one piece.

"Maybe you can tell me how you knew to call your people here?"

"My people?" she said as they began to feel their way out of the canyon.

"Your ancestors. You may not have known them, but I assumed they were, in some way? The ones you called with your prayer?"

The moon was rising, lighting the sky. He saw her shaking her head in disbelief.

"Pratt, you don't have the least idea what you're talking about. Navajo *don't* call the dead. We *don't* ask the dead to rise. You want to know about what just happened? Maybe ask Winn. His people do things differently. They have a different relationship."

"I think the most important thing to understand right now is that behind all of this was a trick. We were sent on the wrong path here." This dead end, this crude site, was no place for a skirt and ribbons.

"Well if it was a trick, it was a damn brutal one."

They were nearer to higher ground, climbing with hands and boots.

"I don't get it," Hogan went on. "What ghost or ghosts would send us somewhere where other ghosts would *save* us? Unless they didn't know or unless they were"—she seemed struck—"trying to teach us something?"

"You can take it as a good sign you're still living," Pratt exhaled and said as they stood on a ledge, "that you don't think like the dead. They don't think that way." They shot arrows into the dark.

"Then I guess we just got lucky, and that's the word I'll put in my report," she said, sounding brusque, staring out into the night.

"Luck we have you to thank for, sheriff. You and your prayer. Your astuteness."

"Astuteness. Yeah, right. I was just scared off my ass, and maybe someone heard what I do when I'm scared off my ass. It's not the first time. Most officers will tell you that."

"That you've had . . . help?"

"No. That we pray. Because"—she went on, striking out ahead of him—"we're scared all the time."

24

I rise and watch the living man I've trusted with every part of me, sleeping, peaceful, quiet, on his cot.

A new feeling, to study a face I've traded love with—that little curl at the corner of the mouth, the way his eyelids rest, each like a soft wing tucked against his body—and know some part of that rest I made and shared.

How did it happen? I only know it did. That for this past little while I have been in a different kind of darkness. And not in the kind to fear. I was tucked against his breast.

And then he slept.

I vanished, for a little while. But I didn't move. Or disappear. My mind wandered.

It was pleasant. To feel peaceful enough to woolgather.

Except now I'm restless. I can't sleep as he does. I won't disturb him. He's seen and felt as much as I have, this night, but he's living and can tire. I leave him and walk out of the empty building meant to shelter machines that fly. I'm lightness itself. The quarter moon has risen over the valley, and out of its tipping bowl is filling it with soft grays and greens. The clover droops and looks a little drunk, tipsy with the water it's been fed. Nothing that I see moves, not even the feathery leaves of the cottonwoods. I can hear the river burbling, like a tap left running.

I'm still flowing, too, I think. Another new thought and feeling. It's living bodies they say are made of water, and that we dead are dry as burned paper. Yet I walk and I feel like rain. I'm a stream moving toward a stream. The stream where we both first plunged together. I might even look back and see a track of mud, so alive I feel.

This is happiness. I remember it now. Even in death, we should have it. Or what's an afterlife for? The way the light falls on the gravel path. This is happiness. The face of a new friend, a lover. The twinge, the delight, at outsmarting a hunter, sending him east to find nothing so that he'll keep moving that way. The night stretching out like a sturdy roof, and look at all the stars, how they follow you wherever you go but mean no bother. Just because a thing seems to chase you doesn't mean it can get close enough to burn.

Closer to the river, the light is rippled and doubled, tripled. It's the moon dancing off shallow waves and whorls, the slickened rocks jutting out, even the wet sand on the banks sparking with tiny bits of metal. The cliffs are coated with light, too, a gleam so bright it seems to step away from itself.

And then it does.

The others take shape. On the bank opposite me. They're staring across at me, looking for a sign.

Is it safe to come across, Emma?

Briscoe is there, his flop hat drooped. If I nod at him, we'll begin to share this paradise. If I don't, then it means we, I, must go. There's a living man sleeping on a cot, and he doesn't know.

234

I should be happy to see them. I am, of course. I nod.
Come.

The moon hasn't changed, but its beam isn't as wide as it was,
now, striking one side of the valley. The noon of the moon is short,
just like the sun of the day.

They float over to me, faces full of hope. Briscoe reaches me
first.

"We were worried," he says. "You hadn't come back. Thought
you might be in trouble. You all right?"

"I'm good. All is well." I smile at him. It's good to see him. "It's
good that you came. Is everyone here?"

"That sad woman, the one we found in the cemetery who didn't
want to be moved, who wanted no company. She didn't make it."

I have to think for a moment. Oh yes. Doris Grunn. I knew
this. So much has happened.

"We left her. We had to. The hunter was coming. We watched
from up on the mesa. There was nothing we could do."

"I know. I'm sorry."

The others have gathered round, plainly eager for better news.

I smile at all of them, brightly. "It's a wonder here, friends.
Mr. Briscoe was absolutely right. And we can make it safe. The
living man here, the guard, I've taken care of him. It's all taken
care of."

"How?" asks the schoolmaster, warily.

What to say? "He has his own dead. Haunting him. Or rather,
he waits for his own dead."

"You mean he's a friend, then?" The schoolmaster wants to be
hopeful. He's seen me make friends with the living. At least for a
little while. There are the living you can trust. And those you can't.
The trick is sorting between them.

And in the end, weren't they all, still, not us?

Briscoe asks, "And where would he be, now?"

"Asleep. At the far end of the valley. In that metal building there. Let's leave him be for now. It will be for the best. But please," I say to the others, "go, and see what you make of it here. Think if we should bide here. If this is our new home."

They flow past me, swift, electric. When I turn, they're roaming through the fields, the children letting out little cries and hoots that sound like burrowing owls loosed from their holes.

Briscoe lingers beside me.

"It's like I said, isn't it, Emma Rose?"

"It is, Mr. Briscoe."

"See, a place like this doesn't deserve just one." He nods toward the hangar. "Or even two or three." He nods at the fields. "It's not right. It needs more."

"Is that why you didn't stay here when you were alone?"

"That," he admits, nodding, "and also, I see a place like this, it cuts too close to the bone. My people died for farmland like this. It's backbreaking work, making men and land do what they aren't meant to do."

"It's all modern here now," I say. "Plenty of machines and only one man."

"So it doesn't cost as much in flesh and treasure. Nice for the masters."

He looks to his left and to his right, and I see how much, in truth, Briscoe wants to take this place for us. And for him.

"Why," I ask, seeing, "did you send me here first when we could have all come together?"

"I wasn't sure you'd want to be boxed up in a valley like this. A man can miss stalls and hay. Not so sure about a woman."

"I like stalls and hay. And if we're careful with the guard, there are animals coming to the barn, too, Mr. Briscoe. Would you like that?"

"They'd be sleeping right now." He looks up at the moon. "If there were animals here, they'd be needing attention. I don't hear any coyotes. But I'll need to check the pens. Even a place like this, you got predators."

He tips his hat and goes.

I rise to the tops of the cottonwoods.

In every direction below me, I see happiness, clear as the stars. Joy is lighting up the fields. The family that washed away in a flood have found the smooth lawn and are standing on it, gazing at the solid main house. The loving couple have reached Winn's cottage, and sit on its stoop, side by side, as though this is a thing they remember. Our newest members, the nurse and the patient, have gathered with the carpenter brothers at the bunker, and are going down into it, curious. The children and the schoolmaster have found the greenhouses and are gadding inside one like fireflies inside a jar.

We dead can make dark places a lantern.

And there's satisfaction in getting what's owed. That can't be denied.

But a man is sleeping on a cot. Alone. And a woman is sitting in a tree. Lying to him. For a little while, I had him all to myself. Only an hour ago.

There came a moment, as we gazed into each other's eyes, when a kind of valley still lay between us, hidden, close. It was cool and fresh like every green and secret thing between our souls and bodies, and we were trying to close it in together, tightly, like a treasure, a box we had made just for ourselves, of ourselves.

"I don't know if I can believe in ghosts anymore," he'd said.

"What do you mean?"

"I don't see how there's such a word, for you. Aren't we the same, but on different parts of the journey?"

"I don't like the sound of that. Different."

"Why not?"

"Because then we couldn't meet anywhere."

It would mean one of us must always try to catch up to the other. And the other must always be chased.

"We've already met, Emma."

"And what do you suppose will happen now, since we have?"

"We'll stay here."

"Forever?"

"For as long as possible."

How deep is this valley? I'd wondered. If you fall into someone, do you carry enough of them inside you that you need go nowhere else? Is that love?

"We'll take," he said, "one minute at a time. That's always worked for me. Take more than that, and the world is overwhelming, hard to think about. But one minute. We could do that. See what happens."

Can we? When some minutes are friends and others are enemies.

25

"This is better," Hogan said in her no-nonsense voice as they left behind the box of Needlestick's canyon, no longer glancing back.

The moon was rising from beyond the thin spire. The flood of light gave them direction, now, a flinty path for their steps. They made their way out onto the open plain again. The air was crisp and night-quiet.

"Be sure to pick up your feet," she said. "You don't want to trip over something you didn't see."

Pratt kept his head down, concentrating. It was like squinting toward a gray sea floor. Something elongated glinted ahead of him.

"Sheriff, you see that?"

She bent and picked it up. "Jesus. My gun. What the hell." She looked to the right and the left before checking and holstering it. Then she bent down again, surprised. "And my phone, too, look at that. Dead as a doornail, but . . . You see yours?"

"No," Pratt said, looking around in the moonglow.

"Ingratitude to dead Indian warriors doesn't pay," she tried joking. "If only they'd left some water, too. We're in deficit but we might be okay."

Pratt also tried a laugh, but his throat felt like paper and the air, though cool, was as dry as after a bitter snow.

"My rifle was in my Bronco. Wish I had both back. I guess a thief would have to cut your arm off to take your weapon."

They would.

On the plateau again, the angled moon painted the landscape in pale grays and oil-stain shadows.

"You making out all right?" she asked in front of him.

"Fair to middling."

She stayed always a few steps ahead, to his left, following the tread previously laid down by her tires. A faint scent of crushed sage dampened the air. Or maybe the night brought it out, the stirring of animals. There were vague rustlings.

"Any nightlife we have to worry about out here?" he asked her.

"No. Coyotes won't bother us. Snakes are in their dens, keeping warm. We're not close to big cat terrain. How about anything you can sense?"

Nothing now of the pounding visitation that had terrified away their captors. Pratt felt, saw, only the grayness.

They dipped into dry washes and out again—the monochrome light made depth perception difficult—while vaguely, more exhausted as the night wore on, Pratt wondered, as he sometimes had before, how it was that ghosts actually saw the world. How could eyes that weren't true eyes take in such moonlight, a grand landscape, anything at all, with any precision? How had the howling band done it? The assumption among some had always been that the dead weren't precise, their focus narrow, tunneled. That was why they could generally be caught and cornered, even if some had the gift of flight. His recent mistake had been that there was no use for all this space, this wide angle, a desert's majesty—not if a remnant was narrowly focused on her own grievances. She might travel through this wilderness but could never really see it.

And then there was the question of how a ghost, every ghost, was fitted for night light.

The dead had never lasted long enough or cooperated enough to be tested.

As his eyes adjusted, minute by minute, hour after hour, Pratt saw Hogan's outline more clearly, her shape and detail. She took even strides through the black brush, steps that were neither short nor long, lifting up her boots, walking like someone who was already used to prowling the night. Part of her trade.

"You're good," he said to her finally.

"What's that?"

"You're good at what you do, sheriff. You were good back there. The belt buckles."

"That was desperation." Her voice sounded exhausted, too. They were both approaching their limits. His need for water was so powerful now Pratt felt he wanted to drink the faintest hint of blue on the horizon.

"Thank you," he said, "for what you did for me, for us, back there. Untying me. For a start." There was every reason to thank the living and no need to thank the dead. "Law enforcement has all my respect." It hadn't always been so. On other cases, so many had been unhelpful. Doubtful.

"Since you're law enforcement too, I would hope so," she said.

"But I'm not." The work of cleaning was the work of balance, harmony, closer to nature than policing. To the soil under their feet. There was an art to it.

"But you are," she said. She was squinting at something up ahead. Were they getting close to some boundary or landmark she recognized? "You're armed. You sort out the good guys from the bad guys."

"The dead are mostly neither." Morals, in any case, didn't come into play. Simply common sense. Necessity. The world, or most of it, understood the dead took energy badly needed elsewhere. It simply wouldn't be possible to survive the current moment, make any progress, with weight tied heavily, so heavy, exhaustingly, at your feet.

"You see that elevation?" Hogan was panting. "That's the paved road. We get there, we wait till someone comes along. Hopefully good, not bad."

They reached the shoulder just as the dome of night cupping the desert was lifting, the horizon behind them reddening.

The first vehicle approached.

"Well, look at that." Hogan lifted an arm. "Sweet Jesus. Darrion. Good boy."

She was grinning into the sunrise, her face pink and cracked with dirt.

"I told him if I hadn't called in by now to hightail it out here first light."

Contingency. What mattered most, with any venture. Imagining alternative plans.

Pratt, having survived his walk through the night, had already come up with his.

26

My lover is awake on his cot. The sun's just risen. He leans forward, rubbing his eyes. He opens them, confused. He must think he's been dreaming.

Yes. No. *I'm here.*

He sits up and drops one hand on my lap, close beside him. Leaving his palm turned open.

I rest mine in his.

"Good morning, Emma."

"Good morning, Winn."

"Well. Everything's going to be different now, isn't it?"

"Is it?"

How, when should I tell him about the others? About what's really going to happen?

He swings his feet onto the floor. He blinks.

"How do we begin?" He smiles. "Do we do ordinary things?" He reaches underneath the bed. "Nope, my phone is dead. Does it even matter?" He says quickly, before I can speak, "It does matter.

We'll have to keep things looking, sounding, ordinary around here. If one of the Halstens' assistants calls."

I don't like it, suddenly, that he's answered a question without me. Then I see his eyes. He's distracted, adding up the night's miracles along with ordinary business in his engineer's mind, trying to sort things out.

"What would you like to do?" He sighs and faces me. Sorted and happy. "Is there anything you need or want to do?"

Such a harbor, that handsome face is. And I'm a sailor come to port carrying pirates.

"You are so beautiful," he says.

Something once said to me in another century. And yet it only seems real now, this instant.

"My love," I say, "there's some news."

"Let's walk and talk."

We move together out of the tall, airy metal nest that saw our lovemaking. We look across the fields of the valley and homestead. I have told the others not to hide, just to be and do as they are, as they like. The children are busy romping through the alfalfa. The elders stand in a row behind the little ones at play, guarding them, waiting.

He freezes.

"What's this?"

"There are others."

"Others?"

"With me. I'm not alone. Any more than you're alone." With his past lover, his dead father, a friend keeping lamb in a freezer for him, a brother, and more ties, many more, no doubt.

He swallows. "I see. So. A group haunting, after all. Who were they . . . are they?"

"I want them to tell you themselves."

I lead him forward. To the edge of the field.

He's tense. I can't tell what else he's feeling. The living don't disappear when they're cold. They stand unmoved beside you.

The schoolmaster comes forward with the others, then waits, hesitating, uncertain, then is the first to break away, stepping out from the tall clover.

He bows politely, as was the way in his century.

"I am Ethan Longhurst. The schoolmaster of White Bar, California."

"Mr. Longhurst," I introduce them, "this is Mr. Winn Towhee."

The two men face each other, one in his plaid shirt and work boots, the other in his frock coat and pencil-thin tie.

The living man nods instead of bowing. He's both looking at and past the schoolmaster, I see.

So many, behind the one.

"Allow me," Longhurst says in his genteel, formal way, "to introduce my pupils to you, sir. Children, mind your manners. Oldest first. Make your bow, Anton."

"I am Anton." The quietest and most polite of them comes forward and bows in his green suspenders. "How do you do, sir?"

"I'm—fine, thank you." The caretaker turns to me, surprised. There's nothing to it, really, being civil to the dead, once you've started. He turns back. "How do you do, Anton?"

"Very well, sir."

"Thank you, Anton," the schoolmaster says. "You may step back. Now you, Jack."

"I'm Jack," the redheaded middle boy says, less easily. Always the most flighty, nervous among them. "Hello, sir."

"Hello."

"And this our Adelaide," Longhurst continues.

"How do you, sir? I'm Addie." A pretty curtsy in her bright pinafore.

"William? Your turn now."

"I'm Willie. I'm six."

"And what do you say?"

He forgets easily. It's helped him, in a way.

"How do you do, sir?"

"Very good, William." Longhurst turns. "Allow me, please, now, to let the rest of our gathering introduce themselves."

I watch as the caretaker faces each new phantom.

"Good morning, sir. My name is Alejandro Santos, and this is my wife, Rocío."

"*Mucho gusto,*" she says, nodding under her bonnet. "Please, these are my children. Alberto and Alicia. They are at school with Mr. Longhurst. Alberto also studies carpentry with the brothers."

"She means us. I'm Tom Rather." The oldest of the blond brothers steps forward.

"And I'm Frank."

"And I'm Danny."

"Danny wants to say more." Frank nudges his younger brother.

"Beautiful place you got here." Danny nods. "Nice lines on that barn."

"Here's another one who's also shy," Frank says. "He just joined us. From the cemetery by the mesa."

"I'm Perry," the once-sick young man says. "And this is my friend, Lodena."

"That's me," the nurse says in her uniform, touching her brown heels together.

Last are the loving couple.

"I'm Bob. My wife is Betty. We've been married for a hundred and ten years."

"A hundred and ten years!" she coos, high-pitched.

"I've gotten used to it," he explains, smiling. "You get used to things," he adds, encouragingly.

"Is this"—Winn turns to me—"everyone?"

"This is our band."

"And they want—to stay?" He looks at them as he says this to me.

"They've already stayed," I say. "All night. And gave you no trouble at all."

We all wait on him and say nothing.

All of us, each of us ready to decide how much trouble we're going to be.

The children, a little afraid, stand with their backs pressed to their elders. And where, I look behind them, is Briscoe? I can't see him.

Winn asks me, low and quiet, "Would they be happy here?"

"I'm sorry?" I turn.

"Will they be happy keeping quiet here, with us? Hidden away."

"Our very littlest ones," Longhurst says, stepping forward and bowing again, "are generally well behaved and reared. They know when not to be seen nor heard. Show him, children. Like this."

Longhurst fades.

All the rest, not just the children, follow suit.

I see the living man beside me understand. What power he has. To make human beings disappear . . . simply by making them fear they might need to.

But where is Briscoe?

"Why are they showing me this?" Winn asks.

"They're finding out who can trust who. Now they want to know if they can trust you."

"I see." There's a queer excitement in him. "May I say something to them? Can they please come back so I can—see them?"

They agree and do. And still I can't see the mule runner.

"Thank you," Winn says, stepping forward, but not too close, sensing, keeping an eye on the wary children. "I appreciate all of your . . . patience, with me. I don't want you to feel you have to prove yourself to me. But this is all very new and . . ." He scans them all, the fields, the cliffs, and seems to be gathering in what he wants to say next.

"This is a very old place," he says at last. "It isn't mine. It isn't yours. And it doesn't belong to the ones who have it now. It's older and deeper than any of us, is what I mean. I've been hired to decide who can come on this land and who can't. That's like saying this field decides what gets to cut it. I've been planted here. If I play my cards right, I can dig in, stay. It's no different than with you. But we both, we all, we have it all wrong, right? We're bartering the wrong things to the wrong people. The people who say they own this place, they see it not as a home"—he points in the direction of the dugout—"but as insurance. They don't care about it. They literally plan on dynamiting the entrances, if they have to, so no one can get in. They've drilled deep for water. They'll bring no one with them, if the time comes. They'll bury themselves like the treasure trove they think they are. They don't come here now, not often, because they just want to know it's here, they don't need to be bothered with it otherwise. It's insurance. That means it's left to me to watch over. I'm insurance, too, see. I'm a plan. You hear what I'm saying? Anything I do to take care of this valley, this excellent valley, it makes me part of someone else's plan. I've done it, and been fine with it. It kept me close to something I wanted to be close to. My old ghosts."

He steps back to stand at my side again. "But now," he says into my eyes, "you're here. And I don't know if you have a plan, Emma. I suspect you do. But what's happened, now that you're all here"—he turns to them again—"is that the plan for this valley is over—or really, it's over all over again. The sea rolls in. It dries up. It rises. It's bigger than us. We don't know how many tribes have been through here. I don't even know how many ghosts might have passed through. I see you want to stay a while. I say you take all the time you need. You could stay here—how long?—and still be just passing through. But I could be dust, and you'd still be here, so I won't bother you, all right? What I'm saying is . . ." He points toward the bunker buried in the earth again. "Go ahead and walk on their backs, with me and this beautiful—"

He looks at me.

A thought has just struck him, hard.

Who does Emma go with now? Where does she belong?

The children have already broken off gleefully and are running like rabbits for the shade trees. Maybe Briscoe is there, for they love him. It isn't at all like him to disappear without warning.

"I have to go," I say quickly, "and look for someone."

The caretaker looks at me, eyes shadowed under his straw hat. "Now?"

"Yes."

"Who?"

"A friend who should be here." Is Briscoe all right?

"Will you be all right?" I go on kindly. "What will you do, with all this?"

He says, after a long moment, "I'm hungry. I have to eat."
"Do, then. Go."
"All right. You too."
Go, we each nod at the same time, lovingly.
Yet not as one.

27

Hogan was waving at her deputy.

"Water!" she called to him as he started from his truck. "We need water!"

The young uniformed man turned quickly and began running, Pratt saw gratefully, back to his cab. By the time they were beside him he was holding out two fresh, clear bottles in the sunrise.

There has never been anything more satisfying in the history of creation. Pratt felt he was breathing as much as drinking.

"Easy there, don't go into shock, sir," the skinny young man said.

"We're fine now." Hogan came up for air at last and wiped her mouth. "You are perfect, Darrion." She turned. "Pratt, this is my deputy, Darrion Silks."

A good name for the thin, clean-shaven, shiny officer, Pratt thought.

Hogan's face looked like a windshield streaked with mud. So must his own.

"You didn't call in, Sherry," the young man said, "so I came. You two all right?"

"We had a little dustup with a restoration militia."

"Where's your Bronco?"

"Stolen. We need to call it in when we get back in range. They'll either be reckless and keep it or else stupid as rocks and post pictures before they ditch it. Let's go. We have to get back to the Halsten Ranch. You got anything to eat in your SUV?"

"Power bars. The good ones," he added helpfully. "The honey kind."

"Great. Pratt, you're in the back."

Astonishing, the luxury of settling into the comfort of worn leather seats. For a moment, all Pratt could do was eat and wipe his face with a faded bandanna Hogan handed back to him. Life. Life. It was in every part of him. Alertness, intelligence.

He had the luxury, as well, of watching the two people in front of him exchanging information, recalibrating their relationship—the hero of the hour, the rescuer, settling back into his role as the subordinate but not quite, while Hogan emptied herself of gratitude and gently resumed authority. Admittedly, he felt a little empty, watching them, and a little distant, giving himself over to exhaustion. But it was still remarkable, how order found a way to right itself again.

He straightened in the back seat—he didn't like feeling himself slipping, sinking down into it—and organized his thoughts around his new plan. He would need to share it—or at least some of it—with the sheriff and her deputy, soon. They were still trying to raise Winn Towhee on the deputy's cell phone.

"Over the ridge and we should be in tower range," the deputy said.

Pratt stared out the windows. No man-made tower, not yet. Only the needles and badlands of the desert. Now he knew what it felt like to walk among that harshness for mile after mile. What it must have been like for the thousands who had crossed this desert on foot, on horseback, in search of whatever it was they yearned for. There could be no greater proof of the difficulty of life and of the earned peace of rest than the fact that the majority of human beings, the vast majority who had lived on this planet, lay down, when the time came, lay their spirits down without lingering and never begged to rise. Or if they did, could easily be shown their error. Like the man in the walls of the governor's house. Or the jaundiced old woman at the cemetery.

When you're tired, you were ready, Pratt thought. When you're not—he sat erect—you got back to business.

He looked again at the two officers in their seats in front of him. Animated, fresh, young. The truck was nearing the ridge.

Pratt said, leaning forward as much as his seatbelt would allow, "When you call the ranch, tell Towhee that we're coming back with excellent news."

Hogan turned her head, surprised. "Why? What do you mean?"

"We're going to tell him we were successful in our efforts at Needlestick."

"And why exactly would we tell him that?"

Because success, Pratt thought, is that which is imagined before it's achieved—although that wasn't all it was.

"I told you once, sheriff, that ghosts hold still for the end, at the end, if you can show them how little they are. When they're forced to confront the charade of their haunting, they shrivel."

"I remember that, but Darrion hasn't heard it, and I'm not sure how it applies right now, in any case. Nothing got shriveled back there."

She was doubting him. Fair enough, after what had happened, and fine. What he was about to tell them was the salient point at this moment and all others: that the greatest advantage of living was learning. Elucidation, deduction, evolution were the purview of those with beating hearts—not simply manipulating objects to terrify, unlocking locked doors or leaving painted messages scrawled on walls or throwing around trails of salt. The dead were stuck, unenlightened in spite of their ability to illuminate. The ones who died hating the world couldn't stop hating it; the ones who were lost were forever lost; those felled by love or deceit or ignorance never trusted again. He'd learned something—and could admit it—while he'd been crouching helpless on the dirt floor of a log cabin as a battle between the dead and the living raged over the earth beyond his sight: it was a great battle he had always given Emma Rose Finnis, and that was his greatest mistake. At their first encounter, by the sea, he had done it. Calling up the rage inside a house, creating a storm of anger that burned and destroyed everything in its path, everything that was beautiful and fine. In the mountains she'd hidden herself inside the grief and battle of others, and thrilled, no doubt, when she escaped him in a burst, a farce, a daring race. But if something wanted, always, battle, drama, because that was how it had lived and died, then granting it that wish must only strengthen the thing, empower it. Maybe even make it feel "alive."

"Hunt something like this," he continued calmly from his seat, "and it will be thrilled to play at hide and seek, give you the scent, lead you astray, give it again. Chase it, and the more it will run in circles, hoping never to stop. With every step, a thing like this, more and more, will believe it's outrun the truth—the truth that it is dead, dead and can make no progress, and no amount of impersonation, no projection she can cause, no living person she can trick or seduce, will make her any more than what she is incapable of learning she in fact is: a mere fantasy of life. An echo that will fade if it has nothing to push against."

"No more giving her what she wants, to sum up," Hogan says.

"Precisely."

"How do we do that?"

"We start by calling Towhee and telling him we're returning with good news." They had topped the ridge, and a cell tower had come into view. Pratt kept his eye on it and assumed that was why the deputy was slowing.

"Whoa." Hogan's voice changed. Confused. "What's that? You see it, Darrion?"

"I do. But I don't exactly get what I'm looking at. Um, whose mules are those?"

Below them, on the other side of the ridge, a pack was strung languidly across the roadway.

"Jesus," the deputy said. "How many are there? How many do you guys see?"

The animals, contemplating him, stretched in both directions to the near horizon as far as Pratt's eyes could scan.

Part Three

THE RUNNER

28

Me, Bill Briscoe, dead a hundred and thirty years, I've got to where I like a good trick.

Plus, it's an old habit, the habit of a mule runner. I see where my animals can do their best work and go there. With good confidence.

You've got to admire a mule. You can trust it.

They're not one thing or the other. Got the git-up of a horse and the sturdiness of an ass. Live longer than both. They need less water, got light, small hooves, aren't apt to spook. In the big battle between the states—I ran away to join it, escaping my bonds before I had a beard to grow, hooked my star to the fight, and got ten dollars a month from the Yankees, first pay of my life—I had me a train of them, and we got to be known as Briscoe's Bloods. I got them through anything. I have the teamster's skill. I've been the familiar of mules since I was a child. My life, such as it was before the war, was stables and slops and keep your head down and try not to get whipped. I never blamed any of it on the animals. You don't want to be a mule, but you can learn a thing or two, being around them. Like being not one thing or the other makes you nimble.

I darted off west after the war, when it was awfully clear some battles don't ever shutter, and I worked supply trains for the forts. I saved my money and bought the spent animals, because the thing about a spent mule is, it isn't used up. No reason to turn something into meat when all that's called for is some affection you've got nowhere else to put anyhow. Everything I ever loved was dead or missing. That's a lot to carry on one back.

It's impressive what you can do with one mule, let alone two, and I always think so, and I think so now, looking down onto that ridge where those modern souls with their guns at their hips are getting out of their chariot, the hunter at the head of them, staring at my pretty train. Get yourself five mules in the desert and you're a twenty-footed raft in a land of snakes. Get yourself a hundred or more, a thousand, who knows what you might do. Maybe dam a river.

I got them doing what they need to be doing. Beautiful line, stretched from here to Kingdom Come. You can trust mules to do what's right. They're sensitive that way. I leave them to it.

Travel gives a man time to reflect.

I came to this desert and meant to stay. I find it hospitable. I know my way around these valleys, at a flying pace or easy on foot, how long it takes to get from where to where, how people meet and greet in all this space. I'm giving them time, back at Pastor Valley, to get acquainted with each other. Prepared. In a war, you need time to work yourself up to doing whatever it takes. You need it afterwards, too. After I came west, I ran supplies for anyone who needed it, didn't matter what side. A man doesn't really have a side when he lives at the bottom, the bottom of anything, including a canyon. Mormons wanted me to bring them their gingham. Colonels wanted their whiskey. Sheepmen wanted dynamite to blast the passes so the ranchers' cattle couldn't eat up the grass in the higher, cooler country in summer. The Indians needed goods as well as news. I always had that. You see higher from a mule's back. You see more. And you're above the mangle of bodies. I say the reason the desert doesn't have more ghosts in it is because the dead are all tangled and piled on top of each other and can't get up.

I lost my mules because I thought I was free of the pile. You might think no one's ever going to come for you because you're useful. It's never so. One day I took my best mount to Hangman's Bridge to meet the postman, and when I came back to my hidden canyon, all my mules were gone. I cried and cried into their feed, smelling it, but then I put my head back on and got busy. I'm no tracker, but it's not easy to hide the tramp of so much heavy flesh. I followed the signs, and at sunset I looked ahead and I saw where the thieves were busy penning my team up on a tall butte, using blackbrush to corral them. That's what the rustlers did, steal stock, drive it up on some table, then leave till they came back with a buyer. I know war. I knew all I had to do was wait, and at some juncture they'd have to leave.

But them and their rifles stayed put. They must have known I'd be hot on their trail. They set up camp outside the brush fence. And sat there on guard. They did nothing for my team. Mules don't need much water, but after being driven all day in the heat they need their feed and cooling off. Night fell, and I could hear my children calling out in the darkness. The bray of a mule isn't like a horse's or a donkey's. There's no complaining *haw*. It's more like the sound of a hot iron kettle being scraped from a grate. The thieves squatted, unmoved, night after day after night. They had food and water for themselves. They weren't about to budge. And then it dawned on me. *They don't want to sell my mules. It's me, Black Bill, they want to torture.* Hoping to flush me out of my hiding place and kill me, for any of the reasons men like that want to kill the business and profit of a man like me.

I had every right to shoot them, and figured I could get a few from my position. But what I also knew about rustlers is that if they don't get what they want, they could drive the whole team, the evidence, right off the cliff.

I should by rights have had them cornered on that butte. But they had me. Because of my love for my mules. If I went off for help, my mules would disappear or die. If I stayed, I would die, and my best mule with me. She was already weak where I'd tied her, far from her own food and bed. I could save her, at least.

When I came back, the men were gone, but the fence was still there, and my mules, too. They'd died for lack of water. The birds were already pecking at them. All that flesh and spent life, lying on its sides, and the thieves got nothing out of it either, except the pleasure of knowing I couldn't have them.

I won't say the fight went out of me then. Not right away. But the places I knew started changing. The Indians were mostly gone or being burned out. The Mormons, getting their feet under them, came back. The sheepmen lost to the cattlemen. Other than cattle, the other life thinned out, the cats and the jackrabbits and the birds. The ground of this country, it's littered with more animals than men, but there are no markers. I thought about starting over somewhere else, maybe Colorado. Maybe I mentioned it to the postman. He and the rest didn't need me now. The trains did more now than a team could. The towns started to grow. People who still knew about my murdered mules felt sorry for me, but that was all. My best mule died of dropsy.

I've always supposed that because I hinted I might be leaving, people thought I had gone, and so no one looked for me when I was walking along my canyon rim one night, staring up at a cut moon flanked with stars, and a boulder gave way under me and carried me to the bottom with it. I've had a lot of time, going over these canyons as I am now, to think about the injustice of me, after all I've been through, being brought low all because the ground couldn't see fit to support me, though I never asked much of it or claimed much of it as mine. That's something to keep a soul up at night.

I was furious as a preacher on Sunday when I found I was a ghost and was looking down at the birds pecking my corpse. But at least I was standing up and understood what had happened. My people live with ghosts. We have a ton of them. There's talk, in life, about how after death you meet all those you've missed; truth is, they're close but also just as far away as they ever were. I was alone. In a dry place. Although soon I got to understanding, being a mule runner made me suited to being dead. I knew how to watch everything. I took no sides, kept my distance. I was duly unimpressed when the town named the canyon that had been my home, and then the depot where they used to meet my mules, Briscoe. Around here, around this whole country, people like to name things after what they remind *them* of, not to honor the reminder.

I try not to get angry, now. Anger gives a ghost up. I've known how to be alone, keep close to places I've known. They call the spot where my team died Dead Mule Butte.

263

From up there, visiting the graves of my animals, I first saw Emma Rose and the rest of them, walking as easy as you please and thinking no one was watching.

I'd never seen two ghosts together at one time, to say nothing of a vanguard. They weren't in a straight line. They were fanned out, like birds. I watched. The girl wasn't always out front. She'd give up her place, as birds do. She was the leader, though. I've been in a war. I know the look. The one with the plan has the eyes that never stop moving.

I came down. I'd never seen a dozen ghosts at once. I thought to present myself as a guide through this desert. It's a habit whipped into you, this feeling you have to be of use or you're not worth diddly. They stopped—not as surprised as I thought they'd be. I bowed and said my name. *Bill Briscoe, dead 1897, mule runner. If I could, I'd like to walk with you a while?*

Queer, how you can lose the habit of talking. But I managed to say enough to show them I was friendly, and that I knew the territory inside out. They made no push to make me overly confiding. I sweetened to that. I walked with the littlest ones at first. It was pleasant, easy going. The thing about children, free children, anyhow, is, where a man like me sees everything as a harness and the question is only who's going to wear it, they see everything like a puzzle only they know the secret to, or think they will one day at least.

When our team wanted a bit of shelter where we wouldn't be troubled, I knew which way to point. The rail manager's house. He collected things in it, and one of my old harnesses was still sitting on a shelf. I had no use for it.

The Irish ghost was beginning to trust me by then. We spoke often.

"How did you know, Mr. Briscoe, about this place?"

"The family that owned it goes a ways back. I knew the way-backs. Rail keepers."

"Where are they now?"

"It's a bust here now. They've gone looking for cover."

"And won't return."

"I've been here a while. I know an empty trough when I see it. It's good."

"Yes, it's good," said the schoolteacher, who cleaved close to her but not too close. The leader of the children wasn't the leader of the pack, nor worthy of it, I reckoned.

I like to think what we did to that old squat rail manager's house was make a flying stagecoach out of it. We plushed it up good. Everyone had an idea of where they were going with it in their own heads, but still all together. I'd never seen ghosts pull all at one time like that, nor how much dead hands can do if you give yourself the permission. That's the whole trick of it, and no mistake. Give yourself permission to build what you're hankering after, maybe you get it. But only maybe. There are still enough out there who would rather let something good rot than let you have it.

I'd never seen anything like that house, and I don't suspect any of us had or will again, but we had to move on when our fun was found out. So I told the Irish about the Pastor Valley, what the Indians called the place of *naat'áanii*, before they all got chased off it by ranchers with guns and dynamite. Now, I told her, there was nobody except one lone guard, although I didn't tell her he was an Indian. I don't know why, except old habits are hard to break. I don't tell on Indians. They know their own business.

In the army, you got to have reconnaissance. So she went on ahead, and the rest I took up to Castle Mesa. From there we saw the hunter she'd warned us about. This devil was slow with the poor woman who wouldn't leave her graveside and come along with us. Like he wanted her all good and ripe before he plucked her.

I made up my mind, right then. If I ever got the chance to slow and ripen that ghost catcher, I would.

But right then me and the others of our band were alone up on that mesa, with the Irish gone ahead, and there was some need of keeping the children distracted. So I pulled them in around me and I said, *You want to hear a story, chickens?*

I've had practice. I used to talk to my mules. When mules are all the company you have, you get to stroking them, to make sure they're all right, especially if you're on a run. You got to make sure each load is settled right, then you whisper encouragement. Never take another soul's willingness for granted. Most of us don't ever have the stubbornness bred out of us. It's there, under the harness. Under the hide it's all thick muscle and forebears and kick and bite. If you want to tell souls ready to bite a story about why they have to keep steady and stick together right now, even if they don't have any choice in the matter, it better be a good story.

Friends, did I ever tell you, I said, *about that time I almost died? Well, that was twenty times over and more, true, but I'm thinking right now of one incident in particular. There was this gal up in a notch called Ladies Canyon*—I omitted to say why it was called that by the gentlemen who went up there to visit the ladies who had set up a good business for themselves, one I partook of myself, plenty of times—*a gal who needed to get down to Hangman's Bridge and meet the stage there. I told her I'd take her for a dollar or else a roll in, uh, well, anyhow, on the appointed day I brought one mule up, not trusting her to mount herself. She made a face about it, but then she just shrugged.* My guess is, she knew a man would pretty much take any chance to have a certain kind of warm body riding up against him, and I'm not saying that wasn't part of my thinking. *Anyway, we started down. The trail was kind of narrow with a drop-off on the left. But it was nothing for my mount. We were heading down and my mule was just fine, the two of us weighed less than a lot of what he'd had to shoulder and stomach before now.* And I have no doubt my mule under me could feel my ease, as what nice company it was, just for a little while, to feel a pair of scented arms wrapped around me and a pair of hips rocking in time with my own. *We were doing just fine. Then there was a sound you don't want to hear if you're on the sheet side of a cliff with little room to spare. A sound that's something between a gunshot and the split of a tree after lightning. I heard the crack and steadied.*

The question always is: where is the rockfall and how hard is it coming for you? Hard to know. Canyons echo in all directions. First you see the small bits rolling down and you know—the big one is getting ready to crash after.

I backed up, steady as I could, no going quick on a trail only as wide as a matchstick, and the gal behind me held on tight—I could feel her breath pushing on my ribs like a wall trying to keep me straight—*but that day was unlucky, and though the first big stones didn't crush us, they were far too close and my mule reared and that poor gal slid off and though I couldn't see for the dust and working to bring my mule down again, I hoped she was busy scrambling out from underfoot, which would be the right thing to do as he tended to calm quick enough, and the dust was already settling except I can't say it cleared, it sort of hung there in a yellow mist like the sun had fallen down.*

And I saw the gal was gone.

My skin felt like it was going to pieces.

My heart was a lump of coal inside me.

I slid out of my saddle. When I looked over the edge, down there she was. Hanging onto a juniper branch, sturdy, both hands, a pretty firm grip. I called to her to hang on. If you're a mule runner you know all about weight and load, what's manageable. But I also saw there was no way she was going to last much longer. Her own weight would pull her hands off. So I told her what she needed to do now was trust me, and to get one hand up to me so I could cantilever her up with my own weight. And the thing was, she was calm as a cold pistol right up until she got aholt of me. Then she screamed. They say a drowning person will pull you down with their fear and weight and will clamber right on top of you. That's exactly how it was, she was hauling herself on top of me now and fighting and grabbing me, and I contrived to lean back and haul her back with both my hands and then she was crawling over me like I was the cliff and the danger and next thing I knew she sets her boot on my shoulder and pushes down and I'm the one sliding and going over and only have enough sense to turn over so I can grab the rocks. I don't have any purchase, though, my feet are trying to find some and losing, when I see to the right of my shoulder the same tree she'd been clinging to, so I grab it and now we've switched places and she looks down at me, her face all scratched and crumpled and ashamed, and she knows she doesn't have the strength to haul me up the way I did her.

I tell her, "Listen, girl, I'm going to whistle to my mule," who hadn't bolted—thing about a mule is, he might lose his head, but he finds it again quick—and I told her to go to him and take the rope coiled on his side and fix a lariat knot—luckily she knew how to do that, she must have come from a wrangling family or maybe shacked up with a wrangler once—and she was calmer now, and tossed the lasso down to me and I got it around me and she tied the other end to my saddle and backed my mule up, and that's how three of us who could have died in a high canyon that day didn't, because just enough of us was mules.

We sat down on the trail, tuckered, and what I don't forget was my mount beside me dropping his head for a scratch between his ears, and the look in that gal's eyes when she looked at me and I looked at her. Our eyes were almost laughing. Like after all this we knew what we wanted, and whatever that was it was bigger even than it was before.

That made the children, up on that mesa with me, sit up in wonder. What does something look like that you can't see because it's bigger even than the eye can hold? I told them, *Well, see, you go a long way and come back, you better not be the same, or it's hardly worth the trip at all.*

When I finished my recital, and when I, when all of us, child and grown, could wait no longer and night fell, we made our way to the green valley guarded only by one lone Indian. I saw the Irish before she saw me. The look in Emma Rose Finnis's eyes. She'd been somewhere and come back bigger. After the others had left us, gone off on a frolic to inspect the premises, and we were alone, just the two of us, standing under the stars, her eyes were bigger than the moon with most of its eye shut.

But I haven't told you the rest of the story, chickens, I'd said to the children back on that mesa. *When the dust settled and me and that gal stood up, what do we see in front of us but a big rock blocking the trail. Turns out you can get out of one thing but not another. You know why that gal wanted to get to that stagecoach, with not much more than the clothes she had on her back? She wanted to get gone. She wanted a new adventure. She was sick of her old life, of doing what she'd always had to. I couldn't help her, not that day. There's always something wants to punch you in the gut, stab you in the back, get in the way if you manage to get up. You won't know what it is till it shows itself right in front of you. But you better get ready for it. And then you'll need some time. The dust in the air, it'll clog your eyes. You'll need some time to*

269

give your situation some thinking. It's what I advise. Or, say, you see someone trying to take time from you, you have to throw something in the way. Some time of your own. It's not always someone else can do the throwing.

The Irish asked me, when we were standing alone under the blinkered moon, "Why did you send me here first, when we could have all come together?"

I said, "I wasn't sure you'd want to be boxed up in a valley, like this." She was always on the move, out front. "A man can miss stalls and hay. Not sure about a woman." What I meant was, you and me, we're not the same, some ways. Other ways, I see how. You got trained, harnessed a certain way, early on, always think it's your place to pull others, carry the load. You got in a habit.

"I like stalls and hay," she said, quick. "And if we're careful with the guard, there are animals coming to the barn, too."

"They'd be sleeping right now," I said, "if there were animals. I don't hear any coyotes. But I'll need to check the pens. Even a place like this, you got predators."

Instead, I went to check on my mules' grave place. Their bones are in the dirt where I left them, on the butte. I've let my mules rest all this time. Life is hard enough. Even doing your best for what's your corner of a hard stall, life is hard, a bit between the teeth.

But sometimes you got to get to where you're going.

I went to Dead Mule Butte. I called, *Git up. We got work to do.*

I waited, curious. I'm their master.

They got up.

29

"I can't find Mr. Briscoe," I return and tell my living lover.

"Who's Mr. Briscoe?" he asks, busy.

He's in his caretaker's cottage again, and by the way he's wiping his mouth, I see he's had his breakfast. He drinks his coffee. He tastes. He breathes. All things I can't do. He's bathed. His long hair is glistening. He'll have toweled like a man. He's wiped his mouth and cleaned his dish, and all at once we're not together, somehow, not in the same way we were.

How does it happen, so quickly? That you're not as close as a moment before.

I remember that, from when I was living, long ago. Surely it hasn't happened again. I remember how a space can suddenly open up, so quickly, so wide the cabin floor might as well be an ocean.

"Mr. Briscoe is someone I wanted you to meet," I say, from across the room. "He isn't here. I asked the others, and no one's seen him. It's not like him to go off with no word."

"He's another ghost?"

"Yes."

"Well. Do ghosts sometimes leave without saying? Do you always . . . stick together?"

It's happened, I think. Jealousy. Now that he's seen me with the others, he feels the distance, too.

"We're friends, Mr. Briscoe and I. We're all friends."

"And friends don't leave each other."

"They can." I've lost so many. Again and again.

"That's not what I meant. I meant I could help."

If Briscoe doesn't want to be found, I think, I have no business hunting him. But if he's in trouble. How would I know?

"Emma." Winn Towhee draws closer to me, without touching me. "Do you notice anything . . . different?"

I don't want to speak of it. Perhaps if we don't remark on it, then it won't be real. Some things, I've learned, if you face them, you make them worse, you drive an ax into the plank that's barely balanced over the ocean between you.

He smiles and looks around the cottage and laughs.

"Look how it's cleaned up."

My eyes follow his. I don't understand. All the papers and careless rummage and bits that were here, there, where Pratt slept on that couch, are gone. The scattered clothing and the shoes left on their sides, the books open on their faces and the hats tossed and the table littered with drained bottles—it's all been tidied.

By whom?

"I wanted to make it fresh for you," he says. "Like when I first saw this place."

I take a step away from him. I don't know what it means to be cleaned and tidied for. I've never known it, my whole life. I was always the maid. The drudge.

The room isn't wide because there's an ocean between us; it's wide because he's made room in it. For me.

Look at that.

I've been a ghost hunted for so long, I think, I see a grave even where there is none.

I could cry at the jolt of it.

"Emma? What's wrong?"

"Nothing," I say. "Nothing at all!" And leap and fall into him.

Oh, if I could make time stop, I would do it now. Or at least slow to the pace of melting ice. This slow lovemaking, on the floor. It should last as long as two souls have the will to give to it. If only nothing would rush us, now. There should be no hurry or worry, all should be well with the world and nothing and no one missing from it, it should be complete, full, full and complete, yes, and if you could reach that, if you could stay in this completeness, if you could just touch him and stay, there would be no more life or death at all.

30

"Jesus," Pratt heard Deputy Darrion saying again, "How many mules is that?"

They seemed to stretch out impossibly, in both directions. A flickering illusion. It had to be, Pratt thought. The heat had to be rising, refracting, mirroring itself into the distance. He stepped away from the deputy's Bronco, into the glare, the slanted angle of morning, and the light was serrated, quivering. Beyond the ridge, the animals stretched out in either direction, hooves planted firmly in the dirt, leather panniers like sagging bricks on their sides, a dangling rope between each animal loose, untied, their harnessed necks easy, turned, heads studying his own, unmoved.

He felt the oddest beating in his chest. Not the ordinary rush and flutter. A lower frequency.

"They're ghosts," he said.

"No." Hogan blinked.

"They are," Pratt said. "Unless you tend to see teams of antique pack animals out here."

The panniers weren't modern. They were rough satchels, closed with awkward leather tongues. The animals were of slightly different shapes. Some looked like mules, others more like horses or donkeys.

"You're certain," she said.

"I am."

"You can feel it?"

"Faint, but clear." His mechanism had always been attuned to the dead among *Homo sapiens* out of necessity and focus. Imagine if, he thought, a hunter picked up the charge of every ghostly animal, too. How disorienting and endless the work would be. How the heart might be blunted.

The question was: *Why were they here?*

"But . . . they look so real," the deputy said.

The nearest animal, standing in a shallow rut just below them, seemed to acknowledge the young man, head turning, gleaming rump tightening.

Hogan said, "I guess I had no idea what kind of day this was going to be."

None of them moved. Not the two living people beside Pratt, nor the dead mule train in front of him. On closer study, the animals appeared almost solid, yes, almost living. Well-formed legs. Short black manes. Faintly lathered shoulders.

He found himself, somewhat surprisingly, moved by the string of them. They looked determined to finish their work, whatever it had been. One last delivery, perhaps? It was something about animals. Their unquestioning tenacity. Their brute consistency, behind all the elegant muscle. He remembered, for no reason, the taxidermied heads he'd seen in Summit, on his journey from Salt

Lake City down to the Canyonlands. Glassy eyes, hard against soft coats. Steady unflinching gazes.

"Any idea where these might have arisen from?" he asked. "What their provenance might be?"

"Only thing," Hogan answered, "I can guess is that we're not far from Dead Mule Butte. That point over there." Pratt saw the high, lonely promontory. "Story goes, it got its name because a bunch of mules got stranded up there and died of thirst, looking straight down at a stream they couldn't figure out how to get to. They got up there but couldn't figure out how to get down again. I guess what we're looking at is not very bright."

That would explain their standing and stalling across a road, in front of a hunter, Pratt thought.

"Not true!" Deputy Darrion bristled, oddly defensive. "Mules are actually smart."

But how could there be so many? More than would likely be in any single team, Pratt mused to himself. "Why would they find their way down now?" he said aloud. "Unless—"

"Unless someone led them here," Hogan finished.

They scanned the horizon. Nothing. Only the animals. No guardian.

"Do you remember"—the sheriff drew closer—"back at the Poston house, I told you about a mule driver named Briscoe? Dead a long time ago?"

The town where they had started. "Yes."

"That looks like his brand. Darrion, stop, what are you doing?"

The boy, making clicking sounds, was walking toward the nearest bay neck. Like a child mesmerized, he reached out a hand. It sometimes happened, the first time someone saw a ghost. A neophyte.

"No farther," Pratt said.

"Wow." The boy marveled. "I just can't believe it. That they're not real."

But they were dead, and anything dead was unhealthy.

"Sheriff," Pratt ordered. "Call your man off."

"Darrion," Hogan said. "Get back here."

The boy stopped but had already reached the closest phantom.

"Ever touch one?" he called back to Pratt.

Absurdity and innocence in the question. *Yes. With my weapon.* There was no need otherwise—only risk, danger, entanglement. There had been one or two, of course, who had reached out foolishly to touch him. He remembered only one clearly, a child in a deep mine, who had hung from a rotting beam above them. Cold fingers had stroked Pratt's hair.

"Get your officer back," he said again.

But Hogan was transfixed now, too. "Darrion, come on, what are you doing?"

"It's all right," the deputy said excitedly. "She's not shying, see?" He lay his hand down.

"No! Son—" Pratt started forward.

"It's amazing!" the boy called, his neck flushing. "It's like, like a breath pushing back! It's . . . aww, it's nuzzling me. It's, like, reacting. I can feel it. It's like it's . . . *flesh.*"

"Enough!"

In three strides Pratt was at the deputy's side, jerking his hand back. But not before he, too, felt the plush of the phantom's outline, the warm shivering.

He felt stung by it.

"Shit," the deputy said, embarrassed. "Sorry, sir. Not sure what came over me there. Except, you know, I grew up with livestock.

I'm fond of 'em." He looked back at Hogan. "Sorry, Sheriff. But I wish you could have—it was pretty awesome."

"You get on back here, Darrion. Let the man do his work."

The deputy tipped his hat, adjusted his gun holster, and obeyed. Pratt remained. The warm shiver was still pulsing through, now finally out of him. Like a wave—not some electric throb—but like a flag, like something rippling, moving but unchanged in itself. Stubborn.

He didn't move, either. He looked down the line, the long mirage of beasts. How suited they must have been, in a way, to this dry country, he thought suddenly. How suited they were still now. Dead, their need for water evaporated. A ghostly mule needed nothing to maintain her. She wouldn't be wracked with choking, as he had been, crossing the desert. A dead mule could wander the heating, ever hotter earth and be no worse for the journey. It could claim the landscape.

He raised his weapon.

The dead responded before he could fire. The line shied away, disintegrating in a burst of wind and shadow, with a sound, a sensation of galloping, telescoping frenzy, until each animal, running until it was safe, stood on its separate hillock out of range, on its own dune, watching, staring back at him placidly.

Ancient memories came to Pratt unbidden. Childhood pictures. Beach ponies running on the Outer Banks. Sloping backs, the sea behind them. Frothy mouths. Damp necks. Eyes as distant and unrevealing as these were.

He should take the time to go after each one of these phantoms. Finish them.

But this would be a distraction, keeping him from returning to the Halsten hideout.

And then he understood.

That's what this is all about.

Distraction. Delay.

This was her doing, somehow.

"The way is clear now," he said abruptly, turning. "Let's go."

"Just leave them?" Hogan was squinting at the hovering shapes. It was clear she didn't understand. She didn't have to.

"Yes," Pratt said. "Immediately."

"You're saying you want us to move on."

"We need to get back. There's no urgency here."

"All right. If you say so."

The watchful, poised animals were already turning transparent, disappearing into the baked country. Only one, on a high mound, pawed the earth, as if digging in, lips pulled back, teeth baring.

"I don't get it," Hogan said as they got back into the Bronco. "You're saying what we just saw wasn't—important?"

"No," Pratt said. "I'm saying the head of anything is what you're after, not the tail." Like the taxidermist's work. The head was the prize.

And if the sting of ghostly, rippling skin was still with him as he sat down on skinned leather again, all that had to be remembered was this, he told himself: A wave is live but not alive. *It might feel like life, like skin. But it isn't.*

31

I think, lying in my lover's arms, that when these days are long past us, and we know more about each other, this living man and I, than we can now, what will most surprise me still about love is that it's like a country you once came from and have gone home to again. I wonder how many in the world already know this. How far and wide it's understood, how close it's held. My family, my own father and mother . . . surely their wandering hearts must have known it, they must have known that you carry love inside you, a soil you take with you that isn't a grave, nor even a garden, but a great rock. A bluff to look out from and know: from here we see everything, and everything we see is ours.

We lie in his bedroom now with the curtains open.

"We're amazing together," he says.

"I think so, too."

"Do you think we're the only ones? Trusting enough?"

"I don't know."

We might be. It's not a story I've ever heard, the spooning of the living and the dead. Not even in the old Gaelic tales.

"Wait." He sits up suddenly. "Is someone watching?"

There's some flutter near the window.

Perhaps. Who can say what the others might do, truly, or what I might do, curious, if I were in their place, and guessed what might be happening between these walls.

I rise and stand and peer through the panes.

Briscoe is on the gravel path outside, lifting his gloved hand, his bowed legs steady.

"It's the friend I've been looking for," I say relieved, already slipping through the window to meet him.

"Emma Rose. Whew there." The mule runner whistles knowingly toward the bedroom.

"Don't be going on about it, Mr. Briscoe," I meet his look and laugh. "It's something, I know."

"Is it?"

"It is."

"You're happy?"

"I'm happy."

"Had some time to sort things out? Keep your eye on the main chance?"

"What do you mean?"

I don't see why I can't have more than one main chance at the same time. I've always had my eye on that.

"I mean you got to know what you want up front and what you want behind you."

I change the conversation. "Where have you been?"

"Out on the trail. Sorry to have to tell you. Unlucky news. Your Mr. Pratt is coming back."

The chill of it.

The fields and cliffs look suddenly smaller.

"You saw him?" I ask.

"Went to visit my mules and saw them coming."

You can push luck and trickery too far, I suppose. I've always managed to lose this stalker before. I thought the lure of the East, of his own idea, would pull him along.

I didn't hoax him this time.

Perhaps the luck was on his side, today. Perhaps I didn't egg him on enough, or perhaps he's learned something, out there, he hasn't before, since it's plain he isn't doing this time what he's always done.

But then none of us are.

"I managed to waylay him for a bit," Briscoe says. "When we got here, I had a strong feeling about a predator coming. Part of my trade, you know."

Then why hadn't I sensed it, I scold myself, when I've always felt so tied to Pratt? I look back at the cottage.

It was because I was busy being tied to something prettier.

"How did you manage to waylay him?"

"Called on my old team. Wasn't sure it would work, but it did. Hurt to see my mules rise after so many years but not for long. That sort of hurt is sweet. And they brought more with them. I had them block the way back, in case I was right about the predator. I was. They're giving him a bit to think about, slowing him down about now. Told them they knew what to do if a man raised a hand to them in menace. I hurried back here since it's time to decide how we go or how we stay, Emma Rose. If you have a plan about how to make him"—he nods at Winn, coming out of the cottage—"helpful in all this or not, now would be the time."

New plans must come. New and quick.

"My name's Bill Briscoe," the mule runner introduces himself. "Am I glad to know you, tall man?"

"I don't know. I hope so. Winn Towhee." They nod but don't touch. "Bill Briscoe? Like the town? The canyon?"

"That's me."

"Then a pleasure to meet you, sir."

"Why is that?"

"I know you helped my people. I've heard the old stories. You were like . . . a spy."

He shrugs as if to make light of it. "I just kept a lookout in the saddle. Still do. Part of the job. Emma Rose." He turns to me. "It's time to put up or shut up. I told her," he says to the living man beside me, "they're coming back. The hunter, and now two with him."

"How much time do we have?" Winn asks.

"Not much."

Choose, Briscoe's eyes are saying to me. *You want this paradise or no?*

Is paradise perfect or a bargain? I ask myself. *What if you have to sacrifice something for it? Is it really paradise then?*

I say aloud, "The others need to know."

"They already do. They're all at the main house, waiting on you and me. I don't know about him."

Winn looks at me. With a long, worried face. This is all so new to him, I think, this hounding, being hunted. Or is it somehow not new enough?

"Emma, where is all this going?" he asks.

This time it will be different. It has to be.

I say, "Love, can you help me? A living man wants to finish me. You're a living man. Can you help me, can you tell me—why does he want to do that? Why does he never rest?" Why won't the man Pratt give up?

"I don't know."

"But you're a living man," I say again. "You move among living men, have lived with them. Why won't he let me go?" *There is a kind of skin you share*, I don't say.

He takes a breath, understanding, and looks past me, through me. As if I'm not there at all.

Be careful what you ask for, Emma Rose.

"It's his work," he says after a moment. Still looking straight by me. "It's his sense of himself. His anchor in the world. He's a hunter. He needs to hunt a thing down. Be done with it. To feel like he has a place in the world."

"But he's already hunted, finished a ghost in this place, this desert." The poor woman at the cemetery who wouldn't come with us. "How often," I say, suddenly angry, "does a man need to bury an anchor in the world?"

"It depends. Some of us, quite a lot."

"And what else does a living man who buries things want?"

My lover looks across the fields. He nods after a moment. "Not to doubt himself."

"What more?"

"If he doubts himself, to go back to a time when he didn't."

"But you can't go back in time."

For all that Pratt loves to say we're different, the living and dead, we mostly travel in the same direction. Forward. But what if it were true, and Pratt wanted to go back—where would he go, how far?

"He can't go back," I say again.

"Let the man think," Briscoe says quietly, watching the man beside me.

Winn looks away. "You can't go back—but you can stop whatever makes you feel you have to. You can hope to meet it and be done with it."

He's looking toward the cliffs where he told me his father had crashed himself into the earth. A man he'd hoped he would meet here.

But what about a man who didn't choose to plunge to earth? I saw Pratt fall once. More than once, in fact. I saw the look in his eyes, as he fell from the mansion by the sea I haunted, as he tried to raise his wrist, his weapon at me. I saw the look of doubt and surprise in his eyes.

He chases me, I see suddenly, *because if he finishes me, it will be as though he's erased that moment and turned the clock back on it.* Is that it? Is that why he won't stop? Is that what he wants, to go back to the sea where we began and smudge out everything that's happened since? If so, then he will never cease hunting me, us. And there can be no paradise. Unless he can be shown, somehow, it can't be done. That it will never be erased and forgotten. There is no going back to being the person you once were before all the things that have happened since have happened to you. Every mistake. Every chance missed. Every bit of life is afterlife, isn't it? Pratt needs to see that. He needs to see there will never be enough ghosts put down to be who he was before he fell into doubt.

"Thank you," I say to the now distant man beside me, looking far away from me. But soon we'll be close again. I'm certain. "We dead need some time to meet alone, my love, and make our

285

plans. Can you stay at the road and wait for Pratt, and when he comes, tell him no one is here?"

"What good will that do?"

It will make him feel proud. That's all. Superior. That he knows what others don't know. It's when we're most certain of something, I think, and look at the handsome living man beside me, that our heart is most in danger.

32

I'm watching, invisible, cold, as Philip Pratt swings his legs out of the dusty vehicle and stands again in this long valley.

He's dirty, he needs a bath, I think. He adjusts the belt at his waist. I can't see his weapon, hidden by his sleeve. He moves more slowly than usual. But some joy, excitement, lifts his chin to the sun.

Two others emerge: the woman who has been with him from the start, and now a thin, clean-looking young man new to my eyes. He ducks his head and stays a little behind the woman, but his head turns, taking in the scene, the green fields in bright daylight.

Winn Towhee goes forward to greet them all.

"Sherry, Mr. Pratt—hey there, Darrion, nice to see you! So how'd it all go?"

"Beautiful. We were eminently successful," Pratt says.

I see my lover's steps hitch, surprised.

The hunter is so certain of himself. Not in the way we imagined.

What trick is this?

My caretaker starts to turn his head toward me, where he knows I'm standing beside the house, but catches himself and smiles and turns back easily.

"Well that's good to hear, Mr. Pratt. Sherry, you okay? You both look a little worse for the wear, if you don't mind my saying. Where's your truck?"

"Car trouble," she says.

"Really? Way out there. Rotten luck. I guess that's how Darrion came into the picture. Want to come inside? Everything's been good here. No more incidents, just restful and quiet. Really quiet. It kind of feels like something's been scraped away. So clean."

"Yes, I'll bet it always feels that way out here," Pratt says, still smiling. "It's such a fine day," he goes on, walking slowly, but not into the house. "The sky is so blue, my god, it makes you feel like you just won something, doesn't it? But I guess we just did. Let's all stroll back out to the field, to where it all started, and celebrate. All right with you, Towhee?"

"Ah . . . sure."

"Winn," the woman officer says, "you don't look all that restful. Got those little bags under your eyes again."

"I've just been anxious for you."

"There wasn't any need."

"There wasn't," Pratt agrees. "It all went like clockwork."

"How's that, Mr. Pratt?"

"That box canyon at Needlestick—it turned out to be a nest. Not just the Finnis ghost there, but others. Blatant. Foolish. Heedless. Overconfident in their ability to fool us. It was easy to see what attracted them there, held them. There's some artwork there—as I'm sure you know, Towhee—that looks like ancient ghosts. Fascinating images. They give you a feeling of being"—he stops on the mown lawn and seems to think for a moment—"not alone."

"So it was a group haunting, after all?" Winn says, polite, I see.

"It was. It might have been all along or simply ended up being one. Hard to know. In the end, moot."

"And you're saying—you got *her*?"

"Cleanly. The Bronco got left behind, but nothing else. Our deputy here got anxious about our whereabouts, but we were fine enough. Just happy for the lift. Thank you again, son."

"Sure. Sure. You're welcome." The young man nods. "Just glad I, I could help round out the, the good work."

"It was excellent work, Darrion," the sheriff says. "And I need to thank you, Mr. Pratt—Philip. I'm not sure I've properly done that yet. I'm so glad we brought you in. We couldn't have done this without you, obviously. Feels so good, getting so much cleaned up. And fairly fast, when you get down to it."

"It's a good day when the dead go down easy, sheriff."

"I don't understand," Winn says. "You say they were . . . blatant?"

"I suppose ghosts that can cast reflections of themselves think they can fool anyone at any time," Pratt says, laughing easily. "Like a funhouse mirror. But we weren't fooled. Not this time. Well. It's all over now. What a sight this place is again. Extraordinary. It's like Eden in the desert. Worth preserving and defending. I'm glad I came here, too, friends. Ah, it was right here, wasn't it? The first projection. The confusion. Now we can celebrate."

Here, yes, my lover saw my reflection for the first time. Here he saw me, and he wasn't afraid. He looks uneasy, now.

"It was here, yes, Mr. Pratt. You got soaking wet, remember?"

"Sometimes you have to get close to the stink to kill the skunk."

"Not necessarily," the young deputy frowns.

"So you're saying"—Winn still seems disturbed—"you got them . . . how?"

"The element of surprise was on our side. It was almost pitiful, really. The Finnis remnant was weak. My working theory is that all the games, the reflection, projecting, they weakened her. Pretending to be somewhere where she wasn't. It must be exhausting. Draining. She seemed almost to be sleepwalking, unaware of her exact location and appearance."

What is this, why is he lying, lying, lying?

"Pretending to be somewhere where she wasn't," Winn says. "Sleepwalking."

"Just a theory again, Towhee. But the fact that she, that they all believed they were safe at that fort, the fact we were able to creep up on them as they sat in a ring near the artwork . . . There has to be some explanation. First time I ever encountered something like it, I admit. In any case, she was the target that led us right to her and to the rest of them."

What can he be saying?

"Weakness is inevitable over time, if you think about it," Pratt is going on. "The longer a spirit haunts, the farther it gets away from its life, its original life-force, surely the more likely it is to weaken, become confused, flighty. My theory is that the Finnis ghost—Emma Rose Finnis," he says, piercingly—"simply sat there and let me finish her, and all of them, because she didn't understand, any longer, that she *was* a ghost. I believe she must have actually thought she was something more. She simply sat there while I erased all the others. As if it wasn't happening. As if she were in a kind of dream."

No. No. This is what they do. This is what he does, I know it is, he's done it before, to me, try to make me feel evil, worthless, blind, but I'm not, no, no, no, I haven't been dreaming, asleep.

The woman officer beside him is nodding—the sheriff who said she came into the Poston house, though I have no memory of her being there.

My lover, he's listening beside her. But it was, is, all real, I want to shout to him, as real as my life was real, as real as dancing with a boy, swirling with the music, as real as a waltz, and his arms were around me and the music made us one, in love there's no beginning nor end, what's inside is outside, and what is outside is in, you see both ways, you see even in the dark, and are afraid no more.

Don't you believe me, love? Don't you trust me?

"The saddest part," Pratt is saying, "is that she didn't seem to care while the others were expunged. As though she didn't think they were real, only *she* was. It was a pitiful group of Indi—"

The woman coughs, to interrupt him, and makes a little gesture toward Winn.

Pratt goes on: "Emma Rose Finnis was finished in a small pool of her own ash. How they all finish. They all burn, in the end. A blaze, a shot, and they're done."

A scream behind me.

Who was that?

One of the children. In the field. Adelaide. Poor Adelaide, Addie. Who remembers the fire that took her young body.

The other children are screaming now too, appearing in the clover where all, all of them are waiting.

We hadn't planned on showing ourselves so soon.

But one by one, now, the light of every pain, each one, shines.

The flooded family of four clutching together.

The loving, grasping couple.

The handy carpenter brothers.

The army nurse, and the boy who died in the hospital.

The schoolmaster, holding his pupils together like a bouquet.

And more.

Pratt's done it. What he wanted.

Yet so have we.

I see his mouth drop open in wonder. It's written all over his face.

He thought it was only me here.

You were wrong, hunter.

The plan, at my signal, was to show ourselves, to give ourselves away. In our hundreds. More than ourselves. Like Briscoe's team.

But how did you get your mules to do that? To be so many more? I'd asked him at the meeting of the dead. *To light not only their own souls but all those they came from and carry within them?*

I found out how, he'd said. *Mules know more things than we give them credit for. They know words. "Git up, whoa, easy, walk on, back." I said "back," out there, because I wanted my team of twenty strung out all over the road, and then it happened. "Back" means something differ- ent when you're dead, don't it? Don't ghosts have ghosts?*

Yes. Ghosts have ghosts.

They needed no signal from me, once Pratt admired our burning.

And so he, and the three living beside him, stare in wonder now at the fields filled with Briscoe's tall ancestors in chains and without them. And the others that fill the fields on either side, too, stretching to the river and even into it, bodies large and small, old and young, in every shape, with glistening faces, in colors warmer than the desert, coffee, honey, and milk, against the streaked red cliffs they stand, from Mexico and the war in France and the schoolmaster's Connecticut and so much more. *Back*, I think, *back, back, back we go*, and there now are my people, too, though I can hardly bear to reflect their memory, my thin-necked mother, from her photograph, my cleft-chinned father, and the thickly dressed kin behind them, woolly, it was cold where we came from, so cold, many of the others are from warmer climes and so they stand bareheaded or under caps and hats thin and light, and the valley is finally filled with people, with more than just the two absent owners who claim it, and all that are present here, all of us, are more than Pratt bargained for, more than he has ever imagined, or bothered to.

He has to see, now, I think, *he'll never burn enough of us to be what he was before he lost me and needed to find me to fix the past. The past is fixed, Mr. Pratt. And deep, so deep, it is, you see. So deep and wide. You can't undrown in it.*

"Holy Jesus, what the—" The sheriff stares and reaches for her gun.

My lover lifts his chin. He knew this would come, we prepared him, but still, he looks amazed and scans, searching for his own people, who aren't there. Only the dead can call the dead, it seems. My lover isn't dead.

The young deputy gaping beside him clutches foolishly at his gun, too. "Sherry—Sherry—what do we do, what do we do?"

And Pratt? He hasn't moved. I've stayed behind him, so close I could climb into his hair and sit there.

He unsheathes his weapon, lifting his sleeve.

Still? Even now? Will you never, never stop? How do you imagine you can kill what aren't even spirits, but the ghosts of ghosts, history, time passing itself?

My lover sees, and in a flash turns and grabs Pratt's wrist, twisting his arm like a knot into itself.

"Got him, Emma, got him!" he shouts. I'm still invisible. He doesn't know how close I am, how pleased.

"Winn!" the sheriff shouts. "What the hell are you doing? Darrion, goddamn it, put your weapon down!"

Neither she nor the young man see the blond carpenter brothers appearing behind them. Quickly their arms, too, are pinned. They're brought to earth. They don't understand how.

Briscoe leaves his people to stand over them.

"Nice bright handcuffs you got with you there," he says smoothly.

He lifts the shackles from the pinned deputy's belt.

Pratt is squirming, shouting, swearing, demanding to be freed. "This is breaking the law, Towhee. You're aiding illegals. You don't want to do this. Trust me."

Briscoe and my lover, ghostly man and living one, easily shackle Pratt.

It's soothing, seeing the devil that wants to finish you in chains. I come and stand in front of Pratt, now, and show myself, in all my fullness. All my glory. The head and the body and the hand and foot and the breadth and blaze of me. He can do me no harm, as he is. I stand before him, and I look into his gray eyes, that gaze that has haunted me for two years, and it's clear he doesn't want me to see anything in them. He's turned cold. The living can do that, too, when they wish. Or how else could some of them do what it is they do?

Over Pratt's shoulder, I look into my lover's eyes. His are bright. Questioning. Even as he holds the hunter in place.

I look at Pratt again.

"Mr. Pratt. How do you do?"

"I'm well enough, remnant."

"It's Emma Rose Finnis."

"You're nothing, remnant. You're a shadow, along with all the shadows here. You have no idea how to get out of this, do you? When you could have rested and made this easy."

I almost laugh. It's a strange thing for an imprisoned man to say. What a hard, hard creature he is. I haven't been so close to him, like this, not in such a long while. His wrinkles are deeper than they were. The salt in his hair is more than it was, and whiter. The salt of the earth, reaching up, ready to take him. He's tired, this man. More than he lets on. He's throwing what he feels, as a reflection at me, when he says *you could have rested*. It's not me that wants rest. I'm only just beginning.

Something in the air changes.

"Oh-oh." The hunter makes a face. "Hear that?"

A whirring sound.

Above us. A buzzing, dropping down.

Pratt grins. "Looks like company."

Winn looks up.

"I don't believe it," he says. "It's the owner's plane."

"Funny," Pratt says, calm. "I thought you said they only come once a year."

My lover's face turns angry.

"You found them and called them."

"Maybe. Or maybe the world is coming to an end, who knows, and they need their bunker."

A gusting breeze. A twist of air skirting across the fields. A dust devil.

Something else has changed. The ghosts in the field have all vanished.

I turn to see the valley. Empty. The purple clover rustling in the wind. And the dust on the long red road leading to the hangar, where we first made love.

Briscoe at least is beside me.

"Smart of the rest to get gone," he says from under his flop hat. "But I think I better lead them on."

"We'll finish here," I say.

"Keep safe."

He fades into the sunlight.

I hear a heave, a harsh grunting, and turn. Pratt is throwing his chained weight against Winn's chest, trying to push him backward and down. The carpenter brothers have swooped in to stop this, leaving the officers on the ground untended. I close in on their frightened faces, their scrambling hands. We have no fear of guns. Only of Pratt's twisted wrist.

"No!" Hogan shouts. "Darrion! Don't!"

A bullet passes through me, like the swooping of a bird.

33

Pratt felt the shot go through him. It was like fire on a leash. It didn't seem possible that he could be torn through so easily. They fell together, he and the caretaker, as if slowly. Knees buckling, legs tangled.

They were both shot. Pratt understood that much clearly. The single bullet had found both their bodies. Hogan was crawling over on her knees, to the caretaker, shouting while compressing the wound in his chest, screaming his name, while her deputy . . . what was his name . . . what was it . . . it sounded like carrion, like death . . . Darrion, that was it . . . pressed firmly below Pratt's shoulder, shoving the searing, acid leash deeper, spreading it, while at the same pressing at a phone, pale-faced, trying to keep his wits about him. Poor kid.

There were no more ghostly forms surrounding them. In the blue sky above, the small plane whirred, banking. The sun was fierce, unforgiving. *I should feel hot*, Pratt realized. Instead, he felt cold, colder than he'd ever been in his life. Colder than a Hatteras lighthouse in winter; than the white fangs of the Pacific;

than all the snow drifts of the Sierra Nevada locked around your knees; than the desert at night, while you searched for her, you had searched.

He turned his head. That plane looked like it would land soon. He hadn't called the owners, no, he'd been improvising. He had no idea why the plane was now circling the valley, preparing to come down. *The runway is over there*, he thought, lightheaded, *nice smooth red dirt, all ready to go.* He looked toward it, and a young woman was standing beside it, in some cut grass. Beckoning, in her white blouse, her antique black skirt, one shoulder raised, a bit of bright ribbon weaving through her hair and over her neck. He could hear her voice calling across the landing strip. The sheriff and the deputy were shouting at each other, it seemed they didn't see, couldn't hear the call. He was dying, Pratt thought. He was listening at a doorway, or through a keyhole, to water rising.

Come to me, my love, the ghost was beckoning. *You must believe now as you've never believed in anything else before. See the sun climbing in the east? Reach for it, my love. Please. Come this way. Come away, and we'll fly, together. I'm here, waiting for you. Please, love, come to me.*

They were the same words, Pratt thought, or very like the words he had once tried himself, when a woman, also a quite lovely woman, lay crushed inside a taxi, her head folded over her own lap. The begging hadn't worked then, he remembered, though he had whispered the words just as urgently, urged with them as the Finnis ghost was pleading now. *It isn't that easy, remnant*, he wanted to tell her, coldly. *Order, for the most part, holds. What is high stays high. What is low stays low.* The plane was dropping lower, about to land. With luck, he thought, it might airlift him out, save him. *Please, love, come to me.* Love? Well. That was a word he hadn't used as he'd leaned through the broken glass toward the woman in the crushed taxi. Because it hadn't been earned, not yet. Or maybe he hadn't trusted enough. But trusted who? Trusted what? You can't just throw love out like a life preserver, he wanted to shout, and imagine it will solve every problem underneath, deep down. It won't. The sheriff was sobbing now over the caretaker's dead body. There it was. Proof that love wasn't sufficient to every occasion. Poor man. Winn Towhee. Good man.

Pratt felt faint. He tried lifting his wrist, now unshackled, in reproof, toward the Finnis ghost. She who had brought all this on. But she was no longer where she had been. The plane was landing instead, in wheeling red dust. What had happened? he wondered vaguely. What was happening? Was it the time for bunkers now? Was the world coming to an end?

He turned his head away from the landing strip. Farther off, past the irrigation stretching across the field, he could now see two figures walking. He could only make out their backs at this distance. A blazing man and woman. Hand in hand. *Love. Love.* The man with long black hair, like a bird's tailfeathers. The woman trailing her skirt in the grass.

The deputy was calling frantically to the sheriff.

"Sherry! Winn's gone. Sherry. Sherry! Listen to me. What about Pratt?"

Pratt watched her crawling on her hands and knees toward him, her face terrible, wet, yet pulling itself together. Good at her job. Good, good woman.

"He's trying to say something," she was saying, hoarsely. "Mr. Pratt. Philip. Philip. Listen. Hold on. We're getting you help."

He felt her putting her soft ear to his mouth. She smelled of damp leather.

His eyes seemed to be going dim.

I want a nice tall gravestone, he hoped she heard him say. *And when I'm under it, fling it down, I tell you. Fling it down hard and heavy, on top of me.*

"That won't be necessary, we'll get you out of this."

Out. That's exactly what he didn't want. Not yet. He wasn't ready.

A surprise that he looked forward to telling the remnant about. That there was something stronger than love, stronger than fear, stronger than anger, stronger than loneliness, stronger than hope, stronger than right and wrong, stronger than rest, stronger than peace, stronger than justice, stronger than all these together.

It was thirst.

He was thirsty. So thirsty.

Before Philip Pratt closed his eyes, he saw the door of the airplane open, and two well-dressed figures leaping down from it. Now they were running, water bottles in their hands, heading frantic toward the river, the bunker, and didn't see the two ghosts standing in the grass.

Finis